The Queen's Rebirth

The Tales of LaRue 2

The Queen's Rebirth

Chapter 1

I lead my horse through the rocky paths of the outskirts of Ambrose. The hills are tall and the bottom of the cliff is endless. Pebbles tumble and bounce down the cliff face. The mountains rise above the cloudy morning fog. Venetta trips slightly as if she too was admiring the view. I fall forward as she regains her footing. I sit on my knees as I try not to think of Luthias; just the thought of him not in my life is unbearable.

I stare at my bloody hands as my general surroundings begin to slowly change into a different, distant memory.

The mountains begin to fade away into the wooden structured halls of Ambrose as I watch a much younger version of myself run through my home's hallways. Her eyes are filled with fright. I follow behind her as she enters her room. I stare at her as she hides under the blankets and I quickly turn towards the opening door as it clicks.

This is a very distant memory. One that I don't exactly remember.

"My little Laerune, what is wrong?" My father asks while moving the blankets away from little LaRue's curled up body. I had not yet been given the nickname LaRue. This wasn't until Avon arrived in Ambrose many, many years after this specific event.

"I had a nightmare with my eyes open." The golden curls shake on her head as she pulls her red blanket closer. The emblem of Ambrose had been embroidered with gold thread in the center of the fabric. That blanket hasn't left my traveling chest since my belongings were brought to Lithien.

He places his hand gently on her face. "It seems that you might have the gift of foresight. Now, can you tell me what you saw?" His eyes glisten with concern and empathy.

"I saw a boy," her voice cracks. "He had red hair, he was of tall stature, a warrior. He carried many weapons and...blood," little me shakes her head. "He was covered in blood." Her innocent, wide eyes stare upward at my father.

I sit on the side of her bed. I am unsure if it is polite to grasp her hands.

I am asking myself if it is polite to hold my hand in my own memory. How ridiculous does that sound?

"What else did you see?" My father calmly asks, but the fear is seen in his face from my new perspective of the memory.

"He had died. A sword through his stomach."

I rise to my feet, shaking the memory from my sight. The vision burns behind my eyes as they begin to water. I wipe my hands on my dress, plucking the loose rocks from my palms as I continue on my way back to Lithien.

Chapter 2

I reach the gate of Lithien. The silver tree carved into the metal gate is the farthest thing from gleaming.

I always thought that Lithien was impenetrable but that didn't keep our enemies away from my kingdom.

It failed the people of Lithien.

It failed the King.

Its last Prince.

I failed everyone.

The sight in front of the gate makes me stop Venetta in her tacks. She gives a slight snort at the scene ahead of us. Even my mare has the same reaction as me.

My eyes widen and begin to water both from the smell and the sight of what lies before me.

Dead bodies of Elves, men, and orcs still lay on the path. The Elves' bodies remain immortal even in death, but the men and orcs slowly begin to decompose.

I step down from Venetta. Carefully, I walk through the maze of bodies, hoping there isn't a familiar face.

But there are known faces and I shiver.

The young maid who had once helped me into my wedding gown.

The guard who had walked me down the hall one night after arriving back to Lithien.

The little girl who had danced on Sentier's shoes at my wedding. What was she even doing so close to this gate?

I can no longer look down, but up towards the sky. This wasn't supposed to happen. The innocent have been killed.

The gate opens for me as if they knew I was taking my time to carefully map every face. Just in case I get the chance to avenge them. Nolan can no longer hurt these people. *My people.*

The entrance takes one final creak before I take one more look behind me.

I regret it instantly.

I attempt to smile as I notice Amar waiting for me on the other side of the gate.

7

"It's nice to see you alive and well." He embraces me quickly as I dodge the sword strapped on his back. "Have you not returned with more?" Amar whispers in my ear as others behind him watch with anticipation. They shift nervously on their feet as if waiting for some news or the slightest bit of information.

They all look like they haven't showered in weeks and are only running on a few hours of sleep.

"More?"

"Your father took many of our people to Ambrose to heal them. I was hoping that some of them were going to be brought back soon. Or at least some healers brought back here. Fifteen isn't enough." His eyes avert to the ground as he pushes dirt with his blood covered boot. "It seems that Nolan knew to go for our healers." *Fifteen is far from enough.*

"I didn't know that. I left Ambrose before I was given any information." I look down, afraid to ask the question I have been dreading since I woke up in Ambrose. "Is *he* alive?" It feels selfish to ask after seeing the dead littered before the gate's entrance.

The answer seems to take an eternity to escape from Amar's mouth. "He is with the healers. I have no news of his condition."

It wasn't the exact answer that I wanted, but I'll take whatever I can get at this very moment. "Thank you, Amar." I bow my head, turning to walk towards the healing houses. Amar grabs my upper arm and I pause while keeping my eyes in the direction of those healing rooms. "I know that you are stressed LaRue, but they need your help there. I know you were taught the healing skills of your father. The healers would appreciate your help."

I think back to The Peace War and how Luthias had told me he always used to want to be a healer, but he was forced to play his part as a protector of his kingdom rather than the more feminine side of recovery. He was talented at healing, but his kingdom needed a commander; someone skilled in weaponry and combat.

I must play my part as well.

Maybe this will be my way to search for forgiveness for not helping during this battle I left them with.

🖋

Elves rush by with blood covering their aprons and hands. They are in a panic as they try to save as many people as they can. Two women run right into each other. The tiredness within their eyes is almost overwhelming to me. They have probably been here for hours with no sleep. Another young girl is asleep with her back to the wall, but her rest is short lived as she is lifted to her feet by another woman with messy black hair and a green apron. They have to be reaching their limit.

I walk towards the closed door knowing that's where they would keep Luthias. The royal quarters should never be used. *Especially for the last remaining heir to the throne of Lithien.* My hand trembles as I reach for the door handle. Finally, I grip the cold metal as I twist it open.

I find Luthias on a bed, tears running down his face and beads of sweat dotting his freckled forehead. Groans escape from his mouth as a woman begins to push a needle through parts of his wound in attempts to close it. Sentier stands before me, blocking the rest of the injury from my sight.

My nails dig into my palms. "Will he live?" I ask while trying to see past Sentier.

"Yes. He will live."

I sigh in relief as a sudden weight is lifted off of my shoulders. But Sentier doesn't seem pleased. There is still a chance that things may head downhill.

"It will take time for him to heal. When you are done here please come find me." He bows and the room suddenly feels lonely even with three rushed healers and their wounded Prince.

The air smells of iron and a healer looks up to me with sad and exhausted eyes. Luthias turns his head towards me.

The words aren't a question when they come from his mouth. "Laerune," he strongly says my name as he reaches his hand out for mine. His freezing palms meet mine as I place my

9

other hand on his forehead. "LaRue." The lovely Prince doesn't stumble over my name as he closes his eyes.

The situation is overwhelming as he rolls his head back to the side. My lips quivers as I fight back the urge to shake him awake for the selfish reason of wanting to hear him speak or at the least listen to me. I pull on my tense shoulders as I turn a fake smile in the healer's direction.

"What can I do?" I turn towards the tired healer in hopes that she will give me something to do in this very room so I can keep an eye on my husband.

She almost seems relieved as she wipes the back of her blood covered hand over her forehead. "We haven't been able to attend to all the children. They are in the other room. Another woman is in there to help." I turn to the next door as her quick words ring through my heart. "Your help is appreciated, LaRue."

There are no formalities here. Death and pain use no formal titles when you are in the house of healing.

🖋

My hands seem to steady themselves as I open the next door. I close my eyes immediately as the sound of crying children echo through my ears. The iron smell of blood isn't as strong in this room, but the sight of all these children in pain sends chills down my spine. They must be terrified.

The healer snaps her fingers in a young girl's direction. The supplies have already been set near the child's bed and all I have to do is help.

The girl keeps a steady pair of blue eyes in my direction as if the pain no longer existed and I was the only thing in the room. She must have been waiting a long time since the tears have long since dried from her cheeks.

"What is a princess doing here?" She questions as I examine her broken leg.

"I am a healer too." I run my hand over the broken bone as I take my eyes off of hers.

"But you are the Princess."

The title stings for a moment as I think back to Sentier's advice before my wedding. *Prove them wrong.* "A Princess can be many things all at once. The healers need my help, so I shall be a healer for as long as they need me." I straighten out her leg as I place the split around her broken limb. I tie the strips of cloth around her leg. "What is your name?" I ask the girl as I place my hands onto her leg in attempts to distract her from any pain. My healing abilities will speed up the process. *It's the only bit of magic I have been blessed with.*

"Bidella."

I place my hand on her arm. "Remember to help those in need, Bidella. No matter your job or title. I haven't always been a Princess and I am far from being just that."

I move onto the next child; their eyes brighten as they notice me. "Help." The young boy pleads. A knife is embedded in his shoulder. I pull the dagger from his arm and I quickly place my palm over his wound. I reach for the bandages as I feel the healing power escape from my body. My stomach turns as I realize that it has been days since the initial battle and this boy still has a weapon in his arm.

I never had to learn how to heal. The gift was passed down from my father. I only needed to be taught how to wield it. The only problem is that I don't use it often and having less experience takes a lot of energy out of me. The task is exhausting.

I move to each child, using my power more and more as I make my way through the room. But, my power is quickly drained. I trip over my own feet and I place my head onto the cold, hard ground. My body is so exhausted I can barely stand. I am drained of my remaining energy.

"Up LaRue. You have helped enough. Don't overwork yourself. You know your limit and you have met it. We don't need a dying princess here, too."

The healer shows me out the door and I reach my hand for the wall to steady myself. Sentier turns the corner and quickly rushes down the hall to hold my body up. "Come on. Let's find you somewhere to sit."

11

I watch as Sentier packs his things into a saddle bag from my cushioned chair. "Are you leaving?" I mumble through my words as I am too tired to function, let alone think.

"Lady Azariah has summoned me to Lindalin and it is urgent."

"What about Lithien? They need their king. I am sure my grandmother will understand the kingdom's urgency in the need of leadership."

Frustration heavily sits in my face. My lips turn downward and my eyes narrow. I feel that whatever reason that my grandmother has for requesting Sentier so urgently is not as important as the wellbeing of his own kingdom.

"That is where I will need you. I need you to take up my duties while I am gone." He places his hand on my shoulder and pulls me into a hug. "I trust you LaRue," he says as he releases me. "I'll be back in two months."

"Be safe," I tell him as he leaves the study. I don't know what else to say.

Chalsarda enters the study and she leans out of the way to not bump into Sentier. When the King disappears from sight she quickly reaches out to me, pulling me into her arms as she lifts me out of my chair. "I am so glad you are safe." She squeezes a little too tightly and I huff as the air escapes me.

"As am I." I share the mutual feeling as I fall back into my chair.

"Luthias?" She questions.

"He will live." I am disappointed in Sentier for not filling in his son's closest friends. It would have at least given them some sort of relief.

Amar enters the room as well. His blue solemn eyes meet mine. "So, Sentier left us alone?" I nod my head. "What can we do?" His tone suggests that Sentier had already filled him in on the prior situation.

"We need to take care of the fallen. Their bodies need to be taken out of the forest. We don't want to attract unwanted creatures anymore. The Elves can be buried in Lithien and the men on their own land." The topic seems to make them both cringe. "I take it back." I think of how Nolan and his army was the cause for this kingdom's downfall. "Let the remaining men take care of their own dead. If they do not retrieve them, burn them." It may seem a tad bit harsh, but things need to get done and I feel no remorse.

"And of the Orcs?"

"They will be burned." *I have no desire to even see their kind treated with any sort of respect.*

Chalsarda lowers her head. "I do think it will be a good idea to address the people of Lithien. They need to know that everything will be alright."

"Yes, Chalsarda. That can be done tomorrow," I reply as I begin to shuffle through Sentier's paperwork littered across the desk in an attempt to look like I know what I'm doing.

I find myself in the dining hall embracing Eldar and Eldrin. They watch my every move as I take my seat at the table.

"Father had taken you and we didn't hear from you or him in days," Eldar speaks calmly while setting food onto my plate. He can already tell that I am exhausted beyond measure. I rub my temples as the tiredness takes over my mind. I feel like I can't focus on any information, let alone their words. "We thought it best to stay here and help around."

Eldar pauses. "Not to make you more stressed, but we don't want to hide any secrets from you." I nod my head, letting him know to go on. "Avon and Tolendeil didn't return."

"And there has been no reports of them being seen in Ambrose or Everford."

I drop my fork on my plate, placing my hands over my face and then through my hair. "I am going to go to bed. We will figure this out in the morning." I would rather think all of this over with a clear mind than one with too many thoughts.

"Goodnight LaRue." They both answer in return.

Walking into my empty room fills me with a sense of loneliness. It is an odd sight to see it so abandoned and quiet. The candles had been lit before I entered my room and I am thankful for the little bit of light. The fire though, has yet to be lit and no wood is there to replenish it. There hasn't been a need. No one has been in this room for days.

I curl up into a ball under the blankets and attempt to fall asleep. *But dreams seem nonexistent.*

I shroud myself with the thought of Avon and Tolendeil missing. Avon's smart and tactful. I can't imagine him being captured or succumbing to an Orc's dirty tricks.

I shiver as the wind blows through the open window. I toss and turn. I am used to the warmth from Luthias. The bed feels too big as I reach over to the empty space, grabbing only a handful of sheets in his false presence.

Chapter 3

My head already pounds from all the stress. I pull on a yellow dress this morning in hopes that the color will lift my spirits. And hopefully, lift Luthias' as well. My only thought last night was that I needed to check on Luthias first thing in the morning.

I make my way down to the healer's house. I open the door to Luthias' room, expecting to find him in the same condition. But to my surprise, he looks much better and healthier than yesterday. He can sit up, eat, and make understandable phrases. I smile at his sudden recovery. It is more progress than I expected him to make this soon.

A sly smile comes across his face as I enter the room.

"You dressed pretty to see me?" He chuckles, hissing slightly at the pain in his abdomen. He sounds like his brother and the flirty comments Luvon would always make.

"Maybe." *Of course, I did. I know how much he loves it when I am in a gown rather than pants and a tunic.*

"You let your hair down. I like that too." He plays with a stand of my golden hair as I sit down beside his bedside. My hair has gotten far too long for it to be anywhere near functional when I leave it down.

"They're going to rush me out any minute now," I tell him, looking at the healers behind me and how they watch my every move. The health of the only heir of Lithien is essential to keep in prime state.

"I know." He frowns and that sideways smirk vanishes. "You have been helping them, haven't you? Healing the children? There has been lots of talk about a golden-haired princess in the Healing Houses."

"Yes. I'm not that good though. But I guess anything helps. I can hear my father yelling at me from Ambrose for not keeping up with my healing studies. You were always better at it."

"I had a lot more practice and I enjoyed learning about it." He did enjoy healing and Luthias would often be the one healing my injuries when we were out and about on adventures together.

As I predicted, the healers rush me out of the room on a moment's notice. And as soon as I leave the Houses of Healing, Chalsarda comes into view.

"I've brought everyone together. Well, most of the people of Lithien. Many of them are busy with repairs and healing." She points towards two healers entering the healing room. "Are you ready to speak?"

Of course I'm not.

※

She leads me to the throne room. The doors are closed and guards stand before them. They quickly open for me and Chalsarda. I look up towards the lofted ceilings decorated with curtains of blue and silver.

The room is crowded with Elves and my heart beats quickly. I step towards Sentier's throne, the Elves become silent as I stand taller in hopes that it will boost my confidence. My hands still shake.

For Electa's sake, why didn't Sentier address his own damn people before he left?

"King Sentier has been summoned to Lindalin and he entrusted me to take care of his kingdom as well as his people. We all have gone through this tragic experience together, but we are still here, we still have our home. It may not be a victory to all, but we are still strong. And I believe that everything will be well. We must be patient, we must work to get back what has been lost and broken. Everything will turn good in time. Don't be scared to take time to mourn your losses."

I bow my head, leaving the throne room and the silent Elves behind me.

There's not much to say to this grieving group of Elves. Lithien is used to experiencing such loss.

Eldar and Eldrin walk beside me as we exit the interior of the castle.

"A storm passed through a couple of days ago and we haven't had the time to clear the path. It would be impossible to get a horse through."

We walk down the path, looking for any sign that Avon and Tolendeil had passed through this part of the forest. I look up at the sun and then to the right of me. Something glistens in the branches. I pull Avon's locket from the tree's branches. The detailed A on the front was the clear indication that it was the only thing he had left of his mother's. *And it is now no longer with him.*

"Well, at least we know that they came this way." It is very hard to track Elves for they are very light on their feet and hardly ever leave tracks, not even on snow or mud. The storm has made it near impossible to see any sign of Elves moving through.

We walk away from the path and into the dark woods. I clutch Avon's locket within my palm as my worry for them increases. Kitsunes and Orcs could still live in the darker areas of the forest or possibly a forest troll. They are near impossible to defeat.

I know that Avon is carrying Caldon's sword, but he isn't as trained as I am. He was trained to be a Lord, not a warrior. And Tolendeil, she is like a child to me, a little sister you could say.

We continue through the woods until we reach a meadow. A thick row of trees guard the open area as the sun drips across the yellowed grass.

I fall to my knees, my head falling into the wheatgrass. I reach my hand up as the vision comes across my mind.

Avon and Tolendeil run through the forest path, the carts of the Dwarves following after them. The Dwarves shoot arrows and their weapons dared to come closer to Avon and Tolendeil. Tolendeil's dress catches on a tree and she pulls it away, ripping the skirt. Avon throws his sword at the driver of the ram pulled cart. They continue to run, only to stop when they are met with another cart of Dwarves. They are surrounded, nowhere to run. The Dwarves bind them in iron chains, taking them to the Mountain Kingdom of Makya.

Although we once had an alliance, Elves and Dwarves don't mix well at all. There is always a petty argument between the two races.

"Avon and Tolendeil have been taken to Makya." I leave the forest, finding my way back to my room. Maybe if I had just listened to the Electa, this wouldn't have happened. *This shouldn't have happened.*

🌿

I walk to my room and I lay onto my bed, still clad in my leather armor. I cry into my pillow and I fall asleep in a daze of depression. *None of this should have happened.*

In the middle of the night, I wake up thinking that my nightmare is real. The God of Death was leaning over me, prepared to take me away from the living world.

My sword is unsheathed and pointed at Luthias, who stands in front of me. He takes the sword from my trembling hands and places it gently on the table. He crawls into bed and wraps his protective arms around my body. I start to shake and he holds me tighter. It has been such a long time since I last felt his warmth and right now I need it the most.

"Luthias, everything is my fault. All of it is my fault."

"Don't blame yourself for the evil that others have done." He runs his hands through my hair.

Luthias soon falls asleep, still groggy from all the concoctions and medicines they have been using on him. I would go to sleep as well, but my nightmares force me to keep my eyes open and my mind awake. I hear the door click open and two Elven women stand in my doorway. I keep my body still as I strain my pointed ears to hear them speak.

"Do not wake them," I hear Etta, my nursemaid, speak. "If he could walk here himself, it will be fine for him to stay. Let

18

them have their little bit of happiness, for I believe that it won't last forever. The world is growing harsher by the day."

Etta pulls the young healer away, closing the door behind them. I sigh deeply, for they are right. Our happiness can't last forever. We have had too many second chances. I am destined to die; *how many battles can one survive that were so close to death?*

🖋

The sun rises and Luthias still sleeps soundly; heavy breaths escape from his lips. I open the drawer of my desk, grabbing my journal. The pages are just about full. I never thought that I would be adding more to this story, but I had left it in hopes that Luthias would find it. I wanted it to be printed so that maybe someone would read my story and find inspiration in it as I did with other tales and adventures. But I guess now is the time to start writing the second part of my story.

Luthias wakes and his hand automatically goes to lightly touch my cheek. He looks better and much more awake. His cheeks are flushed with color.

My husband moves the hair from my face. "I thought I lost you."

"And so did I," I tell him. "Are you strong enough to go to the council that is being held today?" Chalsarda had alerted me sometime yesterday that a council was to be held. I didn't like the fact that Sentier would not be there and neither would my father. *But, this is a step towards advancing my independence.*

"Yes, but what is it for?"

"I am assuming that some Elves are not very happy that I have disobeyed the Electa. They do not agree with what I have done." They're scared.

"You saved my life, does that not matter to them? Lithien wouldn't have an heir without you."

I can't help but think that this is some sort of stab at how I have not planned on producing an heir. I shake my head and then proceed to change out of the armor that I had slept in. I slip on a comfortable green dress because I have a feeling that this council will take a while. And the heat of the day is already becoming unbearable.

🌿

    The courtyard is beyond crowded as most of the Elves are standing rather than filling the many chairs. I take my seat next to Luthias and he looks glad to be able to sit down. His face is contorted in pain as he places a hand over his abdomen.

"Are you okay?"

"Yes, I am fine."

That's a lie. I can feel his pain and panic. The anxiety builds up in my stomach and he closes his eyes, trying to hide it. *Don't lie to me Luthias.*

"You don't have to stay here." I place my hand over the amber stone around my neck that allows me to feel my court's pain and as I am now learning, emotions as well.

"I won't let them harass you for making your own choices, LaRue. There is something about the Electa that doesn't seem right."

An unknown Elf quiets us and I look to Luthias, making sure that he knows that this is his last chance to leave. He dismisses his chance and looks back at the tall, brunette Elf.

"Welcome. We are here to discuss why Laerune is not on a ship right now." He glares at me. I roll my eyes. I was the one left in charge of Lithien. Not these people. "Others will give their opinions, so please be patient." There is no formal language and I can just see my father rolling his eyes at everyone's impolite attitude during this council meeting.

Katar, an Elf that has traveled around here lately, stands to speak first. He clears his throat and brushes unseen dust off of his tunic. "Laerune, will you please tell us why you returned. I think it will be better to know the real story before we start to argue."

I slowly stand up; my joints pop at my stiffness as I clench my fists. The Elves watch me carefully as if I am going to do something very un-elven like. I chuckle at the thought as I clasp my hands in front of me.

"Well if you are wondering, I did plan on going." I laugh, tears filling my eyes at the same time as I think of the whole situation. "You could say fate turned me away from what the Electa urged me to do." I look to Luthias, smiling. "Now if you do think that I am this Pathway to peace, then you will allow me to fight in my own war. I will be a Queen someday. Maybe not to this kingdom, but one day I will rule. If you do not want to listen to me and hear my decisions then you can leave this kingdom now." *I did do something very un-elven like.* "And I don't give a damn about the Electa and their need to control. I am a free woman and I can do as I please. I don't need Gods to guide me! They are selfish beings who only care about themselves. We should start caring for each other and make our own choices in what is right for our path in life."

They start staring at me and whispering to their neighbors sitting next to them. Their voices become raised and they soon rise to their feet, arguing. I stand up taller, crossing my arms over my chest.

"Stop!" I speak rather loudly. They continue to argue. "Will you not listen?" I yell, finally getting their attention. "As I said, if you do not want to listen to me or agree on my decisions then you can leave this council *now.*" I point to the doorway, giving them the chance to leave before they get the chance to feel my wrath.

One stands up but is quickly shoved down into his seat by another Elf. They all seemed to sit down in fear of me. I can't help but smile as I have climbed up another step in the ladder of equality in this kingdom.

"Now, we have greater matters to discuss." I walk around, making eye contact with each Elf attending this council. "Navain has returned whether you like it or not. We can't pretend he is not there, it will make it worse. He is strong, but not to his full strength. He is searching for the stones of the Electa, but he can't touch them like he once used to. He wants me to find them for him because the location is lost from his mind."

"Then find them. You don't have to give them to him. If we return the stones to the Electa, then the light will be restored and the darkness banished." *Finally someone with some common sense. Kind of.*

"I don't trust the Electa." I shake my head as I whisper the words under my breath. I quickly change the subject. "Avon and Tolendeil have been taken to Makya as prisoners. We must decide what to do and leaving them there is not an option."

They began to argue again and I finally walk to the door to leave with Luthias behind me. I put my head in my hands, sighing.

"I didn't know they were taken," Luthias speaks quietly.

"Yes."

"If you do not return in two days I am going to get you myself."

"I am not leaving to get them by myself," I lie.

"I love you." He takes my hand. *He knows it's a lie.*

I smile at him. "I love you too." The grin leaves my face and I start the walk to the stables.

Venetta whinnies a hello as I grab her tack off of the wall. I tighten the strap around her underbelly and I softly comb out her tangled mane. I mount the tall horse and we ride out of the kingdom of Lithien and towards Makya. I will have to risk my own life to save Avon and Tolendeil and I have a plan to do it. *I just hope that it goes well and Amar can keep an eye on the kingdom's duties.*

Chapter 4

I lower myself off of Venetta, slapping her side to make her run back to her home. I watch as she trots away. *This may be the last time I see her for a while.* It pains my heart to watch her hesitate as she looks back to me. "Go." With a snort she continues on her way. I know she can sense my fear and the uneasiness of my situation.

I attempt to keep my back straight as I approach the gate of Makya. The mountain looms over me. I shiver as darkness fills my eyes as the doors of the mountain hall open. Without a single question of who I am, Dwarves clamp shackles onto my wrists. They drag me to their King and I don't fight back.

I am shoved to my knees and I attempt to hide a smirk. I am now the same height. I think the small creatures notice my slight smirk since they shove the back of my head.

My neck cracks and I cringe. I open my jaw in hopes to stretch out the pain rushing through my face. I raise my head up releasing the pain in my neck. The King of Makya stands before me, his hand resting under my chin.

"Lady Laerune."

"Mim.

"King Mim." He corrects me.

"I don't think titles are necessary." I am attempting to hide my nerves with sarcasm. "I mean no harm to your kingdom. All I have come here for is to release my friends from your imprisonment."

He almost sort of waddles in a way and I bite my cheek to stop any sound that threatens to escape my mouth. Laughter in this situation would bring me a quick death.

"I require a price."

He faces the many jewels surrounding his throne. I swallow my pride. *Will my fortune be enough?* His dark eyes glare in the light of the candles as he reaches for the sword leaned up against his throne.

"Name it."

"You." I knew this in the back of my mind when I decided to leave Lithien. But I was hoping that jewels or coin would be more of an option to persuade him.

Mim's hair is braided into his salt and peppered beard and I try to focus on how many times Etta has braided my hair into intricate patterns. *I want to be at home.* This was a mistake.

A chill falls down my spine. I prepared myself for this, but his words make me shudder. "The release of Avon and Tolendeil, in good condition and safe escort to Lithien, for me?" Mim nods his head. "Deal," I speak with as much confidence as I can muster.

"Deal."

I look up at him as the Dwarves bind me with more chains. They push out Avon and Tolendeil and they are set out for their return trip to Lithien. I hope they can find a way to get me out of this before too long.

Avon struggles against his restraints as he attempts to fight towards me. I simply shake my head. "I'll be okay." I whisper.

A look of hopelessness falls over his face as he looks into my eyes. My best friend begins to scream as the throne room doors are closed behind them. I knew when I came here that it wasn't going to be easy for Avon to just leave without a fight.

I turn my head forward, prepared for what is to come.

My eyes narrow in Mim's direction.

"You will only have that fight in your eyes for so long."

My eyes wander around the throne room. Giant walls made out of jewels rise to the great height of the mountain. The color of them bounces off of the light from the braziers.

"Now, your friend Avon told me a few things about you. It took him a while, but the whip sure got him talking." He splashes the contents of his glass in my face. "He told me that you are The Pathway. I expected so. Your name was becoming too popular around the black markets." Red wine dribbles down my face.

Mim then raises his blade; slicing it at my face, sending blood dripping down my cheek and onto my green dress. *Not like it was once of my favorite gowns.*

I turn my head away in hopes that he doesn't see the pain that scrunches in my face.

One of his guards then pushes a barrel out in front of me, its contents containing water. I shake my head, trying to back away from the barrel of water.

This was a mistake.

Mim grabs me by my hair and shoves my head down into the bucket. The world seems to spin and I shut my eyes. My lungs and stomach clench up and I hold my breath for as long as I can. There's only darkness.

When he pulls my head up, water drips down from my face, soaking my clothes. He doesn't give me a chance to catch my breath before I am shoved back into the water. This time he keeps me under for much longer.

He is trying to drown me.

The panic rises in my stomach and air is the only thing I can keep my mind on. My lungs burn like the forges in this very mountain itself. I involuntarily take a breath, letting the water flow to my lungs.

This would surely mean death for me.

"I told you that you would be mine." Mim laughs, throwing me towards the stairs of his throne and chaining my hands to it. "My jewel. My most prized possession. People will pay your weight in jewels."

I'm not the first to be chained to these steps. "You're a bastard!" I yell; my lungs still burn. He walks towards me, his knife in his hand.

I refuse to give up.

It wasn't right to come here alone.

"What did you say?" He growls.

"You. Are. A. Bastard," I spit in his face and he takes his dagger, slicing at my chest. The blood drips down, seeping through my green dress that is already ripped and torn.

"Bring the whip!" Mim screams. "You will no longer be a jewel. But a pile of rubble in my mountain. No longer a beautiful woman. But an ugly *whore*." His voice growls, rumbling through the carved out mountain.

It wasn't right to come here.

He forces me to turn around; forcing the front of my body against a diamond jeweled wall. I close my eyes, preparing for the whip to snap. It echoes, the snap delayed for a moment, but it then rips through my skin, stinging. I hiss, dropping to my knees in pain. I lean my head back. It falls forward soon after.

The whip cracks again and I can feel the blood drip down my back, the cuts burning, searing in pain. The whip cracks two more times before he stops and places his hands on my face. Tears stream down my face as I begin to sob. I don't care about my dignity. I have never been through pain like this. I would take an arrow to my side any day.

"You are still a jewel to me if you wish to behave."

"Never," *I will not let this Dwarf dwindle my spirit.*

He leaves the throne room and I sigh. My body seems numb and I shake. Footsteps echo back through the room. Mim returns with another Dwarf very similar to himself.

"I would like you to meet my son." Mim turns to the other, younger Dwarf. "Doesn't she remind you of someone?"

"Yes. The Elven Queen. What was her name?"

"Lauralaethee."

The son nods his head. "Her eyes are the same. Holding the same spirit that we broke after she was only here a week."

A few windows allow light to shine into the dimly lit room. They are far above me.

Mim's son smiles while unsheathing an iridescent dagger. He holds my shoulder, pressing the dagger into the skin around my collarbone. I would have thought his dagger was made of stars if it didn't hurt me as much as it does.

I bite my lip, trying to refrain from screaming as he pulls his dagger down from my collarbone to the beginning of my chest. I look up as Mim's son moves away. He seems to be admiring the work he has done. Blood drips down from my lips.

I remember Luthias' mother having the same scar that ran down from her collarbone to the end of her chest. Some say that it traced down to her left leg.

I close my eyes as I envision my father holding me in his arms and singing Lyraesel's healing chant.

Earth below, clouds above.
I will fill your dark with love.
Lyraesel will wake the morning sun
And we will be renewed again.

My eyelids burst open as the melody echoes through the hall. A woman escapes the darkness, but she sings a different song; the anthem of Lithien.

Lauralaethee, the deceased queen of Lithien, caresses my face as she kneels before me. She wipes a tear away with her thumb.

"I want to go home." I lean into her touch.

"You must stay strong. I know it hurts." She turns away, a tear running down her pale cheek. "Be strong. Help will be here soon." She walks down the hall, disappearing into the light of the jeweled walls.

I want to go home.

I try to rise to my feet. My legs shake in protest, but I manage.

A Dwarven woman enters the hall. She pauses, her jeweled skirts swishing. She looks at me and then to Mim.

"Husband? What are you doing to that girl?"

"What she deserves."

"No woman should ever deserve this." She rushes to his side, grabbing at his arm. Her large brown eyes are filled with worry.

I would have counted her as pretty if I wasn't in this situation. I would have loved to sit down and speak with her about the ancient history of Dwarves.

I turn to look at her, my eyes filled with sadness, pleading for her to help me. *Please.* I refuse to plead for mercy out loud.

"Do you see this, wife?" He walks over to the fireplace, pulling a metal rod from its embers. I look at the end of it. It's shaped with Dwarven ruins. I look down at my wrist, seeing the other brand of Nadien peeking through my sleeve.

I am simply the property of my enemies.

He takes my wrist, seeing the other brand. "I see that you are starting a collection." He places the iron brand on my wrist. It sears my skin. I only look away; as if the pain is silent and not pushing at my bones or trying to make me scream.

"I will not give in," I tell him, my eyes steady, and my hands shaking.

He only chuckles and then walks away. "Son, you can do the rest."

Mim's son walks towards a cabinet, choosing from different colored vials of unknown concoctions. First, he rubs herbs into my already stinging back and then forces one of those concoctions into my mouth, my head automatically spinning. I blink my eyes, trying to make the dizziness go away, but it seems impossible.

"Please take me home, help me." I beg him, but he only pushes a barrel of water closer to me, forcing my head into it.

My lungs begin to burn again and when I am allowed to resurface a knife is again brought upon me.

I beg him to stop and my mind slightly fumbles at memories. My vision blurs.

I collapse to the floor, my whole body shaking, my muscles screaming for something to ease the never-ending pain. "Please stop. Please stop."

The horrid concoction I was forced to drink earlier seems to wear off. Mim stands before me.

"A week here already and she is still alive. I am impressed." Mim chuckles. "She doesn't look well, does she?" He continues to smirk. "I wouldn't have given her up if Tasar didn't come here himself."

"A week?" *Why hasn't anyone come for me yet?*

"Yes. A week. You can give up now." He caresses my beaten face. "They have finally come to retrieve you."

"No," I whisper and he disappears with his son down the hall. "No," I repeat the word over and over again. *No. No. No.* I shake violently.

My wrists are so small and covered in blood that I can slip out of my restraints. I back myself into the corner, frightened by every shadow that seems to constantly pass by. A shadow walks towards me from the hall and I back away more, but there is nowhere else to go. *No. No.* "No."

"LaRue?" The shadow questions. I look up, seeing a dark haired Elf with familiar, earth brown eyes. "It's me. It's Tasar." He reaches his hand out. "It's time to go home."

I try to rise to my feet, but I fall. Tasar's arms are there to catch me before I hit the ground. "Home?"

"Yes. I am going to take you home."

Tasar picks me up, his hand behind my back and the other under my legs. I cry, the pain in my back is unbearable. "What did they do to you?"

There are other Elves outside of the mountain. Tasar carries me to a cart pulled by a horse. It's filled with soft furs and he sets me carefully down onto them. He climbs onto the cart, sitting down next to me. "Everything is going to be okay." He reassures me while assessing my wounds.

"Is Avon and Tolendeil safe?"

"Yes."

I close my eyes as the cart starts to move, the wheels bumping over rocks and roots. I just want to go home.

As we enter the gate of Lithien I open my eyes, seeing that the courtyards are being scrubbed clean from the blood that was shed over them only a week ago. Maids raise their heads, placing their hands over their foreheads to shield their eyes from the blinding sun. The furs that I have been laid on are now covered in a thick layer of blood, soaking through the back of my dress. *Well, what's left of my dress.*

The cart stops, the horse's hooves becoming silent. "LaRue?" Tasar looks at me. "I am going to have to pick you up." I attempt to nod my head as he again places his hand against my raw back and his other under my legs. He tries to be careful, trying to find the best way to pick me up without further hurting me.

I am then carried to the closest room instead of the healers which is much further down the hall. Healers rush in, their medical supplies in hand. I try to back away thinking that they will hurt me more, but Tasar reassures me that they won't do any harm and that they are only here to help.

He disappears, but then quickly returns with Elora in tow. "Remember Elora, right? She is a healer too. Would you feel more comfortable with her healing you?"

"Yes."

I let them proceed even though they are causing me great pain. I would much rather complain and have them stop altogether, but I know I must be healed. My body is numb, covered in blood and they have to remove my torn dress. It's nothing but rags now, just a tattered piece of silk that used to be beautiful. *I am tattered and once beautiful.*

Elora attempts to keep a smile on her face, but the seriousness shines through her blue eyes. She nods her head as she assesses the damage that has been done to me. I watch her with curious eyes.

Tasar's voice raises from behind the closed door.

"I told you what would happen if we left her there for too long! I barely was able to get her out of there. You owe me Luthias Faen." I have never heard such harsh words come from Tasar before. "The Dwarves rubbed an herb into her back that suppresses magical healing. This means her injuries will have to heal naturally."

Tasar reenters the room. Etta and Tasar help me walk to the next cleaner room.

I breathe in the fresh air as the strong smell of iron dissipates.

Tasar grins as Elora attempts to make me more comfortable. She fluffs the pillows as I lay down. Tasar dismisses himself and Chalsarda takes his place. She sits in a chair by my bedside. She just stares at me, her green eyes saddened yet still curious.

The door opens and I slowly turn my head to see who enters. Elora straightens her back quickly. My mind is put into sudden panic and I try to sit up, trying to back away from the intruder. Why didn't he come save me? He said two days.

"Luthias." Elora raises her hands to signal him to stay still. "I don't think now is a good time." She senses my panic filling the room as Luthias steps closer. "She isn't herself."

"But I need to see her."

"Now is not the time." Her voice is stern.

"No. I need to talk to her."

I place my hands over my ears as I bring my knees to my chest. "Stop. Leave." I tell them as I begin to shake violently.

Luthias' shoulders fall as he exits the room. Elora returns to my side as Chalsarda sets a bowl of soup by my bedside. She places her hand on my lower arm, but I pull away quickly. The brand that Mim gave me is still tender.

"Get some sleep, okay."

I find myself waking with a jolt as sweat pours from my forehead. I shiver and jump as I notice that Chalsarda is in front of me.

"It's just me. It's just Chalsarda." She calms me, my heart beginning to beat slower. "Nightmare?" I nod my head and she walks to the table, returning with a glass of water in her freckled hands. She helps me sit up, placing a pillow behind me. She sits back down, pulling her chair closer to my bedside.

"Do you want to tell me what happened?"

"No."

She changes the subject as my sudden reply. "Avon and Tolendeil made it back safely."

I hand her the glass of water and Chalsarda stares at the brands on my wrists. She quickly adverts her eyes as if they were some sort of sin or imperfection.

"Can you get Avon?" My stomach turns and as she leaves I turn to grab the trash bin at the side of my bed. The contents of my lunch are no longer mine

I pull the blanket closer to my chest. Avon soon enters. His face looks paler than usual and his eyes look sunken in. He has been crying because his eyes are crystal blue. He caresses my face.

"How do I apologize?" I am silent as he speaks. "I shouldn't have told Mim that you were The Pathway. He wouldn't have hurt you so much. He might have even let you go."

"Mim hurt you too."

Avon holds my gaze. "I'm okay."

"No, you aren't."

Avon sits down onto the end of the bed. He grabs his wrist as he rubs his thumb over his brand.

"Did they do anything to Tolendeil?"

"No. Mim didn't think she had any information that would be useful to him." We both sit in silence. Avon's eyes fall to my brands. One from Nadien and one from Makya. "It disgusts me that they think you are like property. No one owns you."

"I only own myself."

Again there's a moment of silence. "What do we do now?" Avon breaks the emptiness of the silence.

"We grow." I let a tear drop from my left eye. "We become stronger than what we were before. We won't let something like this happen ever again." I reach for his hand as I sink further into the blankets. "I don't want to be alone."

"Do you want me to stay here?"

He moves over to the chair, but I grab his arm. I lift the covers and he lays down by my side. We keep our backs together as I pull the blankets closer to my body. "Thank you for being my friend."

"Thank you for not giving up on me," he sighs. "I'm sorry for being jealous, and rude. And immature. And selfish." I imagine him rolling his eyes as he lets out a soft laugh.

I reach over for his hand. "All that matters is that you are still here. I need my best friend."

"I missed your wedding." Avon sighs deeply.

I giggle, the action hurting my back. "You threw a dagger in my shoulder."

Avon chuckles, his raven-colored hair falls over his shoulder. "Did you and Luthias get your wedding night?" His shoulders tense at the question.

"Yes." We both roll over to face each other. "The night I found out I was leaving. I didn't think we would have another chance." I am silent for a second. "I haven't bled this month." I feel embarrassed telling Avon this. "Do you think I could be with child?"

"Do you think you are?" *Elves usually have great intuition.*

"If I am, I'm not sure I want to be. I have this target on my back and I don't want my child to die with me." I place a hand over my stomach. *I know my child is there.*

Avon closes his eyes. "What do you think is going to happen to us?"

"I think I'm going to die," I confess to him the feeling that I have had for a very long time. "One can only escape death so many times. I feel like it looms over me."

Avon chuckles. "No one can kill Laerune Aduial. Not even the Electa."

"Do you think that? You think that they will show mercy if I don't bring them what they want? They are going to use me. I know that."

Avon looks concerned as he searches for the tiredness in my eyes. I nod my head as I roll over to face my back to him. Avon does the same.

"They are going to talk about us, you know?"

"What do you mean?"

Avon again rolls over and runs his hand down the length of my arm. "Us. Together in this room. You dismissing Luthias. They'll talk."

"They always do."

He sighs. "I am tired of the rumors about me. I wish everyone could see that I have the same status."

"Actually a higher status than most. You are the heir to my father's throne. You are his apprentice. My father may call himself a Lord, but his rank is a King. Which makes you a Prince of Ambrose."

"I don't feel like a Prince."

"Look at the garments you adore." I turn over to run my hand down the buttons of his silver tunic. "How many dinners you have attended being my consort. Friend consort." When we were younger many people called Avon my consort. I would get so frustrated that I ended up just calling him my friend consort.

"I've missed this." He tells me. "I miss sneaking into your room to just talk."

"It's been so long." I cry.

"I knew the day that you left Ambrose that our friendship wouldn't be the same. You're a married female and I am considered an outsider. If your father even appointed me to be Lord of Ambrose, I would not be favored by the people."

"Everyone is an outsider in Ambrose. Most of them come from other places searching for new beginnings. I think they would favor you. You are just like them. You have been through a similar situation."

His hand reaches for mine as his fingers fall into place beside my own. "All I care about is protecting you. I took an oath, LaRue. One that I plan on keeping till the day I die. And if I die, then I will carry that oath with me."

I sit up in bed rubbing my eyes as the sun shines through the curtains. Avon is gone as if he never even was here. I look to the chair by my bedside and I breathe in deeply as I notice the room is no longer empty.

I try to move my legs to the side of the bed, the pain in my bones and muscles protesting. My feet touch the floor and I wrap the blanket around my body. I shiver, my whole being telling me to lay back down, but I take a step towards the window. *I have to keep moving to remain calm.*

I don't dare to look back as he swiftly steps towards me, his movements quiet like the wind. He reaches his hand out to touch me, but I feel his arm fall to his side.

"It wasn't my intention to leave you there for so long. They wouldn't let me leave the Healing houses."

"I know." I still keep my back to him. I let a single tear fall down my face and I watch as it drops onto the stone floor. "I am ruined. I am no longer beautiful."

"LaRue-"

"How could you love someone who is no longer beautiful?" *The words from Mim echo in my head.* I am nothing but an ugly whore.

"You are still beautiful in my eyes."

I allow the blanket to dip down my back, showing my scars from Mim's whip. I give him a moment to look before I turn towards him allowing him to see my face and chest covered in scars. "I am ruined."

"No Laerune." He places his hands upon my face. "You are only a map. A story upon your body." He traces over a scar with his fingers. His touch tickles my skin.

I move away from his touch and he backs away. I walk over to the bed, my movements slow and restrained. He watches me, making sure that I am not about to fall over anytime soon.

I lay back down upon the bed, my back protesting, forcing me to lay on my side. I am still healing. I want to stay here forever so no one can see the monster I have turned into. I am ugly and no one should see me this way.

"They're dismissing you today," Luthias says. "You can walk, you'll be fine."

"I'll be fine?"

"Yes. You always are."

"You do not know what I have been through Luthias Faen." I turn my head to look out the window.

"Everyone is going to love you the same LaRue."

"They are going to take one look at me and be frightened. Not even Chalsarda wanted to speak to me."

"They're your family. They won't care."

I roll over, facing away from him.

Luthias stands away from the bed. "Avon was here all night."

I catch his gaze as he dares to step closer. "Is that a problem?"

"No, but you do know that rumors are spreading already. But there is no problem. He's your best friend and I know that you need him right now."

"I know you need time, but you still must prove to everyone that you are strong."

"Then let's show them."

Chapter 5

A fork clatters to the ground; metal against stone echoes through the hall and I flinch. Luthias takes my arm, trying to avoid cuts and bruises as he leads me to the dining table.

I rip my arm from his grip as my back straightens its posture. I don't need to be guided.

I cover half my face with my hair as I try my best to keep my eyes averted from the others. But they all still stare. Eyes wander to every scar that is visible through my clothing. Tasar attempts to change the subject and avert the staring eyes from my face.

"Are the healing houses emptying?" Tasar muffles through a mouthful of what I would assume is potatoes.

"A little at a time." Elora answers. She had been helping there since I returned from Ambrose.

I slouch in my chair, pushing my food around on my plate. But the pain in my back forces me up right. Everyone still stares. Tolendeil clears her throat.

"How are you Laerune?"

"I'm alright. How are you?" I still keep my head down as I force emotion into my voice.

"I made sure all of your things were brought back before they were put onto the ship." She tells me and I nod my head in thanks.

I sit up, dismissing myself as I leave the dining hall. It's not long before Tasar returns to tell me that Sentier has arrived back in Lithien. He guides me outside.

Sentier's smile dissipates as I am led to the courtyard where he has just arrived. His eyes look saddened and I turn away from him, setting my eyes upon two Elves, not from our kingdom.

They are clad in Dwarvish and human clothing, nothing like our own attire. Their hair is a bright red, very much like Chalsarda's fiery tresses. I watch how they walk and how they act. They are undoubtedly siblings. The siblings walk up to Luthias and me, they bow, their heads almost touching the ground. Usually, Elves use a small gesture; a simple hand over the heart.

"I am Deulara and this is my brother Daralien. We have journeyed here from the south."

"It is an honor to meet you, LaRue. We have heard many stories about your courage and bravery on the battlefield." The other speaks proudly. "We are thankful for the sacrifices you have made to appease the Electa."

"Thank you," I speak rather timidly, not wanting to say anything else.

"I would've expected someone as renowned as you to be a little louder." Daralien, the brother, laughs.

I look to Luthias, not knowing what to say to the brother and sister. "She has been through a lot over this past month. She is usually the loudest person I know." He smiles and I smile back. "If you will excuse us." Luthias politely places his hand over his heart and bows his head.

Sentier walks towards us, a smile plastered on his once emotionless face. "I see you are both-" He hesitates. "I am afraid I have spoken too soon." His hand reaches to my scarred arms and then to my face, but he thinks the action as inappropriate for Sentier folds his arms in front of himself. "What happened?"

I am thankful for Luthias' reply. "Mim. He took Avon and Tolendeil as prisoners. For their freedom, it was hers."

"Out of anything you could've done, you gave up your freedom? He could've killed you! You could've sent my whole army to save your friends." I can't tell if he is upset or concerned. But, he wraps his arms around me while placing his head on top of mine. I flinch. "I am glad you are safe."

"I didn't want to make it a big deal."

"A big deal? Losing you would be a big deal."

🖋

The wooden door of Sentier's study squeaks open and he motions for the two of us to sit down. He pours two glasses of wine and hands one of the goblets to Luthias. I attempt to pay attention, but my mind wanders to the ajar window. A cup of tea is placed in my hands instead of the red wine that the other two sip carelessly.

"LaRue?" Sentier asks, worry in his eyes. "Are you okay?"

"Yes, I am fine. Just a bit distracted." My words come out as a cough as I grab at my chest. But I shine a smile in their direction to prove them wrong. Hopefully, they don't see through my lies, I don't want to cause them any more worry. The weight of the kingdom is already on their shoulders.

"Okay." He turns to face the window. Maybe I had drawn his curiosity towards the view of the forest. "As you know, I had journeyed to Lindalin. Azariah and Elender had asked for my council. Rumors are spreading that Mim is currently creating an alliance with the enemy."

"What enemy?"

This stops Sentier and causes him to think. Moments pass as he places both hands onto the top of his desk. "It's hard to tell who our enemies are these days, isn't it?" A huff of breath escapes his throat. "But per usual, the troublesome Nolan still likes to bother us even in the afterlife. It seems as if Mim has decided to take over Nolan's plans to ruin our kingdom. I assume they were allies from the start."

While shaking my head I become slightly more focused. "But that doesn't make any sense. Mim gave us troops for the Peace War."

"Then he must have spoken to Navain or Nolan after the war. Peace maybe wasn't what he ended up wanting."

Sentier straightens his back. "I want to plan a raid on Makya. To show him and the other kingdoms that we still have power."

My husband whips around to face his father. "You can't be completely sure about this," Luthias shakes his head while pointing towards me. "You can't agree with this."

"Mim did try to kill me. If he died, I would have no mercy."

"You can't base on killing a ruler because of what happened."

"I believe in her intuition." Sentier snaps.

I follow their conversation back and forth but they are getting nowhere.

"Trust your wife, Luthias Faen."

"Maybe I could if she trusted me back."

The comment is hurtful, but I push it to the back of my mind. Sentier's eyes sadden as he looks to his son and then to me.

"LaRue?" Sentier almost whispers. "Why don't you go and get some rest." I nod my head, thankful for the excuse to leave. I am led out of the study and the door is closed behind me. I feel so dizzy that I back up against the wall, sliding down onto the floor. I can hear Luthias and Sentier talking angrily to each other through the closed door and I shut my eyes.

"She is sick, can't you see this!" Sentier yells.

"She'll be fine, father."

"Why did you leave her there for a week?" He growls. "She's not to her full strength, physically or mentally. Her mind wanders easily. She is never going to be the same."

"She'll be fine." I still don't know the reason why I was left there for so long.

"You know what your brother went through. You remember how your mother was!"

"Why did you let my mother spend a week in Makya?" The comment sends an eerie silence from behind the doorway.

Sentier pauses. "She was lost. I did not know where she was!"

"And you know what my mother promised after."

Tasar struts down the hall, his hands in his pockets. *Perfect timing.* "Are you coming tonight?"

"Where?" I hate that my voice comes out in an annoyed tone.

"There's a party for Sentier's arrival home. And also for you being brought back from Makya."

I stand up, my head spinning. I reach out for the wall, using it as support. I nod my head. "It seems that I am still out of the loop around here." Tasar places his hand on my back and helps me walk back to my room. Etta smiles as I enter my living quarters and she sets out my clothes like she used to do when I was a child. I proceed to change.

The dress has an open back and I stare at myself in the mirror, disapproving of how I look. The dress showed too many scars; it showed the worst ones. I barely hear Luthias as he enters the room. He hugs me as I start to cry. He places his hands onto my scarred back. His touch is gentle as his hands move from each scar as if my body was a book and my imperfections words.

My husband places his head in the crook of my neck as he mumbles an apology. "I shouldn't have doubted you."

I stare into the mirror. "It's okay."

"You have your reasons for why you have pulled away from everyone and that is valid. I have no validation to not trust you." He rubs my shoulders lightly. "Take your time." Luthias steps back while folding his arms across his lower half.

I stumble while putting my shoes on and I notice Luthias resisting to catch my arm. A knock echoes off the door and I give a thankful sigh as Tasar and Avon enter the room. I have labeled them in my head as my *Saviors* from Makya.

"Change of plans!" Tasar hollers. "We are going to go out and do our own thing."

Avon's approach to the subject is more understandable. "We thought it would be a better idea for you to get out of the kingdom for a night and have some fun with the three of us."

🌿

I was thankful for the opportunity to change out of my more festive clothing and into a more comfortable pair of pants. And it only takes us an hour to escape from the kingdom's borders and to the nearest inn. A few Elves had the same idea, but the area was mostly filled with humans drunk out of their minds.

The activities for the night are found outside around a large fire. Drinks are beginning to be passed around and Tasar makes sure that each of our hands is filled before anyone else's.

Avon watches me closely as I stare at the amber-colored drink in front of me. He turns to whisper in my ear. "Are you sure that's a good idea?"

40

I hesitate as I lower the drink from my lips. "You're right."

I dump the cup's contents into the grass before Tasar returns. Tasar chuckles and attempts to hand me a second drink. I refuse.

He is clearly drunk already and most likely started his partying before we even left the kingdom.

"Would you, my lady, want to participate in a competition?" He burps.

"No, thank you."

Tasar's face drops as he puts his hands up in the air. "If you aren't going to drink, then please, at the least, dance."

"Laerune Aduial." Avon bows in my direction as I eye the men and women dancing around the fire.

My gaze turns towards Luthias. I can tell he is refraining from stepping in, but when was the last time Avon and I got to do something fun? My husband nods his head in approval.

Although my back and body hurt with each movement, I smile. Avon is a horrible dancer and he will take that as a compliment.

But, the dimly lit field and the drunk people seems to make him less self-conscious as he spins me around. He grabs my shoulders as he rocks me back and forth.

It reminds me of when the two of us would sneak into the ballroom in Ambrose and dance absurdly without the fear of anyone seeing us.

I would hike my skirts up so high that if my grandmother ever did see, she would blush beet red and most likely have my head on a silver platter. But Avon, he would sing in the most off tune, horrendous voice the world has ever heard.

The music pauses and my stomach turns. I grab at my tummy as Avon stops laughing.

"You look like you're going to be sick."

"I think I am."

Avon reaches down for my legs and picks me up into his arms. It seems as if Luthias has already gotten the memo and has Tasar wrapped around his shoulders.

We make our way back down the trail.

"Luthias," Avon calls. "I think there is something you need to know."

I wrap my arms tighter around Avon's neck as I brace myself for what Avon is about to say. I don't want Luthias to know that I might be pregnant. But what my best friend says is not what I intended. "We are being followed."

"Aren't we always?"

Avon sets me down onto my feet and I stumble towards the nearest tree. My stomach flips upside down and I brace myself as I lower to my butt.

Avon shoves me to the ground as he places his hand over my mouth. I hear Luthias push Tasar towards the more forested area of the road. I attempt to keep myself calm as I feel the panic rising in my lower stomach.

Something snaps inside of me that brings me back to my time in Makya. I kick my legs in an attempt to escape. I manage to get to my feet as I begin to run through the now dark forest.

I manage to somehow get myself all turned around. I reach my hands out as I bump into Avon. A drunken Tasar stumbles behind him. I fall backward as the wind is knocked from my lungs. Avon's cold hands set me up onto my feet. I reach out for a familiar embrace. But my stomach flips once again.

Suddenly I get sick and it goes all over his shoes. He looks up and sighs. "This is not the first time this has happened."

Luthias comes into view as I finally get the warm embrace I was searching for. Avon slightly rocks me back and forth. He would often do this when we were younger and when I was having a bad day. It was his way of making me smile. Especially since neither of us was that great of dancers.

"Lucky for us, whoever was following us, no longer is."

Tasar lands with a thud to the ground as he begins to pluck the grass from the forest floor. "He'll be fine in an hour or two," Luthias reassures us. "It's not the first time." My husband sighs heavily as he sits down next to Tasar. "Why don't you take LaRue back and I'll stay with Tasar."

Avon seems extremely hesitant about leaving the two of them alone in the woods. "Are you sure?" I hang onto Avon tighter.

"We'll be fine. Just go. She needs to get back. It was a bad idea taking her."

"Come on." Avon places his hand on my lower back as I begin to stumble down the path. He doesn't speak again until we are out of earshot from Luthias and Tasar. "You know that the other night people did end up talking about us."

"What did they say?" I trip over a root growing out of the ground. Avon squats down so he can carry me on his back.

"That we aren't just friends. The word affair rings down Lithien's hallways like a bell. They also are wondering why you haven't produced an heir."

My eyes glance behind me as the forest seems to grow darker than before. "So, us returning together tonight is going to make it worse?"

"I honestly don't care. Everyone important to us knows that we would never do that. The kingdom just likes to make up drama to make their boring lives interesting."

I place my neck onto his shoulder. "I wish I had a boring life."

Avon pauses for a moment while he assesses the fork in the path ahead of us. He takes the left path. "Do you really? All your life you wanted an adventure."

"I don't want my whole life to be boring. I just want a moment to sit down and just, finally, breathe."

"I understand." Avon heaves me up higher onto his back. "It's nice to have some time alone and just reflect. Since Caldon passed I have done a lot of self-reflecting."

I sigh as I wrap my arms tighter around Avon. "Do you blame me?"

I feel his face contort in confusion. "For?"

Saying his name pains my heart. "For his death."

"Things happen for a reason, LaRue. You can't blame yourself for everything that happens. It's all just part of life. Just be thankful. Caldon sacrificed himself for you and your cause."

"That's what makes me feel guilty."

Avon keeps his words simple. "No." I don't push the subject more. The gate of Lithien comes closer to view. "Luthias should start listening to me. I know faster ways of getting back, but he insists he knows everything."

The gate creaks open and the guards' give us suspicious glances. They quickly avert their eyes as I remind them that the Prince and Tasar are on their way.

The walk to my room is only filled with empty footsteps as Avon finally sets me back onto my feet. "Are you staying with me tonight?"

"Might as well. I'll wait for Luthias to come back."

Avon finds a comfortable spot on the couch in my bedroom as I make my way towards the bed. The once green blankets have been replaced with a more cheerful, yellow color. Maybe Luthias had noticed how dull it looked in here when the autumn leaves started to fall this week.

My best friend lounges back onto the couch as he folds his arms over his head and props his legs up on the edge of the tufted furniture. I fold my legs up onto my bed as Avon stares at the painting of Ambrose upon the wall. He points towards it as his blue eyes widen.

"Luthias painted that?"

I nod my head yes. "He thought a piece of home would be nice for me to see every day." I stand back up to my feet as I reach up to admire the painting closer. I set myself into the space between the back of the couch and Avon's legs. "I miss it actually. I think I miss my family more than Ambrose. I haven't actually talked to Eryn in months."

"I was in Everford a few weeks ago. She's huge already. She thinks she's having twins."

"When was the last time you visited Ambrose?"

"Not since you were last there."

I roll my eyes. "My father is probably begging you to come back."

"Actually, no. I think that he likes the thought of me with you. He worries that you are alone here. I've tried reassuring him that you have made friends, but-"

"But he worries about every tiny detail."

He hums his answer as he shifts his legs. Avon pulls the blanket from the top of the couch. "You feeling okay?"

"Just a tad bit nauseous. I'm trying not to think about it."

"And?" Avon pats his belly. "Are you going to tell Lu?"

I chuckle slightly at the nickname. "I don't know yet. Things are tense as it is. I would hate it if this broke the bond between the two of us."

Avon tosses his head back as he brushes through his raven like hair. "Nothing is going to break that. It would be impossible." A small noise escapes his mouth as he stretches his arms above his head. "Just like our friendship. Nothing can break that."

I balance on the edge of the couch as I hang the painting back in its rightful place. I then crawl over Avon's legs and back into my bed. I ignore the blankets as the room is filled with the warmth from the crackling fireplace.

The weather had become much colder in the past few days and it was enough cause for the whole kingdom to start preparing for winter. The door opens as a tired Luthias and a stumbling Tasar find a seat on the opposite couch. Tasar takes up most of the sitting area, so Luthias joins me on our bed. He keeps his distance, but I close the space between us.

"I ran into Elora in the hall. She wants to speak with you in the morning."

I groan slightly as I fall back onto the bed into the heap of pillows. I just about disappear as the pillows swallow me into their comfy abyss. And just like that, I am fast asleep.

Chapter 6

The autumn breeze caresses my cheeks. As I turn the corner to enter the gardens, I see Elora. Her face drops in a tired and worn look, but happy nonetheless. She smiles and walks over to me slowly. Age seeps through her skin. Even for immortals, the harshness of the world takes its toll. For a moment we stand next to each other in silence. *A peaceful, yet short silence.*

"Are you alright?" She speaks softly. I shake my head no. "I am always here, okay?"

"Thank you, Elora."

"I have been helping with the healers as you might remember. It was the only way I was getting news about Luthias." She smiles. "I spoke with your father when he first arrived here to take you back to Ambrose. He said my talent was like no other." She takes my hand. "Avon has also been helping me improve. But he has been busy with foreign affairs lately."

I raise an eyebrow towards her. My father only spoke the truth. There was never, ever any sugar coating from him. If things weren't going to be okay, he would tell me.

"I have the power to fix wounds much deeper than the internal injury. I can heal the scars that come from them." Elora looks down at my arms with a melancholy gaze. "It will take a lot of time for each scar because they might be more difficult than others, but it can be done in time."

"Time seems to be running low for all of us. It feels like death is watching me, hanging over my shoulder. I would much rather keep my scars as a reminder. If I die, then the world shall know what happened to me." A crow sends a shrill call through the forest. It flies away, its wings almost sounding like laughter. The burn marks from where Mim and Navarre branded me are plain as day. My hand grazes across their design. I change the subject. "What of Silevel? Is she well?"

"She is a strong Elfling. Your brother, Eldar, is taking care of her right now. He said I needed a break after all that has happened."

Elora and Eldar have gotten very close from what I have heard. I haven't seen them physically showing affection though.

I have no doubt my brother has feelings for her, but she still holds onto Silvyr. When an Elf's first love dies, it is almost impossible to love another. It's a cruel part of being immortal. We may have all the time in the world, but we rarely love another.

A guard calls our names and we turn around. He rushes over, his breath uneven and heavy.

"It's Avon...he's hurt."

"Hurt? I just saw him this morning?" I last saw him sprawled out asleep on my bedroom couch. I let go of Elora's arm, running past the guard and to the healers. I swing the door open.

I back away, running into whoever stands behind me. They hold my shoulders, keeping me upright.

Blood covers about half of the floor and the healers hands are covered in that haunting crimson red. A dagger lies on the table and I finally look at Avon. His back is covered in blood and he breathes slowly, his body in shock.

"What happened?" I yell while picking up the blood-covered dagger. It had been the one that I gave Avon for his birthday a few years back. *The rise and fall of the Earth shall not separate us for we are bonded by friendship.*

"We don't know." A woman shakes and Elora quickly ties up her hair as she prepares to help. I do the same as we both wash our hands.

The woman pushes me aside. "We suspect attempted suicide."

"Suicide? Are you stupid? The knife was in his back! You think he put it there himself?" I attempt to push my way back in, but the other woman who I assume is the main healer pushes me from the room.

The door slams in my face and I refrain from pounding on the door. I sit down on the floor, the dagger still clutched in my hands. His blood covers my palms.

I walk down the hall; my hands bloody and still holding the dagger tightly in my fist. I have also gotten the staining liquid over my dress. It just about looks like I murdered somebody. The walk down the hall seems to take forever.

"What is the big deal with this princess from Ambrose anyway?" I hear somebody around the corner. "She's weak, only a little girl. She's a coward. I don't see why everyone is praising her so-"

I turn the corner, shoving the person's shoulders into the wall, she pushes me back. Blood smears around her shoulders from what remained on my hands.

"I am not a coward!"

The girl is Deulara and I knew she would be short tempered. She slaps my face, and I go to punch back. I punch her and a steady trickle of blood comes from her nose. She wipes it away, hitting me in the jaw. The taste of blood fills my mouth and I can feel the warm liquid drip down the corner of my lips.

This isn't the best way to release my emotions, but it sure is working. I punch harder, this time hitting her chest. The air escapes from her lungs and she grabs at her stomach.

Castle guards break apart the fight. I know that there will be a lecture in store for me. I am just glad my father isn't around to give it to me himself.

"I don't know what you were thinking?"

My head stays down. I don't dare to meet Sentier's eyes. "I wasn't thinking."

The look in his eyes as he whips his head around reminds me of my father. *I kinda wish my father was here. He might have gone easy on me.*

"I see that." The King of Lithien throws a washrag in my direction. I lean my head onto my right hand to wash the blood off of my cheeks. The quick contact stings and I pull the wet rag from my face. "You haven't even let the rest of you heal yet."

"Did you soak it in liquor?" The washrag plops onto the desk with a wet smack as Sentier chuckles.

"Call it your punishment."

48

I avert my eyes as Sentier crosses his arms. He sits up onto his desk; his blue robes surrounding him like a cascade of water.

He's preparing me for an important life lesson.

"You must have spoken to my father recently. You are following in his mannerisms."

Sentier's face softens. "Not everyone in life is going to like you."

"I know that." I drag out my words. "There is a list of people that would be happy to have just my ears."

"Are you curious about the price now?" He reaches across his desk for a dirty, yellowed piece of parchment. "My scouts came back with this a few days ago from a hidden port in-between Makya and Everford."

My stomach churns as sourness burns in my throat. My hand grips the page so tightly it begins to crinkle. "Twenty thousand and twelve gold pieces?" Our eyes meet as horror spreads across my face. The page flitters to the ground; crinkled edges glide across the hardwood floor.

"They aren't just hunting you either. They are searching for your oath-takers. You are safe as long as you are within the three main Elven kingdoms. Beyond that, you are open game. Warn your friends."

I put pieces together. "I don't think we are that safe in the Elven kingdoms. It has been assumed this morning that Avon had attempted suicide. The knife was in his back. And I don't think it is just a coincidence that Deulara and her brother arrived in Lithien just a few days ago."

Sentier grows serious. "I will look into it."

Chapter 7

A week passes before I can fully speak to Avon in private without healers making sure the stitches in his wound aren't breaking or guards that watch for the current "assassin" that might be at bay.

I grab his hand as he stares off into the garden. There isn't much left of it except for the last of the fall perennials.

Their yellowed flowers are already beginning to brown and fall off.

"Who tried to kill you?"

"I don't know." His responses have been short-lived recently. I grab his hand tighter. Avon's head falls; raven hair drapes across his face as blue eyes gaze west.

"You're lying."

Avon Halen looks up to me. Within his eyes emotions swim. "It was a warning."

"From who?"

"You ask so many questions."

The comment is hurtful, but I shake my head. "Who-"

"I can't tell you."

I sit back in shock as my mouth gapes open. "But this is important."

"You can't save everyone in the world."

I push myself off of the bench as I stand before him. His eyes remain in that westward direction. "I will certainly try."

"But will you spare Mim's life tonight?"

I release the breath I have been holding. The tightness in my lungs remains. Sentier has further pushed the plan of raiding Mim's mountain fortress and I have given my full support. "It may not be my choice to make." I wrap my arm around the still tender brand that Mim had left on me.

Avon lets out a simple scoff from between his pursed lips. "You know that the whole mission is based solely on you getting revenge. We don't blame you either. Mim hurt you in ways that no one here could ever imagine. The world has hurt you in a million different ways and no one will blame you for getting revenge."

I sling my bag over my shoulder as I lock my belt and sheath into place. "Goodbye, Avon."

🖋

The mountain stands before us; grey against the now painted, purple sky. My heartbeat quickens. I escaped death here. *Can I do it twice?*

Five others sit behind Luthias and me as we gaze over the rocks protecting us from the eyes of the guards standing outside. Eyes meet ours as the group awaits command.

"You didn't really give me the rundown of what the plan is." I lower my stance to sit onto my bottom.

The decision was made silently but was well known to everyone. To kill Mim, would be my ultimate choice. My choice of how, when, and where.

But imaging Mim's wife standing in the corner being held back by guards awaiting her husband's death makes me doublethink. *"Will you spare Mim's life tonight?"*

He has a son, wife, and family. A kingdom. Maybe the choice to spare him will change his point of view.

My gaze returns to the mountain.

"A raid is usually stealing something. My father didn't really give much insight. It's mostly up to you LaRue." Luthias returns his gaze to the mountain as well.

"I want to teach Mim a lesson, one that he will hopefully remember."

🌿

I pause in the hallway as steps echo behind me. I slowly turn around, afraid to be caught by a Dwarven guard. But Caolan attempts a smile as he pushes a book into his chest.

"Your thoughts are wanning. To kill a king or to spare one?"

"You're the God of Death, what will my choice be?" I turn back to analyze the rest of the hallway.

"That is information that I can't disclose to you."

"Then why are you here?" It is almost like Caolan is taunting me.

I look to his hands as his grip loosens on his book. "Well, I'm not really a fan of Dwarves and I wouldn't really care to have one like him in my halls anytime soon."

I chuckle at the comment as I reach for the throne room doors. Caolan disappears with a jingle of silky laughter floating on the air.

The throne room of Makya is silent; my footsteps echo across the floor. The room isn't empty though.

"I've been awaiting your revenge. I wouldn't have thought that the kingdom of Lithien would wait this long."

I imagine my blood upon the floor as the diamond wall catches my eye. I attempt to swallow in order to keep down my dinner.

Mim grabs his axe and walks towards me. "I do like you with all the scars. The look fits you."

I unsheathe my two daggers; swinging them in my hands I assume my fighting position. My blades mirror the starlight that now shines through the large windows carved out of the mountain.

I regret leaving my group behind to defend the others and allow me time alone with Mim.

"I made a deal with Tasar when he came to get you. I was okay with him taking you as long as you didn't return to Makya. If you did, I was allowed to kill you. But I see that you broke that deal."

"I was never told of this treaty. Tasar must have had enough faith in me that I would kill you."

Internally, my mind screams. *Protect yourself. Protect yourself.* I make my first move and my dagger hits the handle of his axe.

I lose both of my daggers and I throw my spear into Mim's shoulder. He stumbles in pain and attempts to get away from me.

I grab him by his shirt. "Caolan is watching you ever so closely. Don't make me have to carry out his deed of death."

He shakes violently. I would have thought someone like him would spit in my face and attempt to escape my grip. But he simply does nothing other than let out a soft whimper.

A voice whispers in my mind. *A vow of death, along with the mention of a God is far worse than any ending. Especially the one that deals out the card of death.*

"A daughter of a God." Mim shivers once again.

I ignore the new title. "I hope this makes you rethink who you hold an alliance with. Lithien is not weak and is prepared to bring the downfall of Makya if you make one more wrong move. We won't give out any more chances."

"I promise. Makya will be in alliance with Lithien. I promise." He shakes but continues to keep eye contact. "He threatened to ruin our kingdom."

"Who threatened?" I loosen my grip on his shirt and he rolls backwards onto the ground. "The God. Elbonare."

I move my eyes away from the Dwarf. Why would Elbonare want to have the Dwarves imprison and torture me?

Luthias enters the throne room and I step back away from Mim. I hear the heavy footsteps of another Dwarf enter the room.

"Please Laerune." The voice is thick with an accent. "I know that our kingdom hasn't had the best reputation, but we are creatures stuck in the same world like you." Mim's wife remains at a good pace from Luthias and me. "We attempted to keep our home alive by making a deal with Elbonare. We were more of, well, forced into making a deal with him." Her eyes lower in shame. "We apologize for our actions. But I am sure that you will understand that we were simply protecting our people and our home."

"You have hurt innocent people. I don't care what threats were made."

"We were forced to or our mountain would no longer be here."

"I will let you have your King and your mountain if you promise to never torture another Elf or innocent creature without discussing why this prisoner is being withheld from the world."

"We promise. We will even sign a treaty."

"Come to Lithien in a month and we will work out all of the paperwork," Luthias explains to them. "We would also like you to know that no casualties were a part of this raid on either side."

"Thank you for sparing their lives." Mim's wife replies.

"You should think about having your Queen in charge."

"We shall be off now." Luthias takes my hand in his and leads me away from the throne room and out of the mountain.

Chapter 8

Once a month, mandatory lunch occurs in the dining hall. It allows Sentier to get more insight on what is happening within his kingdom and to listen to the problems of his people. It makes him a much more personal King.

Avon sits across from me and Luthias sits to my side. Our group tends to stick together so the rest of my oath takers are in earshot. But conversation drifts down from the rest of the people of Lithien and it is entirely filled with gossip.

Avon and I seem to be at the center of this blather.

Rumors that Avon was not part of an assassination attempt, but rather he attempted to kill himself. All out of pity at the fact that I am having a supposed affair with him and he wanted to spare Luthias the pain. *Ridiculous.*

I am sure that rumor started when he entered my room the night I came back from Makya. He hadn't left until the sun rose and most would find that suspicious.

"She is still beautiful." I hear someone say down the table. They look at me. "I just wish she would smile more."

"It's sad. Too much has been put onto that young girl."

"Have you seen the scars across her face? Mim deserves to die and we should rage war against him. I wonder why she didn't kill him when she had the chance."

"Maybe she deserved it? Wouldn't the Electa protect her if she didn't?"

"Didn't you hear about her friend? He tried to kill himself and blamed it on an assailant. Maybe he felt so guilty about having an affair."

"Why would he do that? He has a wonderful life here and he should be grateful for all the opportunities he has received."

I look away from the gossiping group. They seem to never stop talking and I plop my head into my heads, no longer having much of an appetite even though it's my favorite dish today. Mashed potatoes with a side of green beans.

"Do you think she is with child yet?"

"She's glowing."

"LaRue does look a little bigger. Look at her belly."

Luthias perks his head up and drops the knife onto his plate. The whole table quiets down as he rises from his seat. "She is not with child." Luthias glares down the table. "Would you want our future heir born during a time of war? To be a target to be taken or killed?"

I was planning on confessing to Luthias about my suspicions on being pregnant, but now I feel that I can't tell him. I was even planning on going to the seamstress today to get more comfortable clothing.

I quickly wipe the tears from my face so no one will see them. I look to Luthias. He returns to his seat and grabs my hand from under the table. "Why don't you spend the day with Avon?"

Avon kicks my leg from under the table. "Will you be joining us Luthias?" He asks as he reaches for the glass of water to his right side. "I would enjoy a little time away from Lithien and wouldn't mind if you joined us."

This is a first. The two could be civil, but never would offer anything to the other.

"We could go up towards the mountains. It's just above Ambrose." He pauses. "My family used to live in a cabin up there before I lived in Ambrose."

I look at both of them. "When do we leave?" I grin brightly.

Avon chuckles. It's been a long time since I have seen him this excited about something. "We leave tomorrow." He rises from his chair, bowing his head in Sentier's direction, before he leaves the dining hall.

The crowd in the hall begins to dwindle; the gossiping group clearing off the table as they go.

"Laerune," Sentier calls. "How have you been feeling?"

"Much better. How are you?"

He grins. "I am well. I have heard that you are heading to the seamstresses today. Are you not satisfied with the clothes that we have given to you?" He raises a thick eyebrow.

"I love everything that you have given to me and I am very appreciative. I just would like something new, especially coming up into these colder months." The need for new clothes was because of the tightness that was growing in my midsection. Another sign that I am with child.

A group of females walk past. He turns around, sensing my seriousness. "What is it?"

I wait for a group of females to walk past. "I have some suspensions."

Sentier raises his eyebrow. "If it's about Deulara and Daralien, I am already keeping a close eye on them."

"No, it isn't that." I place my hand on my stomach, hoping he might get the hint, but he doesn't. "I'll just tell you later." It felt wrong to tell Sentier before telling my own husband.

*

The seamstress smiles as she admires my shape in the mirror. I wrap my arms around my belly.

"I trust you to keep this information between the two of us." This female has been my seamstress since I was barely tall enough to wear a dress and I trust her with this secret.

"Of course. It is safe with me." She pins gold and red material across my shoulders and waist.

I look into the mirror, but this seems to no longer be my memory, but someone who once stood in this very place.

Laura, Luthias' mother, grins widely into the looking glass.

"I am so large." She complains to her own seamstress. "Never did I think I would get this big."

"Hold still, Queen Laura. I don't want to prick you."

The Queen giggles. "But I am too happy." The seamstress steps away as Laura begins to sing and rub circle motions across her large belly. "Silver and brave is the prince who leaves Lithien this day. A many a story will be told of thee. His hair was red and his eye was blue. His arm is strong and his word is true. I wish in my heart that you'll be home soon."

"I haven't even left yet, Laura." Sentier wraps his arms around his wife.

"I am so jealous though. It was my idea to search for Lenair. Not yours." Her lip quivers. "Are you sure you should leave? The baby will be here soon and I don't want you to miss that."

"I can wait if my sweet wife begs me to do so."

I pull the fabric of the dress close to me as someone knocks upon the door. I see Luthias through the reflection of the mirror. His face is contorted in confusion and I prepare to break the news to him.

"There has been an Elf spotted near the East Gate."

"And?' This was the farthest thing I thought would come from my husband's mouth. The information is plain as day, but the seriousness within the lines of Luthias' forehead tells me otherwise.

"We have received information that it could be Malien." There is a pause between his words. "Avon's father."

"He's dead though."

I remember that fateful night. Avon and his parents were retreating to Ambrose for the evening. But an Orc raid had crossed onto the border. His mother was shot with an arrow and died. His father ran off and his body was never found.

❦

I pace down the hallway, folding my arms across my back. "And you want me to-"

"Use your gift of foresight." Luthias exclaims.

"And you want me to do this because?" I wait for him to answer, but he pauses.

"Just please look." Luthias begs as I sigh, letting my shoulders relax.

Using foresight forcefully is a lot of work and often doesn't help exactly the way I want it to. It's tiring and you never know how long you might be looking at the future.

58

I sit upon the bench in the hall. "Force me awake if it takes longer than ten minutes." I didn't need to be exhausted to the point of collapsing in my current condition.

He nods his head and I force my eyes to look past this day and to the future.

I now stand at the door of a small cabin; the blue lights gleam in the forest. Someone shoves future me forward into the house. Black cloaked figures follow quickly behind. The slightest gleam on Avon's face shines in the moonlight as he begins to speak with his father.

But, the vision changes quickly into a pool of blood escaping from a pale figure and then to flowers upon the forest. The images flash by too rapidly for me to fully process what I am being shown.

It slows and I find myself upon a white wall of stone with an army behind me. I turn beside me, looking at future me. I look sad, tired, and worn.

"Protect the King and his heir at all costs." She tells the woman beside her.

"What about you, my queen?"

A king is nothing without his queen.

My eyes then fall to a green forest; the ground beneath my feet soft and warm. Future LaRue kneels down, feeling the grass between her hands. Her hands then go to the crown above her head, three shining jewels glisten in its metal.

"My job is done Luthias. We are home, we can finally be happy." She seems to be talking to no one until I see Luthias enter through the forest. She stands, not looking at him, but past him. "It has been a while, hasn't it?"

"I am sorry for leaving for so long."

"You missed a lot."

"You needed me."

"I needed to see you one last time. Now, I will never see you again." Her eyes are white. *She is blind.* I will be blind.

I open my eyes to see Luthias sitting next to me, the vision is over.

"Did you find out anything?"

"Avon's father is alive. And I saw the two of them together in the future with me."

He nods his head. "In a good way or bad?"

I shake my head. "I don't know. It went by too fast." I leave out the rest of my visions.

I rise to my feet, but Sentier enters the hall. I look at Luthias and then Sentier. "Can I speak with you?" Sentier wraps his arm around mine. Maybe this time he will get the hint.

"Of course you can." Sentier's grey eyes stare into my own, as if he was trying to see if there is still the same light as before.

"What is wrong Laerune?"

I again place my hands onto my stomach. "I think I am with child."

I can sense his smile growing, but he attempts to hide it as I am not smiling in return. "This worries you doesn't it?"

I simply nod my head.

"Have you told Luthias?"

I shake my head no. I change the subject. *I don't have the heart to tell him just yet.* "I have seen my future, but I can't understand it."

"Maybe it's not to be understood."

I look out at the stone carved window. Tasar runs around with Oka at his feet. "What will happen to them?" I ask Sentier while watching Oka jump around in the chilly air.

"They will go on with their lives."

"Will they stay with me?"

"They are a part of your court. They will stay for as long as they feel is needed." I look up at him, searching for his wise smile, but it seems to be missing. "I had a court once. Full of many different people. Some my friends." His complexion turns pale. "But they decided to travel to new places, some stayed, some died. Now, there are few left."

"Why did your wife want to find Lenair?"

Sentier begins to chuckle. "Because she was curious about the stories like the rest of us. And she had just met the Golden Lord, Dehlin, who told her stories like she was a little child. She was extremely intrigued."

"I had a vision-" I begin to tell him, but he sighs deeply.

60

"A vision isn't always right, Laerune." He sighs again. "A vision isn't always clear, even what comes from our eyes isn't always right." Sentier places his hand over my eyes. "You may see darkness, but your mind gives off light. Your eyes still see, even if you are blinded, but is that right?"

"We will never know."

"Exactly." He uncovers my eyes.

I shake my head. "Our world is confusing."

Sentier turns me around to gaze at a map. "There used to be many of us. Many small villages throughout Laquilasse filled with Elves. Now, there are only three Elven kingdoms and very few of us left."

"What about across the sea? Where the Gods are?"

"The last ship sailed away empty. If the Electa wants to send another one, then they will. But I doubt it will be for you." Sentier winks.

I pause. "Can we build one?"

Sentier turns his head quickly towards me. "And who would have the mind to build this...ship?"

"I can design it. Tasar can build. I am sure we can round up the people to help him." I place my hands in my dress pockets. "We aren't far from a port. Maybe two miles to the North."

"Port Nala."

"It's empty, but I think it can still be used."

His face again twists in confusion. "How do you know this Laerune?"

"I have studied your library quite often." I grin.

"Go, have fun with Avon and Luthias. And I'll think about the port. And don't stress about possibly having a child. It could just be a coincidence of having the symptoms. You have been malnourished." He leaves the hall, his hand touching the brands on my wrist. He pauses, turns back towards me and grabs my wrist. "Who did this?" He pulls up my sleeve.

The two brands are just as clear as the first day I had received them. "Navain and Mim. They each gave me one." I pull my arm away. "It's just a reminder of their power."

"Of ones who should not have power."

"I am going to go pack." I tell him, leaving the hall. I wrap my hand around the brands, trying to hide them.

I raise my head as the aura of the room begins to change into something dark. My heart beats in protest and I grip my wrist tighter.

The figure before me removes its hood, revealing long black hair that cascades down his back. Pale skin and a grey aura rather than black haunts the hall.

"Hello Laerune." His face is best described as kind, something I wouldn't have expected from this *God*. "I am Caolan, the God of Death." He places his hands up. They are scarred, yet they look warm and welcoming. My soul feels as if it is melting into a puddle of sunshine. "I've come to help you."

My stomach finally drops, the puddling feeling leaving my body. Death isn't here to take me. Not today at least. I didn't think that him appearing in front of me in Makya was real. I thought that I had only imagined Death before me.

"You are nervous, why?"

My words don't seem to form right. "I…uhh. Umm."

"Come on. Spit it out."

I gulp down my courage. "Why are you here?"

"I have always been here. I am here to help and wish for your help in exchange." He takes his hands in mine and I shiver. Not at their coldness, but at the fact that I am linking palms with death himself. "All those visions of yours are people that you will need. When you see them die, I am giving you a chance to save them in the future. But there is someone, that I need to die and I don't see you failing to save them in the future. You must kill them in order for me to continue to help you."

"Who?" Curiosity buzzes within me.

"Send me Avon and you shall receive my army and support. His death won't just be for my mere amusement. I need his aid within my halls."

"Kill Avon?" I whisper, but Death no longer stands before me. I scan the area, but it seems as if he has vanished in thin air.

And the child as well. His voice echoes through my head.

Luthias touches my shoulder, making me jump. "I heard voices. Who were you talking to?" He asks; his red hair shining in the sun that beams through the windows.

"Myself." I whisper again, still searching the hall.

Luthias wraps his arm around my waist. "I'll help you pack."

We enter the parlor of our room and Oka jumps on the bed. Tasar must have brought her back just before we entered. I move to the dresser, pulling out warm clothes since the cabin is in the mountains and winter is approaching. I look at my bow that is leaned up against my armor stand.

"Do you think I need it?" I question him.

"It would be best if you brought it. I don't know what the forests of Ambrose are like at this moment."

"They have always been quiet. Would Orcs make their way down there if my father still rules?"

"Of course they would. They don't have well working minds like us. They don't care if they die."

I ponder for a minute. "And they only have one short life."

I continue packing, leaving my bow near my bag. I haven't used it in months it seems. All it has been doing is collecting dust along with the other weapons of mine spread across the room. Luthias' weapons look like they have been kept free of dust, but he has had more chances to use his.

I set my bag on the table, stopping to look at Luthias. He's been staring at me. "What?" I lift my hands up and they fall to my hips with a slap.

"You know something."

"Know what?"

Luthias shakes his head. "Something."

The offer the God of Death has given me is impossible.

"I am going to go see Avon."

The guest hall seems lively and I notice that the Elves have replaced their summer colors for autumn. Even a few girls wear wreaths of leaves in their hair to announce the new season. Avon's door is open and I find myself greeted to a mess.

"What happened?" I avoid stepping on the clothing spread across the floor.

Avon appears from the clutter with a mouthful of bread. "I haven't had time to clean."

I pick his cloak off of the ground, draping it over the chair. "This is disgusting."

"It's just clothes."

"My father would be so disappointed in you. He raised you better."

Avon chuckles. "Yes, but he is not here to see my mess. So, in his mind it doesn't even exist."

I open the curtains and the windows, letting light and fresh air clean out the darkness of the room. "Have you packed yet?"

His eyes point to the bag on his bed and he nods. "How have you been?" He sits upon the bed, meeting my blue eyes.

"I've been feeling better." I sit down next to him.

Avon motions for me to drape my dress's sleeves over my shoulders so he can examine if the scars on my back are healing. "They look a lot better, but these scars will last your entire lifetime." He then points at my belly. "And I think your suspicions are right."

I avert my eyes to the hallway. "I don't know how he will react. He has been reminding everyone that I am not with child because who would want a child to live in this current world?" I stop mid-sentence. "What if-"

"What if it's not alive?"

I nod my head.

"Then I guess we will find out eventually." He shifts nervously. "I have a surprise for you."

"A surprise?"

He sits up. "Okay, I can't keep it a surprise." He grins. "There is a pianoforte at the cabin."

I sigh, thinking of how long it has been since I played. It's a rare instrument to find, especially after my father sold ours to a king in the south. "You know how long it has been." I tell him.

"I know." His smile gets bigger. "Are you bringing Oka?"

Avon would always give Oka treats and that's who I imagined she stayed with when I rushed off to Lithien. They seem like best friends. Avon would always carry her when we went for walks like she was a child. She would just lay back with her tongue out, her tail wagging.

Two females pass by Avon's door, one of them waves and he immediately blushes. "Who's that?" I ask him. "What have you not been telling me?"

Avon places his hands up in the air. "I do not know her."

"Well, she sure seemed to know you."

He shakes his head. "I don't think so."

"Avon," I sigh. "She didn't wave at you for no reason. Now, go and find her for the love of the Electa." Avon should be married by now. *But that's partly my fault.*

He is the heir of Ambrose, so of course many young ladies are going to be interested in him. I assume they have been scared to approach him since I have kept him so close to me. But I want Avon to finally be happy even if that means that my best friend isn't as close as I would like him to be.

He grins, rising to his feet. "Okay, okay." I watch as he leaves the room. I missed him and just having these short talks make me smile. It's like the way everything should be. *But, it's not.* There are still problems to take care of. *Why does Caolan want Avon?*

Avon is smart beyond his years and he is one of the greatest healers my father has ever taught. He has accomplished much in life. I don't seem to understand why Caolan would no longer want him to live.

Caolan mentioned an army and that he needed Avon to aid him. Avon is skilled in battle tactics and strategies, but still. Why Avon?

I enter the hall, staring at the other woman who skips by. They seem so happy; their smiles not yet frowned from war and destruction. Their minds not yet broken by torture.

It's odd to think that everyone left in my generation has banded together and have become friends. We are all there is. Some of our homes have been lost, destroyed, burned to ashes. Yet we still stand for the forgotten blood of ended kingdoms.

"You seem lost." Elora speaks quietly with Silevel in her arms.

"Just lost in thought."

Lenair, rings within my head.

She steps closer, her green eyes bright with motherly love. Elora frowns. "What is on your mind?"

"I want to travel."

"To where?" She bounces the child in her arms.

"The Hidden Kingdom."

"And that is? You have to remember that the servants of Lindalin were very sheltered to the stories of the First Age."

"Lenair was once the greatest stronghold in Laquilasse. It was protected by, in my opinion, a rather great King. King Greythore ruled for many years, only allowing the purest and truest Elves to enter the kingdom, hence the Hidden Kingdom. Only the worthy could find it let alone enter. But, mistakes were made of course and secrets of the kingdom's location were revealed and Lenair fell into ruin."

Elora smiles. "So, you wish to find this Lenair, but do you wish for your court to follow you? We don't like being away from you, if you haven't noticed. If you get hurt, we feel it too through the oath."

I lower my head as I remember what they vowed. My pain is shared with them and they must have felt everything I went through with Mim.

She nods her head as if understanding my guilt. "We knew of the consequences and what we might have to go through. Your physical pain is only dull and achy to the rest of us, but we feel the pain that resides in your heart." She takes my hand as her other arm rocks her child. "I hope you will be patient with us as we figure out how to handle this new type of pain and find a way to comfort you at the same time. I won't lie to you, it isn't easy."

It seems as if all my life the people I have been closest to have kept the most secrets. So, to have Elora be completely honest in front of me is both admirable and heartwarming. I feel that I, too, can share how I am feeling with Elora.

"Is it hard being a mother?" I ask her as I look at the child sleeping in her arms.

"Every mother you ask will say yes. It is rewarding, but tough. Every choice you make has to be for their benefit. Currently our world is harsh and I have friends who have a high price on their head, but all I can do since I made the decision to bring her into this world, is to try to make it a better place for her. And I believe that you play a strong part in changing this world."

I blurt my words out, because I feel that I won't be brave enough to say it if I wait a second longer. "I think I am-"

"I know." Her smile is soft. "I have paid close attention to your change in wardrobe, your appetite, and your habit of placing your hands on your belly."

Elora has me reach out my arms. She carefully places Silevel in my arms and then smiles at me. "Hold her for a while, but promise me not to get too attached to her, please."

"I won't." I have never held a child before and Silevel looks up at me with bright silver eyes. She seems curious about everything and she reaches up to pull on my hair. "No. Don't do that." I whine and she listens.

"Etta is supposed to be watching her, if you would like to take the liberty of bringing her to Etta."

"By myself?"

"Yes, go. And be quick, we have a council to attend soon."

Elora disappears and I take a moment to stare down at the tiny thing in my arms. It fills me with the greatest amount of joy, but sadness at the exact same time since I strongly believe that the little being inside of me is no longer alive.

I begin the walk down the hallway to Etta's residence. I changed this child's life because I was unable to save her father in war, but I still have the chance to make this world a better place for her.

Etta seems cheerful at the thought of getting to take care of a child. She tells me that she hasn't taken care of one since I was a toddler.

I rock the child in my arms, pulling the blanket away from Silevel's face. I smile at her and she seems to return the gesture with a giggle. The door opens and I watch as Etta bows. I turn, facing my father. His hands drop to his sides and he rushes towards me.

"Is she yours?" He quickly dismisses the fact when he sees that Silevel's eyes are silver, not blue like mine and Luthias'.

"No father. Silevel is Elora's." I hand her over to Etta.

Elender quickly grabs at my arms and looks over my face. "What happened, my Aduial?" His thumb brushes against the brands on my wrists and I flinch as the one from Mim is still very fresh.

"Imprisoned in Makya." I don't give him any more details. "Why are you here?" I gracefully walk over to the table, keeping a straight posture like he always told me to do.

"I felt the need to be here."

"I'm leaving tomorrow to go camping with Avon and Luthias."

"But you wished to have a council with your court?" I hated the fact that he always knew my plans, that he could see my future even before I knew it. It was a gift but a curse for others. *I am sure he knows about me possibly being with child.*

"You are impossibly overbearing."

"Not overbearing. Just watchful."

"Sometimes you need to be. Have you seen how much trouble I've gotten into?"

My father places his hands upon my face and I lean into his touch. "LaRue-"

"Yes father?" I smirk as his hands return to my shoulders.

"Lenair has been mentioned to you, right?"

"Just today."

"You go and find it. Okay. Right away. Don't delay."

I shake my head as I widen my eyes. "Well, it's going to have to wait. I am going camping."

My father sighs. "I know." He tugs at the sleeves of my dress. "Eryn told me to tell you hello and that she misses you dearly."

"And I return the same kind gestures." I roll my eyes. "Father-"

"I just wanted to let you know. I figured I would stop here in Lithien since I was on my way to Everford. Eryn had her child."

Excitement builds in my chest. "Finally!"

"I am getting old." My father sighs even though he doesn't look a day over thirty in human years.

Elender places his hand onto the small of my back as we reenter the hall. I find it hard to make conversation with him unlike when I actually lived in Ambrose. I would ask him questions nonstop when I was younger.

"You know, that Lithien is out of the way from Everford?"

His face softens and seems to lower his posture. "I see your sister more than I see you." He pauses. "I take it back, I see your brothers more than I see my two girls."

"I've heard they stray closer to home."

We turn the corner into a gathering room, a long table is parallel to the blazing fireplace. I sit at the head of the table and my father takes the seat closest to mine.

"But, they shall not inherit Ambrose." My father looks at me.

"Are they upset?"

"No. They strongly believe that Avon has always been the rightful heir to Ambrose. He has been my apprentice since he first arrived and I knew that he would be able to take my place if I so wish to retire. Or get killed off." He winks. "Plus, your brothers have no comprehension of a single place being home. They would feel trapped in their position if they were heir."

"And that's why, even though you knew that I loved Luthias, that you wanted me to marry Avon. So, he would therefore inherit the kingdom without anyone making a fuss about it because he isn't a part of our bloodline?"

"Exactly. And I had hoped that you wouldn't make a fuss out of it because you two get along so well. Ambrose would have been honored being ruled by the two of you. It would have brought great prosperity and a sense of safety to Ambrose."

"But in all certainty, father, if Avon has inherited your kingdom, then he therefore is basically my brother."

"Correct. In writing, Avon is your brother in a way."

I think back to earlier today and how Luthias had warned me that Malien had been spotted. "Well, I hate to say it, but it may seem like the biological father to your son is coming back to possibly reclaim him."

I am surprised that my father is shocked. I half expected him to already know what I am talking about. "Wait. You don't know?" I think this is the first time he hasn't seen something in those visions of his. But I didn't see them either.

"Malian is alive?"

But before we can further discuss the potential problem at hand, Luthias enters the gathering room with Elora and the rest of my followers behind them. "We can discuss this later."

I smirk at Elora in attempts to hide my anxiousness. I didn't think that Malien would be that important. I wish my father knew why he is here. *That's what I hoped for at least.*

The space in the room begins to fill up as my friends and family take their seats.

The doors close and are locked from the inside. Guards assume their positions, watching both the doors and everyone's every move. It has seemed that Sentier has been taking extra precautions when it comes to council security.

I rise to my feet in a swift motion. For a second I meet eyes with Avon and he smiles as he props his head against his hand. I debate bringing up my encounter with the God of Death and his current wishes.

"We have yet to find a stone. Let alone have any inclination of where they might be. We are going to have to step up our efforts in this search."

I've had enough with the formality so I lower myself back into the chair. I plop my head into my hands as my eyes glance across the room.

"I don't know much about these stones other than that we have to find them. I am not sure if I want to even place them back into the God's hands." *Why would I place such power into the hands of someone that wants me to kill my best friend?* "Lenair. That is where I propose we search. It was one of the first Elven kingdoms on this land, it is bound to have something that can aid our search."

Tasar meets my eyes. He mouths a single word. "Lenair?" I nod my head.

"We are going to find Lenair."

"Lenair is nothing but ruins." Amar speaks up. I haven't seen him since I first returned to Lithien.

"It's not even real. Just a fairy story." Chalsarda, his wife exclaims.

"It's real." My eyes quickly find the voice. I meet Dehlin's crystal-like eyes. "I lived there in the First Age."

"Please tell me more." My voice pleads for answers. I have always been curious about the Hidden Kingdom. But it was told to me as if it was a fairytale. I didn't think much more of it other than that it was a bedtime story when I was younger. Everyone knows very little other than what is written in the book. But that is even hard to tell what is fact and what is fiction.

"It is not in ruins. Well, parts of it. I seem to be the last resident of Lenair. And you will need me to help you get there. I know its secrets and how to get you there safely."

Elora pipes in. "You could rule it Laerune. It can be your kingdom."

"The Queen to the Hidden Kingdom." Eldar and Eldrin say at the same time. "The prophecy is coming true."

"You are my family. But I have been neglecting the fact that you are also my oath takers and my court. I have to appoint positions. And Luthias," I look towards my husband. "If you disagree please tell me." We haven't had the time to really sit down and talk about the possibility of granting positions in our court. Most of them were already known though.

I lean forward knowing that the people surrounding me will not care for formalities.

If I am to have an heir, then I will need someone to protect my child at all costs.

71

"If I were to die-"

"You won't die."

I growl at Elora. "If I were to die, then Elora will take the title if my heir is nonexistent or not of age." I lean back in my chair. "Eldar and Eldrin, my brothers, you will be my eyes. You will keep track of the other kingdoms around us. Tasar you will take Luthias' title if he were to die."

The thought of planning this all out makes my hands tremble. "Tolendeil and Chalsarda you will be the women of honor in the court." I turn to Avon and Amar. "You both will be my closest advisors and in charge of our armies. I trust you two the most."

They bow their heads in gratitude. As of Luthias, he already knows the part he plays as King by my side. "Not regarding your titles, you will all be Princes and Princesses of our home."

I nod my head and they dismiss themselves. My father, Luthias, and Avon remain. Avon, who was seated farther away, places himself into the closest seat next to us. I grin at him; his face looks happier than usual. "Are you excited to leave?" I ask him.

"Very." He seems restless. "Could we maybe leave tonight?"

"You are in a rush aren't you?" Luthias asks him.

A rush. Perhaps a rush to see his father? Or does he even know that his father is still alive?

I look at how energetic his blue eyes are and how they are no longer filled with greyness.

To appease the unusual happiness of Avon, we agree to leave tonight. I exit the hall to return to my room.

Deulara, the awful girl I encountered a few weeks ago, shoves her brother into the wall. "You need to speak to her. You are kind! She would have taken a liking to you."

"I don't want to." His lip quivers. "I can't put false words in her head. She already has been through enough."

Deulara whispers. "Malian gave us a job, Daralien. He expects it to be finished." She growls, shoving him one last time before she continues to walk down the hallway.

72

"Another mention of Malien. Does that worry you?" Luthias takes my hand as we walk down the hallway.

"Of course it does, but I would rather not confront Deulara once more."

Chapter 9

I clasp my cloak around my neck while pulling my bag over my shoulder. Avon enters the room without a knock and Oka slips past his feet. She jumps into my arms and attempts to lick my face.

"Down Oka." She obeys me, but still grins. Her tail wags back and forth and Avon feeds her a treat from his pocket.

"Ready?" Avon's eyes plead for us to go. His outfit is very plain compared to his usual attire. He often wears elaborate robes because he is a part of my father's council. Even when he travels he is expected to look his best, especially when travelling to other kingdoms alone. He needs to look as important as he actually is. He needs to look like the heir of Ambrose. But now, he is just Avon; the Avon that could sit in libraries for hours and read endlessly.

His clothes are plain; simple layers with a grey cloak over the top. He holds a book in his hands, hiding it beneath his cloak. He smiles at me and then turns down the hallway, Oka nipping at his heels. He feeds her another treat and Luthias and I follow him down the hall.

🖋

Avon doesn't need a map, he just simply knows the right direction to go. We make twists and turns out of the kingdom and then the forest. Although he hasn't been to his home in ages, Avon tells us that he still knows the exact direction to go.

The day fades into night and Oka begins to search for the moon. She howls as it begins to rise over us. Other howls echo through the forest in unison with her. Her fur is like starlight plastered against the dark woods. Luthias goes to pull out his sketchbook, to maybe draw the image before it fades from his mind, but another howl echoes. One that is not of a wolf or dog.

It growls, the sound coming from deep in its throat. Even Oka is smart enough to back towards us. She lets out a whimper as I turn to Luthias and Avon.

"Wargs." Avon simply says and begins to climb up the limbs of a tree. I quickly follow in suit, remembering my last encounter with those awful creatures.

Oka jumps into Avon's arms and he hoists her up to the next branch. Once we reach a high enough spot we begin to see the glowing eyes of the creature before us.

Luthias and I are clearly on edge with the situation, but Avon makes himself comfortable. He knows that I should not be fighting Wargs in my current condition.

He leans against the crook of the tree branch and pulls out his book and begins reading in the moonlight. Oka shakes for an animal like her shouldn't even be in a tree.

"Just get comfortable. You don't have to be so paranoid." Avon whispers. His eyes glow in the light of the moon. He notices Luthias' hand on his bow.

"How often have you spent time in the woods alone?"

"Often enough." Avon shrugs his shoulders. "Where does someone go when they are not wanted in the kingdom?" He knows what the people in this kingdom say about him. They think of him as a disease after I left him alone at the altar.

"How long has this cabin been in your family?"

"My grandfather built it around the First Age."

Luthias stares down at the ground below us. "Who was your grandfather?"

"Doran."

"*The* Doran?" Luthias is surprised. I just simply bow my head.

Doran committed treason against the great King Greythore in the First Age. He killed the King's children and brought ruin to his once great kingdom. He had told Navain the location to the hidden city and then destroyed it.

Nothing was left. What remained was a shattered King and a broken kingdom. Twelve children taken by the God of Death. A Queen struck with grief, overcome by sickness, died; not even the Goddess of Healing could spare her.

It is said that each of the children were reincarnated and brought back to the world, but no evidence has been found and no one has come forward saying that they are the children of Greythore.

"Doran had built the cabin to hide."

"Hide from what?" Luthias continues to question. "All the King's men were dead."

"The King wasn't dead." Avon growls. "He came for vengeance, but spared my grandfather out of misery. The King was too sad to kill Doran."

"The King soon died of grief." I continue to tell Luthias. "Saddened at the fact that he couldn't save his wife and children." I jump as another Warg howls through the trees. Dehlin had once told me parts of the story, but never the full account of things.

Avon goes back to reading his book and I lean onto Luthias' shoulder. "I wish to visit my sister after this."

"Did she have her child?"

I just simply nod my head. "My father is going to see her today. She had a boy."

Avon returns to the conversation. "A boy? About time. I feel like the amount of males in your father's bloodline is slim."

"Not really. Only two girls compared to the now five boys in the family."

"Five boys?" Avon counts on his fingers.

"You are forgetting that you are a part of my father's bloodline as well."

He grins. "I am an Ambrose boy, you know."

The air nips at my nose as we reach the mountains.

"How much farther?" I question Avon who is far ahead of Luthias and me. I pull my cloak closer around my shoulders as the chill finally finds my bones. I attempt to swallow the tightness from my throat as my stomach turns.

He turns around, lifting his hands up. "We're here!"

The cabin comes into view, hidden from sight by the forest and the mountains behind it. A creek runs through the path leading up to the porch of the cabin and a little bridge gives you access across.

Little patches of snow are littered across the piles of pine needles. A swing is also tied onto a bigger branch placed between the crooks of two trees. It sways in the mountain wind.

The porch creaks as the three of us step onto it. I hesitate for a moment. This is the cabin from my vision. I wonder if maybe this is a trap and that Malien will come out at any minute.

Avon and Luthias both sense my worry, but they just smile to reassure me. I enter the cabin and Avon immediately goes to the fireplace. It's freezing and an even colder breeze blows through the open doorway.

The cabin seems to have a personality of its own. It's a lot smaller than I thought it would be and I can't imagine that a family of three lived here.

The living room, kitchen, and bedroom is all one open space. I see a staircase to a loft, but I assume there isn't much up there. There is also one small room to the left which holds enough room for the essential bathroom things and a large washtub.

The bunkbeds to the right are enough to fit two people each. "All three of you lived here?" I turn to Avon.

"My father was often gone. So it was just my mother and me." He pulls a wooden box from under the bunk bed. "Everything is still here." Avon begins to examine each toy like he is a child again. A somber look falls onto his thin, pale face. "It's weird being here and they aren't with me. My mother and I used to have so much fun."

Luthias leans up against the ladder connecting the two beds. "I felt the same way Avon." He crosses his arms; perhaps not to look too emotional at the fact that he is probably reminiscing about his own mother.

But Avon's father is still out there. *I wonder where he has been hiding out.* I gaze across the room. It's not dirty and actual looks lived in. But by Avon's emotions to coming back here, I don't think he's been here in a long time.

"When were you here last?"

"Not since I was taken in by your father."

I wipe my hand across the counter. "Well, that's been many years since then. It seems awfully clean and put together."

Luthias pushes himself from the ladder of the bed and to the cabinets in the kitchen. A sound escapes his mouth as he bites his lip.

The shelves are stocked with food. Enough to feed three people through the winter time.

"Well, I guess we wait and see if anyone decides to show up." Avon attempts to diminish the anxiousness in the room. He sits cross-legged on the floor. "You both worry so much even though you are literally the strongest people in Lithien. You carry that bow and that sword," Avon points to each of our weapons. "Like it is another appendage."

I drop my bow onto the kitchen table and Luthias places his sword next to it. He must know that his father is still living here since he doesn't seem fazed. That is what I assume at least.

"You two need to relax." Avon quickly rises to his feet. He begins to shake my shoulders. "Loosen these!" He then proceeds to shake Luthias until both the two of them are filled with laughter. "We are here to get away, not fill our minds with whatever is going on in all these other places."

I take a seat on the bottom bunk bed. "I had a visitor today." I need to get this off my chest and maybe I will be able to relax like Avon wants me to.

The air seems to get heavy in the room and my chest struggles to rise. "Who?" They ask in unison.

"Caolan, the God of Death." The tension rises.

The attention is now fully directed on me.

"Are you just talking about seeing a raven and thinking it is Caolan or actually the embodiment of him? Because those stupid birds tend to follow you." Each of the Electa is represented by a bird. Well, that's the rumor. Each bird matches their talents and their personalities.

"I saw him and he spoke to me." I breathe in heavily. It is not the first time that the God of Death has presented himself to me. "My visions, the ones of people dying; he changes them and Caolan told me that the people I see die are the people that he wants. He mentioned an army-" I hesitate for a moment. "And one of the people he will take-"

Oka whines at the door and Luthias lets her out. "I'll go out with her." I don't know if it is an excuse to get away for a moment or if he really felt the need to be on the lookout for Oka.

"Avon? I thought you said that there was a pianoforte here."

"There is." He pulls a sheet from what I assumed was another table. Dust shudders through the air and floats slowly to the ground. The sun shines through the window, illuminating the dust specks. A yellow finch perches itself upon the sill; it cocks its head slightly.

I stare at it oddly. I shake my head to see if I am just imagining things, but it still sits there staring into the window. I turn to face the pianoforte, ignoring the small bird.

"Are you going to tell him?" Avon questions as I place my hands onto the keys.

"I don't know. I have a strong feeling that my child is gone. How do I tell him that I am with child just for me to tell him a moment after that it is gone?"

Avon lowers his head. "Either way it is going to be tough on him. The longer you wait the more he might feel betrayed at the fact that you didn't tell him."

I breathe in deeply.

Avon decides to leave me alone. Perhaps he knows that I would be more nervous if he watched me play and that I needed the time to process through what I must do.

My fingers dance across the keys as I try and remember the songs that I once played every morning. I sit down; the ivory keys are cold against my hands. I sit up straighter. *No music can be played without proper posture,* my father once told me. He would always sing in a playful voice while he taught me how to play. Often, he would go through all the old books in search for notes drawn across the paper.

I would find little tunes written in the margins of his paperwork. My father has always been a lover of music and it was something we could enjoy together.

That was when my father and I were at our closest. That was, until he sold the instrument to someone in a distant, small kingdom. My father didn't even have to question whether to get rid of the large instrument or not. It simply was packed away on a horse drawn cart to never be seen again. It is a rare instrument and not one that was easily made, let alone moved.

I didn't speak with my father for the longest time after that. He took away the one thing I loved most in Ambrose. And it seems that he continued to do so for the rest of my life. My father forced me into more lessons to keep me busy and used those studies to keep my mind off of the fact that I may never get to feel the ivory keys under my hands ever again.

But I learned many things. I learned languages, astronomy, and the cultures of faraway lands.

I search my mind for the songs that I had learned so long ago. Only a few come to mind.

I begin to play; my hands dance across the piano's white and black canvas of keys. My hands only stumble for a moment and then it seems that life becomes renewed in them. The music plays out evenly and perfectly.

I jump as Luthias sits down beside me. The loud sounds of the lowest keys rumble through the instrument. Luthias sets his hands down onto the instrument. His touch is heavy, not delicate. He bangs out a tune upon three keys and I hit his shoulder.

"What in the world are you doing?" I growl at him.

"Playing the pianoforte." He continues to rack out angry tunes that have no rhythm.

"Your mother, a lover of great music, would be ashamed that her son would hit this instrument so loudly."

He straddles the bench. "I didn't know you could play?" He tells me; his eyes are curious as I watch as they wander across the belt of ivory. "And quite beautifully in fact. Not an easy instrument to learn." Luthias looks up to me, his eyes blue like the covers of the books on the shelf behind him. "My mother would be proud of you. She wanted to learn too, but no instrument could be made in the right way to get that exact sound."

He continues. "My father tried so hard to find one for her. But by the time he really began his search, she passed from this earth."

"The pianoforte is rare. My father once had one in Ambrose, but it is now long gone." I look at the keys. I run my hands over the sheet of music. "This has been the first piano I have touched in years. It's amazing that it is still standing, let alone in tune."

"Are you worried about whoever has been here recently?"

"I have my suspicions." I tell Luthias.

His eyes wander from the end of the keys to the kitchen. "I have the same suspicions."

Avon announces his presence by clearing his throat. "I was searching the loft."

I close up the pianoforte; protecting it from the dust and age of the cabin. The yellow finch is now gone and I am afraid that Luthias' "music" scared it away.

Avon shuffles through a wooden box full of parchment. He finds a letter and rips the red seal open. He begins to read. His eyes dart quickly as he takes in the words.

My dearest Avon Halhen Orthien Elendir,

A God spoke to me about your future today. She came upon the trail of our home and placed her pale hands upon your hair. You are only a small Elfling, still able to fit in the metal tub that your father keeps upon the wall of the kitchen.

The golden woman spoke with a gentle, soft voice. She told me that you would become a great warrior and an important figure among Lords and Kings. Maybe even a Lord yourself. An heir even!

The woman even spoke of a girl. I want you to know how joyful that makes me. It makes me want to dance with delight at how amazing your future will be.

The woman continued telling me about this girl, for I pleaded to hear more. She says that this woman will be important and that you will protect her and love her with all your heart. And you will be Lord and Lady of great lands. But be careful, my young one. I am told that she is very stubborn and could possibly be the strongest warrior in Laquilasse, but I must warn you of something else. Danger threatens her path, so keep watchful eyes on her.

My own future seems blurred, my son. And I am worried that I may not be there to witness all that you will accomplish in life. But always remember that I am in your heart and I will love you with every breath in my life.

> *Love your mother,*
> *Anerin Orthien*

"I see that you have changed your path." Avon tosses the letter onto the table. "It isn't every day that your deceased mother tells you about the future and it is wrong." There is a sort of harshness within his voice.

I lean across the table to reach for the parchment. "I wouldn't say she is wrong. There is only mention of you protecting me. Not marrying me." I know that is the harshness that he speaks about. I think it is still a sore subject. I lean forward. "Tell me about her."

"There isn't much to tell. I don't quite remember her very well other than she had that motherly kindness, but that's normal." He ponders for a moment as if racking his brain for any memory of her.

"And why did she take you here?" I look around the cabin. Avon's family could've had a whole community and a life in Ambrose.

"This was our home. She always told me it was temporary, but we never left until I was around a teen. We travelled to Ambrose without my father."

I bow my head in respect. I know what happened that fateful night. Avon watched his mother die right in front of him and there was nothing that he could do to stop it.

Avon's father was searched for, but he was presumed dead. My father then made the decision to accept Avon as his newest apprentice all while taking him in as a son. Avon even looks and acts as if he was reared from my father. But, without a doubt, the descendant of the Dark Elf, Doran, nonetheless; in resemblance mostly and the way he was able to come up with these hundreds of plans in mere seconds.

I look to the two males in front of me. Luthias is my light while Avon is my darkness.

I am in between. I am after the sunset and before the moon gives light. I was both of them; having both qualities. The moon and the sun. And we shined.

I place my chin on top of my palm. Caolan's words resonate in my mind. *"Send me Avon and you shall receive my army and support. His death won't just be for my mere amusement. I need his aid within my halls."*

I bite the corner of my cheek. What sort of aid does a God even need?

Avon glances up at me with a soft smile upon his face. The questions continue to pour into my mind.

How does Caolan even expect me to kill Avon? That would be impossible. I can't even imagine myself doing that. Avon's life outweighs an army and a God's support.

But does it?

I pull my hair at the current conflict within my head. I grab at my stomach as sharpness pushes through it. *And the child as well.* The voice rings in my head.

A wetness seeps between my legs as I rise from my seat. My body cramps as I reach for the floor and finally falling on my side. I grab for the pain, but it resides within my whole body. Avon and Luthias are above me. The God of Death is behind them.

"No. Not now." I repeat. I know what Death is taking from me. I am not ready. I take back everything I ever said about not being ready to be a mother. I don't want to lose my child.

I scream through the pain as I reach for Luthias' hand. Avon knows what he must do and lifts my skirt up. I have the most skilled healer with me, but I still don't feel reassured.

Luthias places his one free hand over my stomach as he begins to heal me and Avon yells for me to push.

My feelings puddle as Death places his hand onto my shoulder and Luthias' healing powers rush through my body. Avon and Luthias can't see him. "No."

"Let it happen Laerune. It is what is best. Trust in me. Trust in Death."

I shut my eyes, forcing tears from their corners. "No."

"Trust me. This child shall grow and prosper within my halls."

Caolan's hand grazes across my freckled cheeks as he reveals my child's future.

"I will never trust Death."

Avon yells at me once more to push. Luthias seems utterly confused, but still continues healing.

Never could I imagine a child happily running around the Halls of Death, but he does so with such a free spirit. I gasp at his strawberry hair and shiny blue eyes. The breath is being choked out of me as I continue to gaze at my son's future.

How he continues to grow during death is beyond me, but he is beautiful and I watch as he ages in seconds.

Tall, like Luthias, glowing like his Ambrosian ancestors. I beam with proudness. Sword work, books, artwork, the skills of my son are revealed to me. A warrior of Death. A commander of an army of kindred spirits. Battling Gods for the rightful power.

My eyes are released from this vision.

Luthias rushes around the room while ripping it apart in search of any healing supplies. Avon's hands are covered in blood as he wraps what has come from me in a white fabric.

I sit up. "Stop." The pain begins to dissipate as I feel Caolan's hands onto my back. Or perhaps it is the Goddess of Healing, Lyraesel, who now has her hands upon me.

They both stare at me with shock. But not exactly at me, but behind me. I rise to my feet with the help of two sets of hands behind me.

The hands of Death and Healing hold me up. "Be brave, dear. Everything that we do is in order to help you." I can't look at Lyraesel, but her warmth seeps through me. "The God of Death isn't trying to hurt you."

"How can I not hold resentment in my heart for what you have taken from me?" I place both of my hands around my belly. Lyraesel has healed me entirely and only a puddle of my blood remains upon the floor. "You have taken my child away from me."

"You will understand in time."

Luthias' brow furrows as he forces words from his mouth. "Child? You were with child?"

"I wasn't sure if I was. I was malnourished and tortured. But Death has forced my baby away from me and he will now grow in the Halls of Caolan."

I move my eyes to meet his glance but he glares at Caolan behind me. Both Avon's and Luthias' swords are unsheathed in the God's direction. Blood drips and splatters onto the floor from Avon's hands.

Caolan chuckles and tips his hooded face backwards. "We are trying to help. Elbonare is in search of all of you. Your child is going to help build and lead an army of the dead. That's our only way of defeating Elbonare."

Luthias' sword arm doesn't waver, but Avon's shakes terribly and it seems as if it threatens to slip from his hands from the amount of blood that coats them. *Has Death spoken to him?* It lowers slightly and then returns to its straight, steady position. His feet waiver.

"We aren't here to fight, young one."

Avon's eyes meet Lyraesel's and he tilts his head at her. Fear wells within his eyes.

"You are being followed by Malien and other slaves of Elbonare."

"What does Elbonare want with us?"

Death answers my question. "He is hunting down your Oath-takers. He wants the stones, Laerune. And you possess the power to control all of the peoples of this world simply by your spirit and brightness. Elbonare doesn't like that you have so much sway over the creatures of this land. He is becoming fearful that you might find the truth."

Lyraesel continues. "The God of Wind keeps our friends, other members of the Electa, under lock and key. Caolan and I are being watched constantly and we must be careful of how we go about things. Elbonare wants all of the power to himself. We are no longer an equal group, but a dictatorship. We need you, Laerune, and your friends in order to stop him."

Lyraesel walks me over to the nearest chair. She props herself onto the arm of the same chair. She places a soft hand on the top of my hair and beings to follow the twist and curl of my tresses.

I flutter my eyes close as the touch is warm and reassuring. It seems that all the pain in my chest disappears with her trace. Oka plops herself at Lyraesel's feet.

The Goddess sits next to Oka upon the floor. "It has been a long while, hasn't it?" She places her hand between Oka's grey furs between her ears. My familiar grins up at the Goddess of Healing with understanding within her eyes.

"What do you mean?"

Lyraesel merely chuckles. "Oka isn't a normal wolf. She is part of the line of Wolf Gods. We agreed upon a contract of partnership when the world was new. I sent her to watch over and protect you. How else could she have lived this long?"

It was something I wondered, but never out right questioned. I feared that if I went snooping around about Oka's age or life span I would be disappointed or that there would be a chance that she is mere days from the end of it.

They both grin. "She gets much, much bigger."

"How much bigger?"

The Goddess measures with her hands. "Think horse size."

Oka places her head into my lap. "I hope you don't plan on being a lap dog forever."

Avon and Luthias finally lower their blades as they begin to realize that these members of the Electa are not planning on harming us. Rather they are sitting comfortably in the chairs around the room.

Luthias hands out the first set of questions. "How does Elbonare not know that you are here with us?"

Caolan looks to Lyraesel. "Let's just say he is preoccupied."

"If we are going to trust you, you have to tell us the truth."

Caolan rolls up his sleeves as he places himself upon the pianoforte's bench. It is quite a picture and I notice Luthias admiring how it might look as a painting. "He is being preoccupied by another Goddess. She is on our side and makes sure that he has other things on his mind other than where we are. As far as he knows we are still within our halls."

Lyraesel runs her hand down Oka's back. "Our servants are disguised as each of us so Elbonare's own spies don't suspect anything. They wander everywhere in search of something out of place, so we take the utmost precautions to keep everyone safe in the situation." She reaches to place a piece of wood into the fireplace. "We have our servants within your kingdoms as well. They have been keeping an eye on all of you. LaRue, you must love getting into all sorts of trouble. And you, Avon, you are one to sneak around. Your mother wouldn't be too fond of that, would she?"

Avon's blue eyes perk up at the mention of his mother.

Luthias growls. "Why did you have to take our child?"

"We can't reveal everything." Caolan confesses. "But he will lead an army. Even though he is dead, he will still grow and he will still learn. I will keep him safe. I promise that. And one day, we hope that we will be able to return him to you."

"Return?" The word is repeated by the three of us.

"Yes. Reincarnated. Rebirthed."

"Is this what you are planning on doing with this army?"

Caolan beams. "Exactly that. I have the ability to bring these warriors back. The people who wish to be returned, who have a kind spirit, unfinished business, they shall all come back."

I think of my mother. But Luthias gets there before me.

"My brother? Mother? Will they too, be rebirthed?"

"Absolutely. If they want to. I will not force anyone to return if they don't wish to."

Death has feelings. He cares about his people. He is willing to let his people go in order for his fellow members of the Electa to be safe. He is the only one with a group of people to look over other than Elbonare, who I assume likes to keep people under his domain.

"Elbonare has forced enough people under his rule when that choice should be entirely to the self. We aren't proud that The God of Wind has chosen to go in this direction, but there is nothing we can do other than to fight back and keep those we love safe." Lyraesel's bright composure turns dull. "Far too long has he made our lives miserable."

"Why me, out of all the rest of the people?" A typical, everyday question that I ask myself. *Why me?*

"You have been chosen from the very start. Even before your birth." Lyraesel rises to her feet. An owl perches itself onto the window sill and the Goddess opens the panned glass. "We need to go, Caolan. Elbonare is asking for us." She then turns to me. "We suggest you travel to Everford. This place isn't safe."

They disappear with a flash of light and the room feels suddenly empty of any sort of feeling. Luthias breathes in deeply and Avon's sword finally slips from his hands and clatters onto the floor.

I place my hands around my belly. Nothing is there and it saddens me. I wish I could take back all that original fear and guilt when I found out that I was with child. I would take it all back and have him born into this world if only I could have him alive and with me. I would protect him at all costs, no matter what I would have to endure.

I am thankful that Luthias doesn't bring it up further. If any more talk about my child was to be brought up within this room, tears would surely be dropped. I try to shove the thought of him out of my mind.

He doesn't even have a name.

Lorindel.

It keeps with the naming tradition of naming your first child with the first letter within your name or your significant other's name. Lucky for Luthias and I, it is both "L."

Avon takes the spot that Caolan once sat. He places his elbows onto his knees as he stares at his blood covered hands. "Malien is my father." He takes a deep breath in. "He used to do a lot of work for Navain, but I didn't think he was a part of Elbonare's spies and servants."

"When was the last time you saw him?" I ask Avon. There is a huge chance that he decided to switch to a more powerful evil since Avon last saw Malien.

"Not since my mother brought me to Ambrose." He sits up straight. "Elender and his guards searched for Malien, but they presumed that he was dead. I wasn't the biggest fan of my father so I was thankful that Ambrose was able to give me a new start."

Avon was good at lying, but I knew him for so long that nothing could get past me. He is hiding something and I am almost positive that it is about his father.

Luthias props himself onto the arm of my chair. "Is there a chance that he would want to reconnect with you?"

A simple shrug of Avon's shoulders announces that he doesn't know a thing. "Maybe. Who knows? He might just be filling out whatever task Elbonare has given him."

"We have to keep our eyes open for anything out of place. And I think we should leave as soon as possible. If they Electa thinks that the cabin isn't safe-"

Avon butts into the conversation. "I agree."

Luckily, we haven't had the chance to unpack yet. I run my hand across the pianoforte. I wish I had more time for my hands to dance across its keys.

"Malien could be the one that has been hiding out here."

Avon sneaks us out of the backdoor once we get all of our belongings together. We set ourselves up along the tree line as we begin to notice figures emerging from the path and the creek.

They each hold torches and the cabin begins to be engulfed in flame. It is like I can feel Avon's heart sink. I wrap my arm around his side. "I'm sorry."

Avon watches as the flames grow higher. There is nothing we can do.

"It's not your fault Laerune." Avon keeps his eyes steady on the last bit of memory he had of his family. "Blame the Electa." Avon grabs both Luthias' and I's shoulders and pulls us closer. "They are all to blame, but we must cherish what they have given us. They have given us love." He finally looks at the two of us. "And friendship. A family. We are our own creators, but the Electa puts us through struggles that will make us stronger."

"He is right. For once." Luthias whispers the last part. "We do have members on the Electa on our side. We can't forget that. Death is on our side."

The scent of war drifts in the wind. The future holds a battle that I am not sure we can win.

Chapter 10

Being stopped at the gates of Everford sends a nervous rush through me as we repeat our names to the guards. The last time I was here, I was on the brink of death and they were hesitant to bring me within their gates.

Today, my heart threatens to implode from my grief. I again feel on the verge of death or combustion from my sadness and rage.

"Luthias Faen, Prince of Lithien."

"Avon Halhen Orthien Elendir, Lord and apprentice of Ambrose."

"Laerune Aduial, Princess of Lithien, Lady of Ambrose and Lindalin."

The guard backs away as he lowers his head in respect of our titles. He scribbles our names into a book. I wonder how many names are within that journal. Do they even do anything with them? They must place them in some sort of records.

As we walk down the road of the market I notice that I haven't had the time to enjoy the riches this kingdom has to offer. The colors of the market are almost overwhelming. The flowers, clothing, and the jewelry makes the castle look bland in color. Its stone looks stark white against the rolling green hills of Everford and the bright orange flags that hang from the turrets.

As if my father knew we would arrive at the gates this very instant, he appears in front of me. His golden robes catch up with him, blowing past his feet. My father reaches his hand out and his fingertips brush against my stomach.

"Yes father, the child is gone."

Of course he knew. I knew the moment that he thought Elora's child was mine that he had seen this future for me. But, maybe not quite this horrid fate.

He breathes in deeply. This isn't something that he has foreseen happening; the death of my firstborn seems even too much for him to bear.

I find my father's embrace warm and welcoming as he pulls me into his arms. Usually he finds his condolences in words rather than actions.

I let myself sink into his golden robes. Dread fills me as I struggle to keep the tears behind my eyes rather than dripping to my cheeks.

As my eyes fill with darkness for the mere second it takes to blink my tears away, I see my fate. And it is not a happy one.

My father plants a kiss onto my forehead. "I will see you very soon-" He pauses and then nods his head in reassurance. "Soon, my daughter." He has seen it too.

"I am going to die, aren't I?"

He kisses my brow and then brushes a piece of hair from my face. I then watch him leave. My father passes through the busy crowd in the market, disappearing amongst the colors.

My mind wanders to the thought of never seeing my father ever again. I want to run after him and hug him one last time.

How soon will my fate occur? My vision could come true in a matter of minutes, months, or even a hundred years from now. But, this dread that sits in my heart causes me to think that it will happen rather soon.

I smear the tears across my face with my sleeve as the sun beams across my face. Perhaps I am more helpful being dead.

I watch as Avon wanders over to one of the market's shops, searching through the ancient books. "Keep an eye on Avon."

"Where are you going?" Luthias questions.

"To see my sister."

🖋

I search the halls of the palace. They start to seem like an endless maze of white and orange as I search for Eryn's room. I have only been here once and I didn't spend any time exploring this kingdom.

I notice an open door and I curiously look through the door frame. Arms grab my waist and a hand is placed over my mouth. *Curiosity killed the cat.*

Everything goes dark as they tie a blindfold around my eyes.

I have no time to fight back.

I have no time to think.

I am led through the hall and practically dragged down the stairs.

I have no energy left. I gave it all away when I gave up my child.

A horn echoes through the hall. It's a warning. A battle is ahead of us. I manage to shake my blindfold off and my eyes try to adjust to the bright sunshine that I enjoyed only moments before. Elves dressed in black and red attempt to take over the troops of Everford. Humans are no match for elite trained elves in which I assume these are.

Daralien is the one who holds me as Malien walks ahead of us. I search for Luthias or Avon, but they seem to be nowhere near me or within my sight. I slip off my wedding band and I watch as it falls to the ground, clinking against the cobblestone. Hopefully Luthias will find it and know that I have been taken. I cringe at the thought of it lost forever; the sign of our binding commitment stepped upon this battlefield.

I am now being led like a dog from the gates of Everford.

🌿

I attempt to turn my head to take in my surroundings or perhaps someone coming to rescue me, but my head is pushed forward. No one is coming for me.

Branches underfoot snap and I look in the direction. I meet Avon's eyes.

I say a silent prayer that he won't run out to meet his father. But, it seems that whatever God I am praying too isn't on my side.

Have I been betrayed by my best friend?

"What are you doing to her?" He rushes out onto the footpath and rips away the fabric that keeps my voice sealed away. Malien quickly grabs my shoulders and tilts my head back. I can bear the pain, but the fact that Avon is here and not back in Everford fighting with Luthias breaks my heart in two.

"This is the one that will kill you." I am shoved closer to Avon's face. "The God of Death has sent her out to kill you."

I shake. *How did anyone find out?* I told no one and I doubt that Caolan would go about blabbing about it.

Avon ignores the subject entirely. "Did you hurt her?"

"Does she look hurt?" Malien pulls my head farther backwards. "Come with me Avon and I can guarantee your safety."

"Why would I go with you?"

"Because she dies if you do not come with me." Malien unsheathes a dagger from his belt and places it against my throat.

"As long as you swear to not hurt her."

The grip on my hair releases and I am shoved forward into Avon's arms. "I swear, son."

I feel betrayed. I look at Avon's eyes. "Go. I'll be fine. Just get Luthias and he can help."

"I have to protect you. That has always been what I have been taught and my first priority. It's you. It has always been you." He frowns. "I will figure a plan out. I promise. I will get you back to Luthias at all costs."

🌿

I am led back to the remains of the cabin. Deulara returns to her brother's side. "I see you have captured the bitch. Surprised she didn't put up much of a fight."

"She won't be fighting for much longer." Malien throws rope in Deulara's direction. "Tie him up." He points in Avon's direction.

"What?" Avon attempts to back away, but Daralien corners him.

93

I am shoved to my knees. I refuse to look at Avon. There is no way for either of us to fight back and there hasn't been a single sign of any savior to come to my rescue.

Again, my hair is grabbed and my head is tilted back. I am forced to look forward, but my gaze remains past Avon. Death hides in the shadows of the forest. He simply nods his head and I feel reassured.

Avon screams. "Father, no!" He attempts to move, but he tumbles to the ground as he watches helplessly. Avon is shoved to the ground; his face pressed into the dirt by Deulara and her brother.

I look up at the nighttime sky. Thousands of stars are watching as I, *Laerune Aduial, Princess of Lithien, Lady of Ambrose and of Lindalin,* takes her final breaths.

I finally take my last minutes to look towards Avon. Tears shine within his eyes. "You know everything that I would wish to tell Luthias. Make sure you find him and tell him for me."

He remains calm. "I promise." He knows that this is the end. "I'm sorry. I made a mistake."

Malien's blade slides across my stomach and I topple to my side. I keep my thoughts on those twinkling stars and the thought that Death is at my side although I am not sure if I can trust him.

My blood seeps through my dress and into the dirt.

Those twinkling stars die out. And so does *Laerune Aduial.*

Chapter 11

Avon's account an hour after Laerune's death:

Her eyes stare upward with blank emotion. I force my eyes to blink away tears for my hands are still covered in her blood. I drop to my knees; the movement shatters through my bones. The ground brings me closer as if it calls my soul to come lower.

I reach for her cold hand expecting for her to return the tight grip, but I only find those lifeless eyes searching upwards. The sea does not rage within her eyes, only placid stillness shines brightly.

I run a hand over her scar covered cheek. Her soul seems so far away. Caolan must be celebrating her for the great deeds she accomplished in her life. I can imagine her dancing with her ancestors as they praise her with gifts.

But an emptiness in my heart causes me to wish for her to return. *How will I tell Luthias?* The thought of the Prince mourning his wife's death sends a chill down my spine.

The dark forest is no place for the Princess' body as I look around at the shadows dancing around the light of the moon. So, I reach my hands under her back and knees, carrying her just like I did so long ago.

Those times seem so simple. Broken bones, scratches, and what adventure we were going on next was all that we thought about. Now, death and war circle through our minds day and night.

My mind seems blank as I carry LaRue's body to the hilltop. In the summertime golden flowers grow there and I place her amongst where they would grow and where my mother and I used to play.

I look back to her as I walk to the clear stream to wash my hands. I reach for the metal pail to bring water to her body. I return to her. Her eyes shine more brightly as I wash away the blood from her face and arms. I then rise, the wind blowing the small amounts of snow around us.

"May my call be answered," I speak quietly as I reach for the horn at my side. "And may it be heard by all." The horn echoes through the hills and the faintest of sounds answer back.

"Alas, the Great Laerune has passed." The cloaked man wanders through the shadows. "Her soul will be carried gracefully to my halls and she shall be treated like royalty."

"That is not what I fear." I look into Death's cold eyes. I find kindness in the eyes I imagined would be filled with darkness.

He grins, but sorrow fills his grey eyes. "You fear what all others fear." Death's silvery voice floats along the breeze. He kneels down next to LaRue and grazes a hand over her cheek and then to her golden hair. "You fear that she may not be great enough to return back to you, Avon." Death chuckles, his voice light and airy. "You fear that she won't want to come back. Or you fear that I have taken her far too early."

I stand taller as Death sits below me. "I fear you have." I look out to the towering mountains in the distance. "You loved her. Gave her gifts, guided her, and this is what you do to her?"

"How do you know that this isn't a gift? An opportunity, perhaps?" Death places his hand onto her chest. A smirk appears under his cloaked hood.

"How is this a gift?" I growl, throwing my hands to my sides. "You took her life. She can't get that back."

"The children shall be rebirthed when they have proved themselves." Death walks down the hill. "Her soul shall be cared for, Avon Halhen Orthien Elendir." He disappears.

I look back down at LaRue. Her eyes don't shine as bright as they did a moment before. My hand reaches down to her face to close her eyes. I must bring her back to Luthias.

Luthias' account three days after Laerune's death:

I stop my pacing as Avon enters through the main doors of Lithien. His head is turned to the body he carries so delicately in his hands. He has been missing for a few days, but had sent a messenger to let us know that he was on his way back.

"What news do you have?"

His raven hair drops over his shoulder as he places the body onto the floor. He brushes her golden hair away from her pale face. Avon then places his hands into his lap.

I hesitate to lower to LaRue's side. What I have feared has come true. I knew the moment that Avon was carrying LaRue's body, but I didn't want to believe that.

My blood goes cold as I stare down at her. My hands reach for Avon as I shove him to the floor.

"What did you do?"

"It wasn't me, Luthias. You know I would never touch her."

"Then what happened!" The tears begin to fall. My anger rises as I shove his shoulders harder onto the stone floor. Tasar attempts to pull me off of him, but I push him aside.

"Malien murdered her and Caolan took her soul."

Avon's account six days after Laerune's death:

Luthias' red tresses fall into his hand as he runs his dagger through them. I prepare for the loss of my hair and the loss of my status. I am hesitant. This is not an Ambrosian tradition and I know that Elender would not approve of this. The heir of Ambrose shouldn't be doing such things.

I grip Luthias' dagger in my palm. "I don't understand why we have to show them that our loss is affecting us. I think that they would already know."

"Even in death we must show our devotion." Luthias' face is cold as stone, but with his words my raven hair falls into my palm. The rest of the court's males follow in suit.

"This is an ancient tradition for Lithien's men." Elora comes around and places a daffodil in each of our hands. "We have more important things to mourn than our hair." Luthias clutches the flower and his braid in one hand.

I pull Luthias around the corner of the hallway. I want the chance to speak with him before the start of the procession. I attempt to keep my emotions intact for the rest of the court. It seems that most of us are all either in shock or scared that if one of us releases our emotions the rest of us will quickly follow.

"She wasn't scared, Luthias. She knew. She must have known this was going to happen to her." I run my hands through my short hair. I know it won't do justice to my looks, but that's selfish to think about right now. The short hair doesn't suit Luthias either.

"She didn't tell me." Luthias' words come out harshly. "She would have told me."

I know LaRue kept many secrets from Luthias and from me. "There are a lot of things she never told you."

The Prince of Lithien pushes my back into the wall.

"She told me everything!"

There is nothing but rage in my heart right now. Rage for Luthias blaming me for what happened to LaRue. Fury for what my father did. Wrath for Caolan thinking that what he gave LaRue was a gift.

"The baby? Did she tell you that?"

This catches him off guard and I await the punch that I rightfully deserve. His grip on my jacket tightens. "Bastard." He shoves me backwards once more before attempting to storm off down the hall to rejoin the rest of our mourning friends.

"She kept secrets from all of us. It wasn't just from you."

He pauses as his hand goes to his sword.

"Caolan wants me, but he can't take me until LaRue kills me."

His sword gleams as it is aimed at my stomach with Luthias' other hand around my neck. "Then let me finish what she couldn't."

Footsteps echo down the hall and Luthias regains his princely attitude. "LaRue would laugh at the two of you." Dehlin, the Golden Lord, crosses his arms over his chest. "Those haircuts don't suit you. A shame that you have to present them at the most attended and public event of the century." Dehlin's voice lowers to a whisper. I assume he saw the actions that had occurred before he announced his presence. "And for you," he points a slender finger in Luthias' direction. "I would have expected better from you. We all lost her. Not just you."

Dehlin shoves the Prince of Lithien aside as pulls me by the arm.

"Thank you."

"Don't worry about it. It is my duty to protect my friend and the heir to Ambrose."

I have to admit that I feel honored to have Dehlin count me as a friend. LaRue and Dehlin spent many hours filling me in on Ambrose's traditions and how things worked in the kingdom when I first arrived. Occasionally a few private sparring sessions without LaRue.

The music lofting through the hallways aren't as somber as the situation actually is. I think LaRue would like that and it reminds me of when we would dance around the ballroom when no one was around. She would smile and laugh. When it was just the two of us in Ambrose, we could be ourselves.

Luthias shoves past the two of us.

I can't blame him for his harshness.

Luthias' account six days after Laerune's death:

Although LaRue is now with death, she still shines as I place golden daffodils in her tresses. I caress her face. Three pieces of fabric are draped over her body. One of red, blue, and green; representation of Ambrose, Lithien, and Lindalin where she held high titles.

I am angry that the Gods didn't allow me to say goodbye or at least be there for her as she took her last breaths. I turn my head as I make eye contact with Avon.

Instead of me, he was there. And he did nothing.

If I traded places with the Lord of Ambrose, I am sure that LaRue would still be with us.

Avon lowers his head as he steps towards LaRue.

My shoulders sag. He watched her die. I can't be upset at him. He loves her. Avon always has. If there was something that he could have done, he would have.

Avon keeps a decent distance between the two of us, but I close that space as I take his hand in mine. He doesn't pull away and his whole body drops to the floor. I follow in suit as my knees buckle.

For once we push our titles of heir to our kingdoms aside.

And we cry.

Our petty rivalry and differences are pushed aside for the sake of remembering and celebrating the great woman that has touched both of our lives so dearly.

Avon's account six days after Laerune's death.

LaRue's body is lifted and the gleaming platform she lies upon is set onto our shoulders. To carry her through the three Elven kingdoms is an honor in itself. Dehlin sits upon his steed as he leads the procession.

With Luthias and me at the front, Amar and Tasar take up the back while the rest of our courts female members follow behind.

Although four of us are holding the weight of LaRue upon our shoulders, I forgot how light she was. I remember all the times that I have held her in my arms; how I carried her up to her room when she fell asleep in the library amongst a stack of books or wounded after taking the wrong step through the ruins of the old Ambrose castle.

It is hard to keep my emotions intact. Especially with the hordes of people flocking to see the great Laerune before she is finally laid to rest. It is almost obnoxious and I am not sure if LaRue would actually like all this fuss.

Snow begins to fall when I feel it should be raining. The world should be crying, yet it is only getting colder. It won't rain for many months.

I attempt to breathe as the memories I shared with LaRue flood into my mind. This is far worse than death and I think Luthias can agree on that as well. What do we live for now that our light is gone?

The Prince of Lithien is one to seek vengeance and I can already see it brimming in his eyes. Once this procession is over, I know that retribution will be the only thing on his mind.

I can't hide that it is already on mine, though. But I know better on what LaRue would have wanted us to do. Finding the stones was addressed in her very last council and that is what we must do.

The world is without Laerune, but it still needs protecting.

My father is working with Elbonare. I never wished to share it and swapped the name of the God of the Wind with Navain. LaRue believed me and I ultimately brought her downfall.

101

I know of the reasons why Caolan wants me in the halls of Death; he would rather have me in his grasp than in Elbonare's. My bloodline is notorious for working with the most feared God. It was never a path I wished to follow and my mother didn't want that for me either, hence why we ran away to Ambrose.

If I had stayed in that cabin with my father, I could have potentially been the one to kill LaRue. And I fear that I wouldn't have cared because I wouldn't have known her the way I do now. How could the heir of Ambrose not fall in love with the shining lady that resided there?

Although the raid for our revenge is small, we carry her banner into battle; red, gold, and embroidered with daffodils. A lock of her hair has been braided into my own red locks for we will always be one. The red ribbon that she had given me as a token when we were younger still remains tied around the pommel of my sword.

I turn towards Avon. We all seemed to carry something that reminded us of her, but I wasn't sure what the heir of Ambrose carried with him.

But, I watch as he twists the ruby ring around his finger. The ring was bought at the black market when we were barely of age. And for some time, that ring resided on LaRue's finger as an engagement ring.

How all of our lives could have been so different if LaRue hadn't run away from Avon on their wedding day. Maybe I would have had to love her from afar like Avon does today.

The rage in Avon's eyes almost seems to overpower mine. I let him know that he could be the one to give the killing blow if his father even appeared in this battle. But, Avon assured me that Malien was not here and that he was smarter than that to show his face near any of LaRue's Oath-takers.

Avon prepares his stance as Malien's men begin to notice that we stand at the border of their makeshift camp. How this Elf managed to build up such a following is beyond me. What could Malien possibly promise to all of these Elves and humans in order for them to blindly follow him like this?

Avon was never one to fight in battles. Elender kept him locked away in councils and occupied with his studies much like he did LaRue. How and when did he learn to wield a sword with so much power?

It dawns on me; that fighting style was so familiar. How the heir of Ambrose fights is identical to LaRue. I think back to the hundreds of sparring matches that my wife and I shared at a young age and Avon was always there to watch.

He must have trained with her and Dehlin for years. He must have wanted to be able to protect her at all costs if he needed to. I take back all the times that I ever thought Avon was weak and helpless.

I think it makes it hurt so much more that he couldn't do anything to save LaRue when it counted. I have been trying so hard not to blame him, but it has proven difficult.

I can't even find satisfaction or relief as we cut through Malien's men until nothing remains of them, but a few that we are going to take in for questioning.

None of this will bring LaRue back.

Avon wipes both blood and tears from his face as Dehlin keeps a close eye on him. The Golden Lord has watched the heir of Ambrose very closely since I threatened him at the funeral. It seems that my ties with Ambrose are growing thin. Even Elender has shied away from my presence after I demanded that LaRue be placed in Lithien rather than with her ancestors in her home kingdom.

Of course it is selfish. But no one seems to be thinking about how I might feel about my wife being so far away and laid to rest in such a quiet and cold place like Ambrose.

I flick the blood from my sword. Tasar stares at me. "What?" I growl at him.

He simply shakes his head and walks away. I know I am not being the strong prince that I should be, but why should I be the only one that has to remain calm and unaffected by this horrible tragedy?

No one should expect me to be handling this well, do they? *I'm angry. I am angry at the world. Everything.* Avon attempts to put his hand on my shoulder. *I am angry at Avon.*

"Get off of me, you traitor."

"Traitor?" He doesn't sheath his sword and I count this as a threat.

"You probably worked with Malien from the start. You planned her death, didn't you?" I shove him away from me.

Before Avon can say a single thing Dehlin steps forward and pushes the two of us away from each other.

"I would watch that attitude." Dehlin keeps his hand firmly on the pommel of his sword. "We get it. You are hurt and you don't know how to handle such emotions, but that doesn't mean you can take it out on someone else that is going through the same thing."

I'm furious. "I don't want to see the two of you step foot in Lithien's borders ever again." I point towards Dehlin and Avon.

"You are making a mistake, Luthias."

The rest of LaRue's court surrounds us. I don't know who they will side with, but Elora steps forward.

Her eyes meet the ground. "Why don't we just head back home and discuss this in a more orderly fashion. We don't need a feud between Ambrose and-"

"Shut it."

Elora's head tilts up and I don't even feel regret. "If I want a feud, then I shall have it. I wish to break all ties with Ambrose. I don't need them."

"Then you don't need us." Tolendeil growls. She had insisted that she come into battle with us although she had no prior experience. She only can grip a dagger tightly and that is all she does now. Her hands shake in my direction.

This quiet, young elf feels that she can stand up to me. She never played a big part in any of LaRue's plans. She hardly spoke up and remained solely in the background.

"I don't feel like you should have an opinion. You haven't done much."

Elora grips Tolendeil's arm and Chalsarda follows in suit. Within moments everyone but Tasar stands beside the three women.

"You don't need us."

Their words hurt, but I dare not show it. I sheath my sword as I turn away from the people that LaRue trusted the most. While mounting my horse I notice the glance shared between Tasar and the rest of the Oath-takers.

"I will stay." He tells them, although I know that he would much rather stick with the rest of them. Tasar is loyal. At least I have him to lean on.

I turn away from them as they cling together. My hands grip the reigns tighter.

Is this really what LaRue would have wanted?

Avon's account two months after Laerune's death:

The stars glisten as their light dances across the waves. I am trespassing on Lithien borders, but this view is a welcoming sight; one that LaRue would have loved.

Port Nala was in her list of plans, but now it will sit empty like it already has for many years. The planks of the dock are nothing but stumps sticking up from the water.

I wish that LaRue's spirit would be here tonight, but it seems that she is probably farther away than this. That would be too simple for her taste.

"You know that you aren't supposed to be here."

I turn around. I swallow my fear as I meet the eyes of a God and not a Lithien guard prepared to detain me.

She bows with a smile plastered on her white face. "We have not met properly, but I have watched you from afar for quite some time. I am Catoneras, Goddess of love."

I scoff. "It seems that you have not gifted me with much love, have you?"

Her smile grows. Although her attire was grey and quite dull, she gleamed with beauty. "Then you still have yet to appreciate my gift. I don't just give out romantic love, you know?"

This isn't my first encounter with the Electa, but I had expected Catoneras to be much more formal. Her frail hands have a red ribbon wrapped around them and she reaches out for my own palms. She grasps them tightly as she kneels to the ground and then places my palm to her forehead.

"If you had paid attention your entire life you would have noticed the types of love I gifted you with." Her eyes gaze upwards at me. They are the brightest blue I have ever seen and it reminded me of the flags in Lithien; ocean blue and rimmed with ribbons of silver. "I gifted you the love of a father. Although he was not of your blood, he still cared for you the same. I gifted you the love of friendship with the Laerune; a friendship that could withstand battles and eras of this ever changing world. Don't you see, Avon? Look what I have gifted you and there is so much more coming your way."

Catoneras rises, but she still grips my hands tightly. I find that my palms are sweaty and I debate on pulling away from the Goddesses' grasp, but she must notice my anxiousness and pulls me tight into her embrace.

"I know that your love is away, but she will return bright and new someday. And she will always be your friend. Not even death can part the two of you."

"Well, what do I do in the meantime?" I know what I need to do, but I don't know where to start.

"Do what she wanted to do. Find what she was looking for."

I begin to speak, but Catoneras silences me.

"He listens to the wind. Always remember that." Her back goes rigid. "I'm sorry that I can't help you further. You will have to find your way out of this one."

Within a blink of an eye she turns into a chickadee and flicks herself into the tree branches. I sigh as the Lithien guards surround me on the bank of Port Nala.

LaRue was not happy when Tolendeil and I were captured by the Dwarves in Makya. I can't imagine that she would be a pleasant elf if this occurred when she was alive. She would surely have Luthias' head on a silver platter before he could even lock the dungeon door.

But, with the rekindled rivalry between me and Luthias, I can't imagine that I will be getting freedom anytime soon.

🌿

This dungeon is far worse than Makya because I know that no one is coming to my rescue this time.

Red hair catches my eye as the Prince of Lithien descends down the stairs.

"I warned you." There is no remorse in his eyes, only resentment. "This is where you belong anyways. LaRue should have left you in Makya to rot."

"But she didn't. She would have done the same for anyone that was an Oath-taker. And LaRue would have expected you to have the same heart being her King and all." I pause in order to calculate my words. But, I throw all caution to the wind. I am already stuck in this dungeon and I most likely will never leave as long as Luthias' heart is in the place that it is. "Why did you leave her in Makya for so long?"

LaRue had asked me the question once, but I didn't know either. LaRue's time in Makya was kept behind closed doors and between The King, the Prince of Lithien, and Tasar; their only tie to the Dwarven kingdom.

A softness resides in Luthias' eyes. He lowers his head and his red hair cascades over his face. His hair had probably grown an inch over the last two months, but the look still didn't suit him.

"Because the Queen of Lithien promised us that if it ever happened again that we remain quiet. She had been imprisoned in Makya for the same amount of time. My mother felt it was better to endure the pain rather than start a war. We could not afford one when my mother was released and we were in no shape for battle when LaRue was brought back. We didn't want to be set back further than we already were."

"But, you still ambushed the Dwarves."

"I planned it as a warning. It wasn't a war or a battle even. It was LaRue showing that she was still strong and that the Dwarves of Makya did not break her."

It sort of makes sense and I nod my head to let him know that I understand. "We all should have listened to her more."

Luthias sits himself onto the dungeon floor. Although we seem to be rivals we always have a sort of understanding between the two of us.

If Luthias even had a change of heart and released me it would make him look weak to go back on his new set of rules that he somehow managed to get by the King of Lithien without question.

"Don't release me until you have to. I know the importance of your reputation. Once you let me go I will resume my search for the stones. I won't come back here."

108

"I don't plan on releasing you until Malien resides in that cell with you. Then we will have a trial."

I must have misinterpreted his feelings. Luthias rises from the floor and turns away from the cell's door.

"Trial? For what? Trespassing on Lithien borders?"

"No. For the murder of the Princess of Lithien."

My words and my breath escape me as Luthias ascends the dungeon stairs. The Prince of Lithien will never find my father for he resides close to the God of Wind.

Maybe this was my immortal punishment for letting LaRue down; to be locked away and hidden from the stars, the sun, and the moon.

I no longer seem to be able to keep track of time. My immortal days drag on and my internal clock can't tell from day or night.

Food is a rarity. Conversation has been even scarcer. I don't know what the Prince has told his people, but I can't imagine it is good things.

I can only be thankful that the guards have not pursued a more violent punishment. I grasp at the brand that the Dwarves had given me; one to match the two that used to reside on LaRue's forearm.

Soft footsteps echo down the hall and an angered voice follows it. "I do think that I, the Lord of Ambrose, should have been alerted about his imprisonment. He is my heir. Release him."

I sink into the cold, stone floor as the cell clinks open. I thought that my father figure had forgotten about me, but knowing that he simply was not told causes my legs to buckle.

Elender embraces me as he helps me rise to my feet. "Let's get you home."

I blink the sunshine away from my eyes as we enter the hall and once the rays become less harsh a flash of blue, silver and red appears before Elender and me. That freckled face is pale and consists of no emotion unlike the last time I saw him in the dungeons.

The air fills with tension as Luthias keeps his hand on the pommel of his blade. They stand close together and I ponder the thought of the spirit of LaRue being the only buffer between them.

What would she make of this mess?

"Taking a prisoner from Lithien's dungeons is a crime to my kingdom."

Lord Elender breathes in deeply as he assesses the situation at hand. "Lithien did not take the right steps to inform me that an Elf from my kingdom was being held in your grasps. It is clearly stated in our treaty that you must inform the prisoner's Lord of their crime and punishment."

Luthias unsheathes his sword and points it towards Elender's neck. I wish I could step in, but with my lack of sleep and food I would be nothing but a wreck. I know that Elender is strong enough to fight his own battles.

"You can't take a prisoner from within our kingdom without permission from the King and as the King is not around today then that responsibility falls onto the Crown Prince."

The Lord of Ambrose shoves Luthias' blade away. They are now mere inches from each other's faces. "A Prince shouldn't be making such threats."

I have never seen Elender so angry. He never got this angry even when LaRue and I had snuck off to explore the kingdoms outside borders.

"What would LaRue think of you? When did you forsake yourself?"

Luthias sheaths his blade and turns away from Elender. It seems that he has nothing else to say. I can't blame him for hurting. We all are. We are all just processing this differently.

Elender takes my hand as we leave behind the mourning kingdom of Lithien.

Luthias remains in the hall with his back turned to the two of us. I pause.

The Prince of Lithien has lost so much. I doubt that he was ever prepared to lose again after his mother and brother died. I regret not reaching out to him when we were younger and perhaps sharing a connection over our lost, beloved mothers.

But, I know when someone doesn't want help. So, I continue down the hall.

Ambrose brings a light to one's soul and I dread the fact that I will be leaving my beloved home today. LaRue's court seems to still be at a loss, but I refuse to let my sadness get in the way of the path that I must follow.

I pull at my hair. It is not quite at the length that it once was, but now it looks a little less awkward.

I don't often think of my mother, but I am reminded of her braiding my hair so I wouldn't tangle it so much as it grew. She would give me words of wisdom that didn't make any sense to me at the time.

'A soldier, poet, or king. You will have to choose one day, Avon.' I would always choose soldier.

But today, I must be all three in order to find the stones of the Electa and to fulfill what LaRue could not.

I clasp the last two buckles on my healing kit closed when Elender enters my room.

"I'm not very happy that you are leaving."

I smile. It is reassuring that I will be missed by someone. "You are never happy when any of your children leave."

"I'm feeling lonely lately. My sons seem to be off somewhere else and Eryn is now a mother. All I have had lately is you to keep me company." He avoids the topic of LaRue. I know that it hurts him since I am sure he knew of her fate long before it actually occurred.

"I will come back. It is not like I am going to be gone forever. This is my home and I plan on keeping it that way."

Elender buckles the clasp of my cloak together and I am reminded of when he would do that for LaRue every morning that she went out.

"You would tell me if I wasn't coming back, right?"

It almost seemed as if Elender and LaRue had some sort of understanding when it came to her fate when the two met for the last time in Everford.

"I only make a mistake once. I regret what my visions showed me and what I did not attempt to stop. I will regret my mistake for the everlasting years of my life. LaRue should be here with us now. But, yes. You will come home."

I sigh. At least I know that I will see Ambrose and Elender again. Elender moves gracefully across the room to where my messenger owl is perched.

"Write to me when you can."

"Boudicca's wings will safely deliver my words at least every month." I place my hand over my heart in promise to him as the owl perches itself onto my forearm. She ruffles her golden feathers as Elender pulls me into one last embrace. "I will find the stones and hopefully LaRue will forgive me."

'There is nothing to forgive.'

I blink as the soft words float like a whisper causing me to smile. I won't allow the guilt that Luthias has put upon me to wreck me further. I believe that LaRue would not find me guilty.

Avon's account a year and four months after Laerune's death:

The sea meets the sky as I once again find myself at the edge of the land. I have traveled as far west as my feet could carry me.

Information about the Electa's stones is few and far and I am almost tempted to head towards the mountains in hopes of finding Lenair. The possibility of it not being in ruins is farfetched, but perhaps some remains of a library might aid in my search.

But, my feet remain planted in the sand of this beach. The air is warm here compared to the cool breezes that loft through the valleys of Ambrose.

The beach is littered with colorful rocks smoothed down from the embrace of waves. The green stones stand out the most as the sun shines down upon the expanse of the land.

Perhaps it is simply my mind playing tricks on me, but in the glimmer of the sun's rays a woman dressed in white plucks rocks from under the ocean waves. She holds a length of her dress in the form of a makeshift apron to carry her treasures.

She turns, waves, and pushes her golden hair away from her face.

"I knew you would find me." Her voice is soft as it dances upon the air.

I quickly drop to my knees as I take her hand and place it against my forehead; an Elf's most respected gesture.

"LaRue-"

"No. I still reside with Death." She turns to face the ocean. The waves seem to calm as she tilts her head to the side. "It is out there." LaRue turns back to me and with a delicate smile she fades into the sunshine.

I unclick my belt and my sword drops into the sand. I neatly set my healing kit beside it and hastily remove my shirt. My boots are soon kicked off and I am left in nothing but my pants.

I have never been in the ocean before. I know it is not like the lakes near home and far from the healing hot springs within Ambrose.

Although the waves are much calmer than when I first arrived I can still feel them sway around me. I place my hand gently over the water as I breathe in deeply.

A light shines beneath the surface and I descend into the water's depths. The stone shines brightly as if it was a flame dropped from the sun.

It is warm as I grasp it in my hand and rise to the surface. I drag myself to the beach and I take a moment to lay in the warm sand.

The stone could be a star itself with how bright it is, but that gleam slowly dissipates and turns into a duller iridescent color. I hold it tightly to my chest as the heat from the stone seeps into my chest.

"What do I do now?" I never thought I would get this far and my goal was to simply find the stone, not what to do with it.

I open my eyes and a shadow is casted over me. His hair came down in colors of blue and white, resembling the crashing waves of the sea before me.

His hands, feet, and pointed ears are all webbed, but he slowly seems to be looking more Elf-like by the minute rather than a foreign sea creature.

Seaweed is strung over his shoulders and waist as if the ocean itself has just clothed him. Seashells hang from his pierced ears and a crown of coral is swept through his hair.

"Who are you?" I sit up quickly.

"Taillefer. It seems as if you ordinary Elves have forgotten about me. There aren't many that reside by the sea anymore. Not since the fall of Thia."

Taillefer, God of the Sea.

"I don't mind though and Elbonare tends to leave me be. But, when it comes to the importance of that small stone in your hand, I must reveal myself."

"Are you here to help me?" The idea of having a God help me with what to do next is reassuring.

"No. I am here to tell you a story about how that stone got there." He points to the ocean. "And perhaps that will aid you to what you shall do next."

My whole body sags into the sand. A story is not what I need. But the God begins to speak.

"This world has always been riddled by war and destroyed by the need for more power. When the stones were hidden away from Elbonare who craved power as if it was air itself, us Gods did not know where they were. The son of Death took them and wiped his mind clean of their locations. One stone resided somewhere on the island of Thia where the young Lauralaethee soon discovered it. She had an idea of what it was and what that would mean if anyone found out she possessed it."

The waves crash angrily against the rocks upon the beach.

"So, when Thia was invaded and it was no longer inhabitable, Lauralaethee knew what she needed to do as she left her burning kingdom behind. On this very beach she stood with what was left of her once ancient people and casted the stone into the ocean so the evils of this world could no longer follow her with their destructive intentions. But peace did not follow her. In Lithien, she married King Sentier, but war ravaged that family and kingdom. She had urged Sentier to travel to Lenair in hopes she could come back to this beach and keep the stone in her possession. But, her life was taken before she could even plan for that possibility. And now we are here."

Taillefer folds his arms across his chest to show me that he is done telling his story. I open the palm of my hand to stare down at the stone. It almost beats as if it had a soul within it.

"So, you are saying that it is my choice to keep the stone in my procession or throw it back into the ocean?"

The God of the Sea nods his head. "I know that the choice is hard to make on your own, especially since us Gods have kept so much of the main story from all of you. I wish I could tell you more."

Taillefer disappears into the sand and all that remains is sea foam and bubbles being disrupted by the tide.

Chapter 12

"Welcome Laerune Aduial to the Halls of Caolan."

I open my eyes and bright silver ones stare back at me. Death reaches his hand down to help me to my feet. "Why am I here?"

"I needed to show you my home. I needed you to trust me and this was the only way."

"You killed me." The panic begins to settle within my chest. My feet wobble, but Caolan holds me steady.

"You can return once you understand." He takes my hand once more as he leads me down a dark hall and into the bright sunshine.

"How long will that be?"

"However long you it takes until you trust me fully."

I never expected there to be sunshine here, but the air is warm and sweet. Laughter begins to fill my ears the closer we get to the light.

"Don't be afraid." He releases my hand.

Smells of lavender and parchment reach my nose. Tufted chairs of red sit in front of the fireplace which is empty of its flame. Yellow walls are painted with soaring birds and the reaching arms of trees. I am home. The red banner, the owl of Ambrose, embroidered in gold, makes me grin.

But Death standing beside me is a reminder that I am not alive.

"Why am I here? This doesn't seem like your halls."

"Death brings you home."

It seems wrong to me that I am forced to wander the empty halls of my home while the living world continues to go one without me.

I run my hand across my father's desk. Even the papers littered across it match how it probably is right now.

Caolan walks me down the hall and into my childhood bedroom. It is quiet and lonely without all the people who usually wander the halls of Ambrose. Death appears and places himself on the edge of my bed.

"My halls work in funny ways. They can allow you to see whatever you please." He bows his head. "Anywhere you want to go, you simply ask. Anyone you want to see, just say their name. As long as they are a part of my halls. They will be able to guide you if that is what you wish. An abundance of important, ranking Elves from the First Age reside here."

"Reside here? I doubt that they had a choice."

"Sometimes Elves welcome Death. Very much like you did. More of them attempt to fight, but they soon embrace me with open arms."

The yellow walls of my bedroom feel somewhat welcoming. I push down on the red blankets upon my bed. Everything feels real, but things look brighter and clean.

I pace the halls outside of my father's study. My white gown drags across the floor as I patiently wait for the important guest that should be arriving in Ambrose at any moment. I stare down at my bare feet.

The days have been boring and bland. They have been blending together into a jumbled mess of time and different places that I have been drawn to.

Death still finds that I do not trust him, but I have asked him to send me someone that might be able to give me more information.

The flash of blue, silver, and red catch my eye at the end of the hall.

"Silver and brave are the princes who leave Lithien this day. A many a story will be told of thee. His hair was red and his eye was blue. His arm is strong and his word is true. I wish in my heart that you'll be home soon."

It is useless to think that this Elf could ever be Luthias. Rather it is Luvon, Luthias' older brother who perished in battle.

"Hey Princess." He smirks as he lowers himself onto the bench in the hallway. "I saw that they made a pretty good looking statue of you in Lithien recently."

Although the two brothers were close, they were very different. Luvon was more of a ladies' man and loved to flirt. Luthias was quite shy when he was younger.

"I would have preferred a painting."

Of course the kingdoms were going to mourn me like they would any other Elf with a high status. Ambrose put up my banner and Lindalin covered the treetops with golden lights that resembled my hair. But Lithien, where my body is put upon a pedestal of stone in the greenhouse, has a statue. It seems a bit much.

Open burials are usual for our traditions as Elves don't decompose unlike humans. We are internally preserved and often put on display for others to see if our battle wounds aren't too ugly and disturbing.

"I know what you would have preferred and it is none of what was done." Luvon takes my hand. "I am not proud of what my brother has done. I don't know everything as I can't see it all, but I know that things aren't right."

"I didn't expect him to handle it well."

"And to top it off, my mother feels that one of the stones has been found."

I smile, because I already know. It was the one time I was able to see someone apart of the living world. I had asked Death himself why that has occurred and he only smiled. But, I was thankful to speak to Avon even if it was a short while.

"Avon has it."

Luvon's laughter fills the halls. "Well, he is the best person to have something like that." He turns towards me. "I know that you won't be here forever, but I do feel like you should meet someone who might be here a lot longer than you ever will. He asks about you a lot."

✺

I pause in the courtyard as I stare at a young boy playing by the river bank. Caolan kneels beside him as he plucks different plants from the ground.

119

"He doesn't know his relation to you, but knows about your greatness and Luthias'. He is safe and happy here."

I force my bare feet to move forward.

"This is Blue Vervain. It can help with combating sadness and anger. It will sooth and sedate our nervous system."

I intervene. "Teaching him the healing ways?" My eyes are drawn to his red hair and blue eyes.

"Yes. Lorindel here is a fast learner."

My heart sinks.

This young boy is my son. I didn't believe Luvon at first, but the resemblance is uncanny. I never knew that my son would grow here. I thought his soul would remain unborn forever. I am thankful for Caolan for giving him the gift of growth even if it is without true life.

I must trust Caolan that he has a plan for my son. So, I refrain from embracing him, no matter how hard my arms wish to enfold him within my grasp.

"Who is this?" Lorindel asks. Curiosity fills his eyes. *He has my eyes.*

Caolan kneels beside him. "This is the Great Laerune Aduial. She will only be with us for a short time."

"Why? I have heard so much about her. I want to learn more."

I kneel down in front of him. "Because there is a lot left for me to do back home." I attempt to count the freckles that line his cheeks and scatter across his nose.

"Matter of fact, LaRue here, will be going *home* as we speak."

I look to Lorindel. This might be the last time I see him for many years. I place my hand onto his warm cheek. He blushes.

"Promise me to be brave in everything that you do. We are always thinking of you and loving you. You have parts of us within you, don't you forget that. Your heart will guide you. With fire in your hair, the ocean within your eyes, and the stars in your heart, you are a child of love. You are the child of warriors and rulers. Rise above us all."

I stand tall. I smile to give the God of Death my thanks and my trust.

One Hundred Years from the Time of Laerune's
Death

Chapter 13

I rise from the stone platform I am laying upon. With tired eyes I look around at my surroundings. The high glass ceilings of Lithien's greenhouse towers above me. I roll to my side as I admire the freshly grown daffodils and pansies to my right. It must be spring.

I rub my chest as the pain where Malien stabbed me still resides. There is certainly a scar, but I don't dare to look at this very moment.

My legs shake as they meet the floor and I struggle to hold myself up. I quickly reach for the stone table as my knees threaten to buckle. My sword clatters to the ground as I knock it off of the edge of the table. The metal to stone sound echoes through the greenhouse as I finally am able to rise to my feet.

I reach down for my sword. I am adorned in blue and silver rather than my white gown. I look to my feet expecting them to be bare.

Sadness fills my heart that I wasn't buried in Ambrose next to my ancestors. Did my burial create a rift between the kingdom of Lithien and my father? I am sure that my father wanted me to be placed within Ambrose.

My grip tightens on my sword as I race to the stables. *I want to go home.* I must see my father. I must see Avon to make sure he is still safe and still in possession of the stone. I have no time to tack the horse so I simply pull the stallion from its pen and towards the forest.

I can't be seen.

🪶

The gates of Ambrose are like a beacon of hope as they stand gleaming before me. I drop to my knees before them. It has been far too long since I have been home.

I open my eyes and my father stands before me. He grins. "I knew you were coming back." He drops to his own knees and his golden robes pile around him.

"I'm home." I cry into his shoulder as he embraces me. My father rubs small circles across my back.

"You're safe."

I laugh as the sense of relief fills me. I lift my head from my father's shoulder. The wooden buildings of Ambrose stand proudly against the Erutan Mountains behind them. The red banner snaps in the wind as it welcomes its Lady home.

I sink deeper into my father's embrace. He allows me the time to cry before picking me up to my feet and guiding me back into the main pavilion of the kingdom.

"The riff between Ambrose and Lithien has been growing."

"I know. Only parts of it at least."

My father fills me in on the entire situation and my court's banishment from Lithien.

"I am sure that Lithien guards will be here any moment because your body has gone missing." My father sits down upon the bench. His gaze is out towards the lake and the waterfall that flows into it. "Avon tried to get Luthias to have your body placed in Ambrose instead. They fought and fought."

"Where is Avon?"

"I have no idea. Occasionally he sends a letter to tell me about all the things he has been doing." My father returns his gaze to me. "He is in the west."

The horn of Ambrose echoes through the kingdom. "Lithien is here again." My father rises.

🖋

To once again be adorned in red and gold is refreshing. I straighten my golden circlet as I strain my ears to hear what is being said between my father and whoever has arrived in Lithien to confront Ambrose.

Luthias' voice of course echoes through the great hall. "We suspect that you have taken LaRue's body."

"We have not taken anything from your kingdom that isn't rightfully ours." My father's voice is calm and collective.

123

"Do you suspect that she just got up and walked away?" Luthias steps forward towards my father as I peer around the doorway.

"I do actually."

I attempt to stifle a giggle as I step into the hall. "I do think I have the right to go where I please."

The tension drops in the room as I step beside my father's throne. The guards behind Luthias drop to a knee as they place their hands over their heart in respect.

"I would have expected more from you, Lord Elender, then to try and trick me." Luthias growls.

"I can assure you, Luthias Faen, that I am not an illusion. My father is no conjurer of cheap tricks." My palms meet with his cheek and he stumbles backwards. Luthias attempts to collect himself. He pulls his hand away revealing that I had drawn blood with my nails. "When did you forsake yourself? Why did you not stand beside my home kingdom when they needed it most? You imprisoned Avon and never once alerted my father about it. Avon is like a son to my father. How do you think he felt when he thought he lost two children?"

I continue to hit my fists against Luthias' chest. "Did you take a single moment to ever think about what I would have wanted?" The tears rush down my face.

Luthias looks into my eyes as he grabs my fists to stop my next hit. "Everyday." I try to break his grasp, but he holds me tighter. "But I couldn't let you go. As for Avon, I didn't want him leaving and doing something rash and reckless. I was upset at your father because I am sure he knew of your fate and never told you."

"A change in the future can change the world. And changing the world can change the future." My father and I say in unison.

Luthias comes to a realization. "So, you both knew?"

I slowly nod my head.

My husband begins to look around the room. Betrayal fills his eyes. I dismiss the guards from the great hall. Luthias breaks down.

"I had no time to tell you. I figured it out in Everford, but I had no idea that it would all happen so soon." I take my hand in his while giving a reassuring squeeze to let him know that I am really here and alive. "I met our son."

His brow furrows as he sinks into my grasp.

"He has red hair. He is kind and smart. But most importantly, Lorindel is safe with Caolan."

Luthias' smile shines as his cheeks redden. He laughs softly. "That's why Caolan took you."

"Yes. It was so we could trust him and know that what he is doing is for the greater good of this world." I shuffle through my memories. "And Avon found one of the stones."

"Avon is in possession of one of the Saryniti?"

My father rises from his throne. "I do think that going and finding Avon is the most important task at this moment. He has been sending me letters over the years of his whereabouts. He has spoken about Malien trailing him for the majority of this time."

I clench my fists. "Malien can't find that stone. Elbonare can't have it. If The God of Wind is in possession of the stone, the unbalance of power will be beyond our control."

The eyes of my father soften. "So, the Electa has finally come forward and asked for your help?"

"Yes. Both Caolan and Lyraesel."

The doors to the great hall are shoved open. Navarre struts in the hall. He pulls at his sleeves to straighten them. He had helped me while I was imprisoned in Nadien, but I never expected to see him again.

"It seems that I no longer need to address my condolences towards your death." Navarre pauses a safe distance away. "Don't worry. Navain didn't send me. Caolan did." His grey eyes with the slightest hint of orange gleam. "My grandfather occasionally likes me to do his dirty work when Elbonare is watching him more closely."

I scrunch my nose. "Navain is Caolan's son?"

"It's true. Navain isn't as dangerous as you have thought. He is just angry that he was banished from the Electa. Elbonare has been playing the Gods and their servants for years. If you simply speak to my father, he might be willing to side with you."

Navarre watches Luthias intently.

"But, the message I was supposed to relay to you. Caolan told me to tell you to leave Ambrose now. Elbonare is growing stronger. He is sending out more servants every day. Find Avon. You know what to do. Go to Lenair. Leave now. No one will suspect it."

Of course I feel distrust. But Navarre did help me escape Nadien and bring me safely to Lindalin. But what if he is lying?

Navarre lifts the sleeve of his tunic as he rips the sleeve of my dress, revealing our brands. "We are one and the same LaRue. You can trust me."

I turn my head towards my father. In approval, he nods.

"You have saved me before. Hopefully, someday I will be able to return the favor."

Navarre winks. "Let's hope that you won't get into that much trouble trying to fight for my life." The Elf's smirk widens. "If you lose your husband in any battles, come find me."

Luthias sneers through his teeth. My husband's hand returns to the pommel of his blade. "Watch your back, Navarre of Nadien."

"Always, Luthias of Lithien." Navarre turns to face me. "Good day, Laerune of… wherever you decide to go."

Navarre's silver hair falls across his back as he turns from us and canters down the space of the grand hall. We are silent until the doors close behind him.

"He may have saved your life once, but he has the same attitude as the Orcs that run ramped on his homeland." Luthias clenches his jaw.

"Being raised by the son of Death seems a bit difficult. Family get-togethers might not be the greatest."

My father clears his throat. "Yes, he has an attitude. But that might be another alliance that you will be able to count on in the future. Our world must be untied to defeat Elbonare someday." He ungracefully falls down into his throne. My father places his hand onto his forehead. "But you must go and find Avon. He has the stone and is somewhere near Lenair."

I grab at my own head as a sudden pain begins to appear deep in my skull. My vision blurs as I attempt to blink the pain away. I pull at my hair as a vision of Avon appears.

Avon sprints through a lush, green forest. He whips his head around to look at whoever is chasing behind him.

"We are simply trying to help you, Avon! We don't want you to be killed. Especially with something so important within your pockets." Malien appears behind him. "You don't think the Prince of Lithien will follow out his plans of killing you?"

Avon pauses. The wind blows through his dark hair. He pulls his sword from its sheath.

"Never." Avon whispers. "Never would I betray my Queen. Not in a thousand years. Never for another world. Not even for a God."

Malien dares to take a step forward and Avon raises his sword higher.

"Elbonare is trying to help us. If you give him the stone, he can bring her back."

Avon's eyes light up. "Only Caolan could bring LaRue back."

Avon's father chuckles. "Not her. Your mother. Elbonare promised to bring her back if we bring him the stone."

I can see the internal conflict within Avon's eyes. But I don't get to hear his answer because my eyes finally blink the pain and the vision away.

My father swears. "We have to find Avon soon."

"Did he give Malien the stone?"

"I don't know." My father shakes his head. He has more of an inclination as when this vision will occur or if it already did. "The vision didn't last long enough. This will be in the future, rather than in the present. So, we have time to get to Avon before this actually happens." He rises from his throne and walks towards me. "Take this next day to rest. Prepare yourselves for this journey. I will send Dehlin and Tasar to go with you two."

🌿

127

Twinkling lights dance across the hall. Ambrose is quiet like usual. I push my food across the plate. I sigh as I feel Luthias' gaze upon me.

"What?" I drop my fork onto the face of my plate. We have yet to talk about my death and what exactly happened. I know that talk has to come soon.

"Can't I look at you?"

I giggle or at least try to. "No. It's not allowed."

Luthias grows serious. "Do you forgive me for what I did to Avon?"

I slam my elbows on the table. Oh, what my father would think right now. "You imprisoned him."

"I thought he had something to do with your death."

"Did you really think that he would do something like that? Avon told you the truth. And all you did was label him as a trespasser and traitor of your kingdom. He is a citizen of Ambrose and you denied that through and through. You treated him like scum."

Luthias lowers his head in what I would assume is shame. He continues to look down at the book he is reading. But his eyes don't dart across the page. "I'm sorry. I hope you can forgive me someday."

I want to tell my husband that Caolan wants me to kill Avon. But, I simply can't. I am terrified. I can't kill my best friend, let alone someone innocent. How could Death think I could do this?

"You have missed a lot over the years." Luthias changes the subject. "Dehlin almost died about five years ago from a group of rovers passing through. They wanted to take his sword. It was a dumb reason to attack an Elf. They threatened to cut his hair if he didn't give the rovers his sword."

"What happened?" My curiosity peaks. Dehlin prized himself on his golden locks.

"Well he still has his sword and his long tresses. The only one that didn't get to keep his prized possession was the rover leader."

"What did he lose?"

"Let's just say that he won't be having children anytime soon."

I squeeze my legs together as I imagine the pain that must come from losing such things. "Has anything else happened over the years?"

Luthias lowers his head. It won't be anything good. "Unfortunately yes. Your brother, Eldrin, fell off of a cliff and has been paralyzed from the legs down."

I am shocked and guilt flows through my heart. My brother, who loves to run so much, can't even stand anymore. I haven't known him for long, but he often repeats about how he is glad that my father hasn't made him and his twin the heirs of Ambrose because he doesn't want his freedom taken away. My whole childhood they were away, traveling around the world in hopes to find something worthy of telling a story about. "Where is he now?"

"Here in Ambrose. Elora has been taking care of him. She has been doing lots of research alongside your father to find a way to heal him. Your father believes that Avon has enough power to heal him, but he was gone before the incident occurred. Ambrosian healers have even tried to summon Lyraesel with no luck."

I bite my thumb. "I want them to know that I am alive. All of my court."

Luthias smirks. "That would spark a flame of hope throughout Laquilasse. But you also know that it would create fear. You were dead, you know."

"And they would think that you are a God yourself, Lady Laerune." Dehlin drops to one knee as he enters the hall. His hair is much longer than I remember and it just about matches the length of my own. He rises, but hesitates to step forward.

"Did the Great Golden Lord forget his little warrior?" I spread my arms out to welcome him into my embrace.

"Never." Dehlin wraps his arms around me. His embrace gets tighter by the second. "I knew that you didn't deserve your ending. You deserve so much more."

Do I?

"I am just LaRue of Ambrose."

Both Dehlin and Luthias scoff.

"*Just?* Hundreds of people look up to you."

"You should have seen your funeral." Luthias adds. "It absolutely destroyed me, but how everyone came together to mourn you, was almost uplifting."

Dehlin beams. "Your body was carried across the three Elven nations. A ceremony was held each night in those kingdoms to praise you."

"Ironically, they praised you with daffodils." Luthias adds.

That explains the new banners that are hung around the kingdom. Daffodils are the symbol for rebirth and renewal. I was dead and here I am today, alive and rebirthed.

Luthias whispers. "The Queen's rebirth."

I blush. "I am nowhere close to being a Queen." For someone to look up to me like that is freighting. To be in charge of the safety of a whole nation of people causes my heartbeat to quicken and flutter in my chest.

When I was much younger, the idea would excite me. But, after losing so many people in the Peace War, I don't ever want to be in charge of such a thing. I don't want to be the one to blame for the disaster that I'm sure I will ensue.

Even though most of the recent fighting has been because of me already.

I want to throw the title of The Pathway out the window and never hear it again.

Pathway to what? Death?

"So, we are off to find Avon tomorrow morning?" Dehlin senses my tension and changes the subject.

"Unfortunately." Luthias' voice echoes through the hall.

"Don't make it seem like a bad thing." I sneer. "If you had just treated him like the Lord and heir he is, then this wouldn't have happened."

My husband shuts his mouth rather quickly. I know that there will be tension between us. I just hope that it isn't for too long. With one friend missing, and my partner obviously upset with my concern for Avon, I feel lonelier than I did while I was dead.

"I need a moment."

I find the time alone beneficial. I spent one hundred years alone, but wandering around Ambrose with my life still intact is a whole different feeling.

Although Elves live forever if they are lucky, things change often and we fight hard to keep up with the ever-changing culture. Even the food tastes different and the clothes are far fancier and poofy than I remember them to be.

Dehlin is quite happy about that fashion changing as it reminds him of what everyone would wear back in his home kingdom in the First Age.

It seems that Ambrose has grown into the farthest thing from simple. I am overwhelmed by the change.

Golden rays gleam across the dusty yellow of the daffodils. Fresh grass grows along the banks of the lake. Spring has arrived in Ambrose. At least that will never change.

Usually it rains in March, but something has renewed my home kingdom's shine and I couldn't be happier. The rush of the waterfall rings within my ears as I approach it.

The waterfall, well this one in particular, was my and Avon's favorite spot. But there was one time that I was stupid and decided to climb it. It resulted in a broken ankle.

I smirk at the memory. Times were so simple back then.

I step into the large pool of the waterfall as I pull up the skirts of my dress. I reach one hand out to cup the water in my palm. I bring my palm to my mouth.

The healers of Ambrose often believe that Lyraesel will bless and heal you if you bathe in the water of the waterfall. But my wounds seem to be so much deeper.

Large, grey clouds cover the sun. Small drops of rain fall from the sky. "I spoke too soon." I speak to myself.

It begins to downpour and lightning flashes across the sky. I force myself to face the darkening forest. I don't feel alone anymore.

The wind attempts to blow my wet tresses.

"Please know that Caolan will do everything in his power to make sure Avon is happy." Lyraesel appears before me. The rain glides gracefully down her face.

"Will killing him make him happy?" It seems far too normal that the Electa like to present themselves so often and I answer too quickly.

"If he knows that it is something that will make the world a better place for *you,* then yes."

"I don't believe that. How could he even stand the idea of me murdering him? It's sick." I grab at my stomach. "I don't think I could ever hurt him."

"Then why are you searching for him?"

"Because he is family. He is in danger. Ambrose is his rightful home."

"Ambrose belongs to Elender's children."

"Avon is Elender's son. Not by birth, but by soul. He loves Ambrose far more than any of us do."

Lyraesel chuckles. "Silly girl. I gave Ambrose to your father so he could give it to his kin. And look at what he does. He goes on and gives it to a lowly Elf. It is not something that I would imagine he would ever do."

"Then you don't truly know my father."

She sneers. The anger flourishes in her cheeks as she clenches her fists.

I simply fold my arms across my chest. "It seems like the Goddess of Healing can't hold her temper."

"Watch your mouth, girl." She points a finger in my direction.

I can't help but grin. To see someone a part of the Electa get so upset about something so little is entertaining. But, I know that I shouldn't press her too much because she is helping me while I assist her with Elbonare's downfall.

I haven't spent much time thinking about it, due to the fact that death and how to get back to the living has taken over most of my thoughts for the past hundred years. You would think that I would have been thinking about how to defeat this powerful God. I don't even know what I was thinking about.

"You think that you are all mighty because Caolan granted you another chance, don't you?"

132

I shake my head. "No. I just have the confidence to believe that I can do what is right."

I see her attempt to hold her smirk back. But my laughter pulls her emotions apart into her own giggle.

"That is what I wanted to hear from you." Lyraesel confesses. "I was hoping that you wouldn't say anything different. Some people change while they are in Death's Halls. But, you didn't." She pulls the hood off of her golden face. "I do hope you have a safe trip tomorrow. The Electa will be watching over you."

Chapter 14

The sun shines down onto Ambrose. Someone is watching over us as we prepare for our departure. Tasar shields his eyes from the blazing rays. The sun has returned and the rain has gone back to the East.

Fog rolls and curls across the placid lake.

"How do we even know that Avon will be there when we finally arrive?" Tasar questions while clipping his bag to his saddle.

Dehlin holds up the stack of letters my father has received from Avon. "Lord Elender said that if anything new arrives that a messenger bird will be directed immediately to us."

My father walks across the main courtyard and towards me. He places his hand onto my cheek and I lean into his touch.

"I have faith that you will find him."

I have no other words for him, so I simply give him a smile.

"Come back alive this time."

"I'll try." My father lost me, he can't lose Avon.

I lean forward into my saddle. I wipe the sweat from my forehead. The sun is beaming down onto me and Luthias looks over with concern written across his face.

"It was never this warm in Caolan's halls." I explain to them.

"What was it like? To die?" Tasar shifts uncomfortably.

"To die?" He nods his head. "Soft, actually." I pause to actually go back and think about the memory. "I saw the stars until everything faded away into darkness. But there was light. Caolan took me home."

"Was it horrible being there?" Tasar doesn't meet my eyes.

"Our son was taken from us before he even had a chance to live and Caolan gave me an opportunity to see him. So, I guess it wasn't horrible."

"A miscarriage." Luthias further explains as he sees the puzzlement spread across Tasar's face.

"Our son is safe though and is being kept under the watchful eye of Caolan. He even still grows."

I look at Dehlin's golden hair. "Death wants you to be as happy as possible. He doesn't like his job, but does know the importance of it."

"Have you met Caolan?" Tasar squints as he looks towards the Golden Lord.

Dehlin nods his head. "When Lenair fell, I was killed in battle while protecting the King's daughter. Just like LaRue, I stayed in Caolan's halls for many years until I was brought back. Death guided me to Ambrose. He said that I would be needed there."

I keep my eyes on the back of his head. I was desperate to see my home when I returned to the living world. But Dehlin hasn't seen his home for hundreds of years. He died fighting for that home.

I imagine that it will be painful for him to return and remember all who were lost when darkness fell upon Lenair.

I look to my side. The river flowing beside my horse's hooves glisten. I jump down from my saddle and my boots splash in the water.

Lupines bloom across the river's bank as I take a hold of my mare's reins. I turn my head upwards towards the tops of the trees. I will never take for granted the feeling of seeing everything with a living soul within me.

I close my eyes as the wind blows my tresses behind me. The three males in my company begin to whisper.

"She is smiling."

"It's something that I haven't seen for a long time."

"What God gifted her to us? Who thought that we ever deserved to be in her presence?"

I force my eyes open. "If the Electa gifted anything, it was giving you guys to me!"

The three of them chuckle.

"Curse your perfected hearing!" They turn back in their saddles to face me.

"Tell me about him. Our son."

Luthias places his hand onto my cheek as the fire cracks beside us. Tasar is asleep across from us and Dehlin has taken the first watch. I glance over at the Golden Lord as he crosses his arms across his chest and leans against a tree.

"I know very little."

Luthias gives me a half smile.

"Red hair. Freckles. Without a doubt our child. He seems to be humble and smart."

"And you do believe that he is safe?" I see the concern within his eyes with the glow from the fire alongside us.

"Caolan took me in order to show me that Lorindel was safe. His intentions were never to hurt. He just needed me to gain his trust."

"I can't help but be hurt." Luthias confesses. "He took you away for one hundred years. I don't think that is fair."

"Life isn't fair." I think back to all the lives that were lost during the Peace War. It was never fair that their lives were taken far too soon. I hold each of them dear to my heart.

I had hoped that Caolan would have let me see them while I was within his halls. But, I was kept away from others as much as possible. I like to assume that the three of them are watching over their loved ones and that they were too busy to welcome me to their new home.

Vestan, that high spirited boy, deserved far more than death. I have pushed most of the memories about them to the back of my head, but it all rushes back so quickly. Even though Caldon didn't quite like me, I still hold the greatest respect for him. And Silvyr, who was going to be a father, was kind and reserved.

There is a memorial for the three of them in Ambrose. I regret not visiting it before I left.

Luthias leans back down onto his bedroll and folds his arms behind his head. "How do you think that Avon will react when we find him? He doesn't know that you are alive."

"I'm not sure. I hope it goes well though."

My husband chuckles. "He is your best friend. I am sure that he will react happily to seeing you."

I bite my thumb. "What if he tries to kill me?"

This causes Luthias to laugh loudly and Dehlin turns around to check up on us. "That is such an absurd thing to say."

"Quiet down you two." Dehlin growls. "If anyone sees LaRue we will have a lot of explaining to do and I would rather not do that tonight."

Tasar stirs in his sleep. "Yes! Quiet down. I am trying to sleep." He throws his cloak over his head.

Luthias closes his eyes and I know that in a matter of minutes he will be fast asleep. I pull my knees to my chest.

Dehlin sits beside me.

"What is it like there?"

"Lenair?" Dehlin lowers his head. "A whole different world."

"Tell me more."

"As you pass through the gates, you enter into the meadow. In the summer it is covered in every color of flower imaginable. Then you reach the courtyard which leads up to the grand stairs. The best parties started on those very steps."

"Parties?"

"Almost every night. Greythore's daughters loved to dance so he made every excuse to give them the opportunity. I wish you could have seen the clothes." His eyes light up as he speaks. "You would have loved them. Elegant and bright were the women's dresses." Dehlin's grin widens to his ears. "And then at the very top of the palace, there is no roof. It's completely open and it seems as if it reaches past the clouds. I would take Dalary up there a lot."

Dehlin is silent for a moment as he tilts his head back to view the stars. I think to how there is a legend about how you had to be worthy enough to be let into Lenair. So I ask Dehlin.

"There was a book in the throne room. Everyday a new name and location would be found in it. We had a special messenger just to go out and find the people who appeared on the list."

"Did the book ever make a mistake?"

"Only once."

I know the answer already. "Doran?" Avon's ancestor.

"He was kind at first, but he betrayed Lenair's secret to the enemy. He became a traitor." There is hurt in his voice. "It surprised us all that he was the one to reveal our home's location. And that the very next day Lenair was no longer. I think Doran proved that day that words can harm just as much as a sword can."

We both tilt our heads up to the stars. They seem to glitter down into the forest like snowflakes. I keep my eyes on the stars.

"Do you think I'm going to die again?"

"What do you mean?" I sense that Dehlin turns his head to face me.

"Another war is going to occur. I died once. I doubt that Caolan will bring me back a second time." I pull my cloak closer. Even though it is spring, the night air is still chilled. "I feel alone in all of this."

"You aren't. I've been through the same thing. It is a lonely process." His eyes return to the sky. "I died protecting everything I loved. Quite heroically I must say."

I take Dehlin's hand in mine, but it seems that my mind has intertwined with his memories. I have done this once before with Sentier's inner thoughts, but that was completely intentional. This time it is unexpected.

Bright light shines against marble floors as I watch Dehlin rush towards a woman dressed in a violet gown. She holds a golden shield and she shoves it into his hands.

The desperation is clear in her voice as she begins to plead with Dehlin. "You have to help them." The wind blows through her silver hair. If there wasn't so much anxiety in the air, it would make for a beautiful painting. Dehlin seems to only want to protect the woman, but her pleas remind him that he has an entire kingdom to look after.

Dehlin tightens a strap of his golden armor. He is truly a Golden Lord and always has been from the start. "I know Dalary." The woman walks around to his backside to tie up his golden hair. Dehlin's eyes begin to give that same desperate look. "Will you leave? Run? I will find you after."

Her lips turn to a frown, but she quickly gives a genuine smile to Dehlin. "Of course I will."

Dehlin believes her and he turns to leave the too bright hall. He simply nods his head and she lingers in the hall as he disappears into the outside light.

Outside of the palace is complete chaos. Arrows with tips of fire soar through the air. Shields bang against each other as the shadow of the enemy showers over Lenair. They truly have been betrayed.

Dehlin pushes an Elf away from the stairs, sending him tumbling over the edge. He pushes into the crowd, fighting his way to the front of the battlefield. An arm is placed onto his shoulder, the delicate hands far too familiar to him. His dreadful eyes turn to meet her. Her armored frame sends a worry through his body. He shivers.

"What are you doing here?"

"Helping!" She yells over the cries of the fallen warriors and the metal screeching of steel swords.

She gets pulled away by her braided hair and Dehlin throws a dagger at the enemy that is holding her. But within an instant, the enemy's sword is pushed through her back and into her chest. Dehlin is forced to leave.

His heart seems to skip a beat, no, it stops. I can feel it within my own chest.

He rushes through the fallen rubble of walls, buildings, and his fellow warriors.

She's dead. Gone forever. He finds himself facing Elbonare's servant. His eyes are like daggers, reflecting the steel of his sword.

Dehlin tries to fight him off, trying his best to avoid his vicious blows from his sword. But nothing prevails. And all Dehlin is left with is a sword through his chest. He is then sent to the Halls of Caolan.

My chest heaves heavily as I open my eyes to the stars still shining above me. I look to Dehlin as we both attempt to slow our breathing back to a normal rate.

For a single moment it felt as if my soul was escaping through my chest, but it thrums back into place as if it never left.

"I saw you die." We both say in unison.

"Your death was soft." Dehlin confesses. "It didn't feel like mine."

My breath finally slows down to something I can manage more easily. "No. Not at all."

A sudden sadness falls over him as he grips my hand tighter. "It seems like you were prepared. Like you accepted your fate."

It hurts to admit, but I force the words out of my mouth. "I did. There was no way that I could change what was happening. I knew that there was no way that anyone could save me in that moment. And all I could do was embrace the fact that I was dying."

Dehlin nods his head. "Where I couldn't because I knew that my home was still in danger."

The flicker of the fire catches my eye. I watch as it dances across the embers. "Do you think that there are others like us? Who have died and returned?"

He furrows his brow. "I like to think that we aren't alone." The Golden Lord rises to his feet as he begins to pace around the fire. "I kept my identity a secret. But the people of Ambrose are smart. They soon found out that I had many similarities to the Golden Lord of Lenair and began to ask questions. I fear that for you."

"Fear what, exactly?"

"That someone will assume that you are taking up a false identity. That you are pretending to be the Great Laerune Aduial."

I bite my lip as I stuff my hands into my cloak pockets. "I guess I never thought of that."

"You are a very important person and hundreds of people know you. There is bound to be at least one that is distrustful of your rebirth." He continues his pacing. "So, if you take up the crown in Lenair like it is prophesied, then you need to be prepared to convince someone that you are the real LaRue."

I think to my scars and the brands upon my wrist. That could be a way of showing that I am the real Laerune. I doubt that anyone would shove an iron rod to their forearm just to impersonate me. It seems a bit extreme.

I look to Luthias who is now sprawled out on his bedroll. There is still pain in my heart towards him for what he did to my father and Avon. I wonder how the situation would be different if he treated Avon with respect.

What would have happened between our two kingdoms if I didn't come back?

Dehlin pauses in his steps. A branch snaps.

"You heard that, right?"

I point to the branches of the trees above us. "It is my father's owl."

Dehlin lowers his shoulders before reaching his arm out as a perch for the owl. He takes the letter from its leg and hands it to me. I break the seal.

"Avon still remains on the Western Coast and plans on moving towards the main mountain range northwest of where he is located. Hopefully we will run right into him if we are lucky."

"Depends on if he follows the coast up or if he heads inland. If he chooses the coast then we might not see him for a while. It takes a lot more time to go around the mountains then through them which is the path we will take."

I fold the letter closed. "Let's hope that fate draws him in our direction."

Chapter 15

The palace rises over the trees as the tattered flags still dance over the turrets. I now understand why it is called the Hidden Kingdom. The entire kingdom is encircled by a towering mountain range. The forest's great oak trees hide most of the paths and arching gateways.

As we reach the gate, Dehlin places his hand onto the marble arch. The white of the wall can barely be seen as it is covered in layers of vines. He breathes in deeply.

My heart beats in anticipation. What could be behind this gate? Is it going to be ruins of a once great kingdom or will the white walls still shine in the rising sun? I grew up on this place's story and I am not sure if I am prepared to finally witness it.

"Uilos." Dehlin speaks loud enough for us to hear. The word was meant to unlock the doors of the kingdom.

The gate creaks open. Vast overgrown gardens covered in an array of colored flowers line the green grass and a river flows between the grounds. A pathway follows up to the great city where another wall separates the castle and the common living areas.

Lenair's beauty far exceeds my expectations. The White Kingdom still shines, even though it is not in its best shape; towers and buildings are crumbling and the stone wall is stained black from the soot of fire.

I look at Dehlin and he frowns.

"So the stories are true." Tasar tilts his head back to admire the towering turrets. "I thought Lithien had too many stairs."

"But nothing could describe how beautiful it once was in the First Age."

"It smells of dragon." Luthias sneers as we pass the dragon bones that are littered across an expanse of crushed buildings.

Tattered flags still hang from the walls that represent the Houses of Lenair. Twelve there were, each different, yet all important.

I pick up a blue flag with a picture of a flowing river on it. Dehlin told me many stories of the House of the River. Flavel, the leader of that house, was Dehlin's best friend.

The guards of the river were primarily those of the King. They defended the royal family if the palace was under attack.

"Water of silver and blue was their delight." Dehlin quotes.

I hand him the flag, but he refuses, not even wanting to glance at it. So, I fold it neatly into a tight square to place it in my bag.

We walk through the throne room. It is much larger than the one in Lithien. Four large pillars hold up the ceiling which is painted with a beautiful scene that depicts the Electa coming to this earth.

I look up at the walls of stone. Its height is intimidating, but enchanting. I look at the Golden Lord in front of me. His figure seems to shine as we walk through the hall.

It almost seems like he never left this place. Dehlin proceeds to show us the main rooms that we will need to use while we stay here.

I wish I could go and explore on my own, but it seems that Dehlin has a plan.

We ascend many stairs until we reach the royal living quarters. A large gathering room is near the center with doors on every wall leading to different hallways and living spaces.

"LaRue, can you come with me?"

I nod my head as I follow Dehlin out of one of the doors. He opens a violet door and it leads into a wide room with a balcony overlooking the most extravagant garden.

"Whose room was this?"

"It's Dalary's." Dehlin moves towards the wardrobe, unhitching its locked doors. "Everything that is in here, I am giving to you."

I bite my cheek as he reveals shining armor made for a petite woman. Matching weapons hang around it.

"You are the rightful Queen of Lenair."

I am appalled and grateful that Dehlin thinks so. "This kingdom deserves better. Someone less like me and more like you."

"I wish you could see your worth, Laerune." We exit the room. "You and Luthias can take the King's chambers and Tasar and I will take the other rooms in the hall."

He shoves open the door and I look at the bed with a smile. "That could fit ten people." I laugh while jumping up onto the bed. Dehlin had warned me that mostly everything was still intact because the founder had placed a spell upon the kingdom.

"Greythore liked his comfort."

Luthias and Tasar enter as well and I find myself sinking into the bed. I throw my hands above my head, reaching for the pillows. I lift the blanket from the bed and drag it to the window seat. I wrap it around my body and I open the window.

"Is it weird to anyone else that we are the only people here?"

Luthias lays down next to me and rests his head in my lap. I run my hands through his red hair. Dehlin lowers himself onto the window seat and Tasar jumps onto the large bed.

"Would we even notice Avon if he entered the kingdom?"

"He might honestly be here already."

Tasar groans. "It is too quiet in here. I wish I had my fiddle."

"I am sure that there is a music room, am I right Dehlin?"

"Second floor, third door on the right." Dehlin tells me as he follows me out of the bedroom. "And you will be happy to know that there is a pianoforte."

I stop in my tracks as I start to smile. I can't contain my excitement as I run down the hall, almost missing the door as my shoes slide against the marble floor. Tasar keeps me balanced as I swing open the door. The last one that I was able to play on was burned at Avon's cabin.

It isn't a music room, but a dancing room. Mirrors line the walls and a set of instruments lay in the corner near the balcony. I spin around the room as I plop myself onto the bench of the piano. I lift the piano's cover up and I sit up straighter as I place my fingers on the keys. I had begged my father to put the pianoforte in my bedroom so my imaginary ballroom could be complete as a child. This is far from my imagination's expectations.

I breathe in deeply and as I exhale I begin to play. My fingers dance across the keys as Tasar picks up the fiddle. Dehlin sits down next to me as his own hands join in a dance with mine. They chase each other across the keys as Luthias looks around the room for something he might know how to play.

He sits upon a chair and places a harp between his legs. And not only does he play, but he sings. My hands pause over the keys as I listen to him. We all silence our own music to listen to Luthias' song. He has yet to notice our silence as he closes his eyes and smiles.

Luthias stops abruptly and quickly blinks his eyes open. The three of us clap for him and he blushes a deep shade of red that matches his hair.

"When did you learn how to sing?" I rise while reaching out to take his hands.

"My mother wanted me to have lessons. She said a Prince should have some sort of kindness to him."

I grin at him and he returns the gesture with a sideways smirk. I don't know what to say or how to process his exquisite voice. So, I just stare up at him with a smile plastered on my face.

A shadow moves and I quickly turn around to find the culprit, but nothing is there. Dehlin looks at me with a questioning look. "What is it?"

"Nothing." I walk out to the balcony. The curtains blow in the soft breeze as I look around for any movement. The shadow marches up the stairs leading to the next level. I follow after it as Luthias and the others admire the view of the kingdom.

Once I reach the next level of the balcony the shadow appears behind me.

"We meet once again, Laerune."

"I can't quite say that I enjoy meeting Death."

"Yet, you still follow." Caolan folds his hand in front of himself. His steps are silent as he circles me like I am his next meal. "I need Avon and soon. I can't wait any longer."

"I can't kill him." It is not even a debate in my head.

"You must. For the sake of the peoples of this world and your son." Caolan lowers his shoulders and sighs. "Please. Trust me."

"I do trust you, but I don't understand why you even need an apprentice."

"Because even Death can't live forever."

"I can't kill Avon. You can't expect me to do that and go on living. You are asking too much of me."

Caolan steps forward. "I can-"

"What? Send him back a hundred years later? That still doesn't change the fact that I would have killed him."

I close my eyes and when I open them Caolan is gone.

Luthias climbs up the stairs to the second parapet. "It's going to take a lot to get used to all these steps." He points a finger in the direction of the towers looming over us. "Any guesses on how many stairs it takes to get to the top."

"I don't plan on counting." I smirk at him. But behind that smile is a hint of pain. How am I supposed to kill my best friend? I know the reason, but I can't seem to validate it.

"Dehlin told me that they have an astronomy tower. I assume it's the tallest one over there. Apparently there is a type of pulley system so we don't have to climb all the way to the top ourselves."

I walk over to the balcony, gripping my hands on the edge of the railing. "People die here. Our friends die here." I bend down to my knees as my body begins to shake at the thought of killing Avon.

"Maybe things are meant to happen for a reason." Luthias doesn't seem shocked. He has lost too many that it almost doesn't seem to bother him on the outside. It is like he has been hardened to stone.

I collide into his open arms. "He was here. Death was here. I spoke to him." Luthias' hands run through my hair.

Tasar interrupts us. "Malien is within the walls of the kingdom."

I don't feel that I am at my strength, but I force myself to get onto my feet. They wobble in protest.

We rush down the halls to grab our weapons before entering the courtyard.

Deulara and Daralien stand at Malien's side. Two others, masked and cloaked, stand in the shadows of their master.

I pull my bow off of my shoulder as I knock in a silver arrow. I aim it at Malien's face. *If I am going to kill him, he will die painfully.* The arrow releases from the string, but Malien unexpectedly catches it within his hand. Of course I don't expect this to go that easily, but it was worth the shot.

"No, no, no." He scolds me like a child. "We are simply here for Avon. Not you."

I grab my sword once again as I charge towards Avon's father, but Deulara blocks my way. Tasar attacks Daralien and Dehlin and Luthias go for the other two masked Elves. Malien begins his search for Avon and the stone that he has kept safe for all these years. I pray that Avon isn't in Lenair.

Deulara takes my bow from my shoulders and pulls it up around my neck. She is choking me and I slam her back into a crumbling wall. Deulara lets go and I sling my bow back across my body.

I back away, quickly searching my surroundings. Deulara again tries attacking me. Her daggers come close to my neck. I grab her hands, twisting them to keep her blades from my throat.

"How are you still alive?" She asks between fighting motions. "We killed you!"

I manage to knock one blade out of her hands and she staggers. We each take a moment to catch our breath. Everything around me feels slow and I see the flash of Deulara's green eyes as she too is figuring out her next move.

My sword glistens in the sun. Deulara now puts her daggers away and reaches for her own sword. Deulara charges at me with her hooked blade upheld. I dodge her first swing and meet her second with my own sword. My strength makes her stagger, but not enough to knock the blade free from her hands.

Her next swing slices a bit of fabric from my armor, but not deep enough to cause fatal damage. I slice through air and quickly spin around to get another shot. This time my blade finds flesh. Deulara drops to a knee, tries to stand, but drops again.

"You know nothing of this world, little girl." Deulara spits her last words. My stomach knots and churns at the thought that I took an Elf's life.

I walk away, watching as Tasar kills Daralien with a brutal blow to the head. Tasar wipes one end of this sword clean and then brushes the hair from his face.

Luthias and Dehlin now stand back to back with their two enemies sprawled out on the ground.

Avon. I instantly turn away from my fallen enemies and towards where my first instincts send me. I am driven inside of the castle, up a flight of stairs, and into the main library. Fleeting memories of my visions send me flying through the corridors of the castle.

Avon wanders the aisles of books as he runs his hand across their leather covers. I know Malien isn't far behind me, but I have to savor these fleeting moments of Avon simply being himself.

I smile as he immerses himself in knowledge. I feel Caolan at my shoulder.

"Now is the time Laerune."

I attempt to concentrate on slowing my breathing, but my chest still rises heavily as I lean my head back onto the stone pillar I am hiding behind. My grip upon my sword tightens with each passing moment.

I shut my eyes before charging in Avon's direction. This is my only chance. I won't be able to work up the courage ever again.

But, I pause when my blade is barely an inch from Avon's stomach. He places his hand upon my back.

"I know." His voice is soft as I gape at him. Those blue eyes puddle as he pulls me and my blade closer to him. "I know, LaRue."

My eyes don't leave his as I begin to feel the warmth of his blood drip down my own stomach.

A tired look falls over him. Avon's blood covered hand pushes my hair behind my pointed ear. "I hope all of you can forgive me someday."

I can't say anything. His eyes search mine.

Avon places a soft kiss on my forehead. He is struggling to keep himself up and I slowly lower him to the ground. He grips my hand tightly.

I let go of his hand as I pull my knees to my chest. I run my hands through my hair. Avon's blood stains my golden tresses. I place my head into my hands as Luthias kneels down beside me.

"Go!" I scream at Luthias. "Go away."

Luthias rises back to his feet and takes a few steps towards Dehlin and Tasar who have now entered the library.

"Give her a moment." Dehlin's voice echoes. "Malien is still out there. We must find him."

I lean my head onto Avon's chest. There is no heartbeat. Nothing but emptiness and silence. His soul now resides where mine spent so many years alone.

I rise to my feet as I feel the all too familiar grip tighten on my hand. Death once again stands before me.

"Think of this as a gift for your son."

"But you have other motives, Caolan. You don't give things as gifts if it doesn't help you in the future."

"I am also giving you the skill to pass in and out of the shadow world. It will allow you the chance to speak to many people. These people know more than what any textbook can show you." Caolan begins to look concerned. "But use it wisely and sparingly, for it can take its toll on your soul." *So this is what happens when you kill a friend.*

I find myself staring at the placid eyes of Avon. I close them and I give him a soft smile. "I'll bring you back."

Luthias, Dehlin, and Tasar enter the building again. They seem hesitant with their words. "Where would you like to bury him?" They refrain from making eye contact with me. *They already think I am a monster.*

"A royal, open burial."

The royal, open burial is a tradition from Ambrose. Kings and Queens and their kin are placed on top of slabs of carved stone so their families are able to visit and see their glory. Elves don't decay, so they are naturally preserved until the end of time. They simply look as if they are sleeping forever.

Dehlin's eyes turn gray as he nods his head. Luthias bends down to pick up Avon's body. He turns to me with saddened eyes.

Our friends die here.

Chapter 16

It is odd to see Avon so still.

Dehlin and Tasar have cleaned his wound and dressed him in robes of the brightest colors of red and gold. I could not bring myself to help them.

I wonder what he is doing with the God of Death tonight. Are they already making plans for an army or is Avon getting time to mourn the loss of his dear life?

Dehlin doesn't stay long. The King and his kin seem to set him on edge, but Tasar and Luthias stay by my side. Tasar wanders around the stone slabs of the royals, warriors, and kin before us.

Luthias places a kiss onto Avon's forehead. "A brother always."

They had their differences, but I am sure that they admired each other for those abilities that set them apart.

"Thank you." I lean into Luthias' side.

He intertwines my hand with his. "Why did you kill him?" Luthias whispers into my neck.

Tasar shifts his weight as his eyes meet mine. The tension builds within the room.

Instead of shrinking like I want to, I stand tall. But not a single world escapes my mouth.

"He wasn't posing a threat to you, was he?"

A small squeak is the only thing that my voice can expel. I cross my arms around me. A harshness that I never thought I had comes out of me. "I did what I had to do." I do feel like speaking about what Caolan has asked of me.

Luthias furrows his brow. Tasar changes the subject.

"What now?"

"Malien is still out there. I'm not going to let him terrorize us anymore."

"I don't think you should be making any major decisions for a while, LaRue." I turn towards Luthias rather quickly as he speaks. "You are grieving."

I bite my lip.

Tasar butts in. "Luthias, I don't think now is the right time to argue." He notices the anger raging within my eyes.

Luthias doesn't stop. "You will feel the guilt for the rest of your life. Don't hide your pain. You can't heal if you hide it."

I glare at him as I exit the room. I stop before Dehlin who has been waiting for us to leave. "I want you to go back to Ambrose and bring the rest of my court."

Dehlin bows. It seems that he has been at a loss of words. *He's taking commands from a murderer.* "Dehlin." I reach for his arm. "Are you scared of me?"

He shakes his golden head. "I'm not scared of you. I'm worried about you."

I close my eyes as I hear Tasar and Luthias beginning to yell at each other. My heart is heavy, yet I can't seem to make the tears fall. *I must seem heartless.*

"Don't be scared to feel a certain way." The Golden Lord pushes my shoulder slightly. "Wash up. You're covered in blood."

I glance to my right at the mirror upon the wall. My hair is crusted in blood and streaks of it is dried across my cheeks. I bring my hands up to my face. My palms are covered in red and my clothes are stained.

My fist connects with the mirror and I cover my face as I fall to my knees. The glass shatters around me and I hold my bloody hand to my chest. Luthias enters the hall and helps me rise to my feet.

"What happened?"

"I broke the mirror." My voice breaks easily. "I didn't like what I saw."

Luthias seems confused as Tasar begins to pull the glass shards from my hand. "What did you see?"

"Myself."

I scrub at my hands in an attempt to wash the blood from them. I scratch at my palms until my whole body feels like it's burning. The bath water is too hot and sweat drips down my forehead.

Luthias enters the bathing room and quickly pulls my hands away from myself. "Hey, stop that. You washed it all off."

I stare at him as he releases my hands and they splash into the water. Luthias reaches for the washcloth hanging on the edge of the tub. He scrubs at my face and I stare at him as he does so.

"We need to talk." Luthias drops the rag and proceeds to wash my hair for me. "I need you to know that we don't look at you any different." I close my eyes as he pours water over my head.

"Do you think I am a monster?"

"I don't know why you had to do what you did, but I will never think of you as a monster. Please know that when you are ready to speak, Tasar and I are both here."

I reach for the towel when Luthias disappears behind the other side of the privacy screen. I wrap the towel tightly around my body. Luthias hands me a dress and I slip it on over my head. I scratch at my palms. It feels as if the blood is still there, hidden under my skin.

"Stop that." Luthias once again pulls my hands away. "Why are you doing that?"

"Because I feel like his blood is still on my hands." I shove my palms forwards as Luthias examines them closely. Avon's blood will always be on my hands.

"But there is no blood. You washed it all off."

"It still feels like it's there." My footsteps are silent as I move towards the clothes I left on the bed. They are too stained to be salvaged. I ball them up before throwing them in the trash bin.

"Do you think we ever forget parts of our lives?"

"I'm sure there are blurred memories." Luthias cocks his head to the side and then shines his sideways smirk. "You aren't going to forget him." He sits down into a chair and leans forward. His pale hands run through his red hair. "You'll forget tiny things. But never the person as a whole." Luthias again rises and looks out the window. "I lost my mother over one hundred and eighty years ago. I haven't forgotten her and I never will. I might not be able to paint her the same way I did when she was alive, but she still resides both here and here." He points to his head and then to his heart.

Most describe my husband as a powerful warrior and diplomat; the perfect Prince. But most of the people in Lithien don't realize that most of the newest, royal portraits were painted by their Prince.

He paints under a pen name. *Hiraeth.* I found his art enchanting. The portrait of his mother was the first thing I was drawn to when I travelled to Lithien. I would stare up at his paintings and wish to be one of the beautiful women among his artwork.

I attempt to rise to my feet but a sharp pain in my side causes me to collapse onto my knees. I swear as Luthias rushes to my side.

I cringe as my whole head pounds as a blinding whiteness shoots through my eyes. The agony slowly fades to a dull throb.

"Is everything okay?"

"I'm fine." I rub my temples as I finally rise to my feet. I use the edge of the bed for support. "I need some air." I find myself running from the room in hopes that Luthias won't follow. My feet take me past the market of Lenair and out into the more forested area of Lenair.

I stand still as the wind breezes past my skirt. I reach down for the yellow daffodils. I pluck one, snipping its stem with my nail. The sun shines down onto my head as I set myself down amongst the flowers. I begin to arrange them into a crown of flowers and I set them on top of my head.

The air seems fresh as it enters my lungs. I follow the rocks towards the river. I find myself stepping into the water and it comes up to my waist. My hands run over the current that threatens to pull me under. *I needed this air. This time. This place.*

The water pushes me under, but the God of the Sea pulls me upon the shore before I am swept out towards the sea.

The pain settles deep in my chest. I had taken in too much water and Luthias, like always, hovers over me as I cough up the remaining water that had entered into my lungs.

I sit in front of the fireplace, my hair soaking the floor as Tasar wraps a blanket around my waterlogged self.

"What were you thinking?" Luthias growls as he crosses his arms and paces in front of the fireplace.

"I wasn't."

"You're lucky that the God of the Sea helped you."

Tasar pulls on the length of my tresses. "Did he say anything to you?"

I shake my head. The God had only smiled once he carried me to shore. "I took his actions as a sign of his willingness to side with us."

"You shouldn't have gone, Laerune. What if he didn't want to be on your side?"

"I just needed a moment to breathe and get my head on straight."

Luthias interrupts me. "You don't know how to grieve, Laerune. You can't just run away from everything."

I rise to my feet quickly. "You don't get to decide how I grieve, Luthias. Is there even a right way?" My eyes fall to the fire in front of me. It flickers and dances. It looks so free, but it must never leave its ashes. "I'm going to lay down."

🪶

The staircase looms before me as I pause at its white steps. This is not the way to my chambers, but rather to the hall where the dead are held. Where the King and his kin, and now Avon lies.

It's quiet here. Too quiet.

Maybe Luthias is right; the pain in my heart is just the pain from losing my best friend. We watched each other die, but only one returned to the living world. My heart beats loudly in my chest as I kneel down beside Avon's body.

155

I take his hand and place it upon my head. I don't know why I do this, but it lessens the guilt that burns my heart into ash. Light pours into the room casting his face in golden rays. Ravens flock towards him; Death's Guardians are now watching him. They perch themselves upon the arms of the stone statue that looks down upon Avon.

I rise to only wander further down the hall. I brush my hand over each stone table. Runes are carved over each slab of stone, telling the story of each person.

King Greythore's crown gleams upon his head and I look down at his soft face. His wife lays beside him and their children surround them.

The silver haired woman from Dehlin's memory shines as the moonlight glistens against her pale figure.

Dalary. I lower to my knees to see her titles. *Lady Dalary of the Eastern Wood. Shield maiden of the Iron Gate. Princess of Lenair. The Silver Lady of our beloved kingdom. Her and her dancing will forever be missed.*

Next to her is an empty slab. I lean my head onto the cold stone. *The Golden Lord.*

They had prepared a spot for Dehlin next to The Silver Lady for him to rest beside her. It hurts to think that he died protecting what she cared most about. He died to only come back for entirely different reasons.

With Dehlin the last remaining resident of Lenair, I can only assume that he was the one to bury the dead when he was rebirthed.

I look back to Avon's resting place. I kneel down before his stone table once more.

"I hope you don't hate me." I cross my arms over the stone as I speak. "I know that what I did was extremely wrong, but I know you know why I had to. Make sure my son is safe. I don't think I need to tell you that. You'll know who he is the moment you see him."

I wipe my nose with my sleeve.

"I feel dumb talking to you like this. You are probably laughing at me." I chuckle slightly as my nose begins to stuff up. "Probably wanting me to shut up or something. Like just stop talking, Laerune. You are bothering the rest of the dead people with your nonsense words."

I remain silent for a long moment.

I shiver. The hall suddenly becomes chilled. I follow the breeze back down the stairs and across the hallway to Dalary's room. I shudder as I grip the silver doorknob.

Dalary, who seems much taller in her paintings around Lenair, stands before me. But the setting sun shows that she is not a part of this world, but rather a translucent spirit wondering who has entered her bedroom.

Dalary seems very similar to me and roughly around the same size. Her armor would fit perfectly and I would assume so would her clothes. The clothing I brought along with me is too worn and already in the trash from being covered in so much blood. *So much of Avon's blood.*

"You are Dehlin's friend, right?" Her voice is like a whisper and it sends shivers down my spine.

"Yes. He is like my brother."

She glides closer. "Are you here to protect my kingdom?"

"I...Yes. I am here to make it flourish."

Dalary smiles and nods her head. "Then you have my full permission to use any of my belongings." Her spirit disappears into the sun's rays.

I open up the wardrobe in her room. Gowns of deep purple and lavender fill the closet. I step into the purple material as I drop my slip onto the floor. The nightgown was made from flowy material that lets the warm summer air heat up my chilled bones. I slip on a pair of shoes as I wander down the hallway and down the hundreds of steps.

My eyes wander around each corner, searching each shadow as if someone was following me and I was being watched. But no one is here.

The large doors entering the courtyard creak open as I push them. The sun has set and my heart yearns for the gardens as I can see the lamps light the way to them. Fireflies flicker down the paths as they bounce from leaf to leaf. The moon lights up most of the walkway and I can easily find my way around.

I sit down onto the stone bench near the center of the garden. I feel my eyes start to water as I look down at my shoes.

"Out for a midnight stroll, are you?"

I look up at Tasar as I attempt to wipe the snot running from my nose. He just simply sits down next to me. Tasar picks his nails for a moment before placing his hands back in his lap. He bumps his shoulder against mine.

I stare awkwardly forward as he continues to bump my shoulder. "So?"

I continue to stare forward. "I'm tired." I speak in a monotone voice. "And I'm not really in the mood to talk."

"It takes up a lot of energy, doesn't it?" He slaps my back a little too hard and I fall from the bench as my hands meet the gravel.

Tasar quickly reaches down to pick me up, but I wave him away with a bloody hand. I stare at the rocks buried in my palms as the blood seeps around them.

Tasar is reluctant to leave me on the ground so he grabs my arm. I close my eyes as we are sent to a memory. *No.* Not a memory, rather a different view of Lenair.

Elves wander the gardens, some hand in hand and others laughing and joking. I am seeing what I can only assume is the Halls of Death.

"What are you looking at?"

"You can't see them?"

Tasar shakes head. "I don't understand what you are talking about."

"Caolan said that I would be able to cross into the shadow world, which is his halls, but I never thought it would be like this."

Tasar lifts his hands up. "You're going to have to explain a little bit further."

"I see the Elves that are in Lenair in the Halls of Death. When you die you can go where you please, but you can't see the living. You can't see the dead around us, but I can."

He pursues his lips. "Okay. This would be far fetched coming from anyone else, but I believe you. How about we set this aside and talk about a few important things. I know it sucks, but I have to ask for my best friend's sake." Tasar sits himself down among the tulips. I go to lay down next to him to look up at the stars. He folds his arms over his head and lays back into the dirt and grass.

"Did you and Luthias ever talk about your death?"

"No."

"The grief topic is hard for him, you know?" Tasar shifts his back and it cracks slightly. "We all knew when you died before Avon told Luthias. Luthias just refused to believe it until he was told."

"I know that it didn't go well."

"No. Not at all. He was all strong for everyone in the beginning. A bit over helpful. He never left me alone, but I think that it was because he was scared of being alone. But, he then grew distant and almost mean, in a way. Especially when we went into battle to try to avenge you. He made everyone choose a side and I am the only one that stayed with him."

"So, that's why our court was banished from Lithien?"

"Yes. He took most of his anger out on Avon. When King Sentier was away for council, Luthias took a lot of the political matters into his own hands. And Sentier didn't have the heart to tell his son no." He shuts his eyes. "He didn't care what your father wanted. Or Avon for that matter. He didn't even care about what you might have wanted. And it broke all of our hearts to see him fall apart in such a way. He knows that. And I think the reason why he is treating you so harshly is because he doesn't want you to be the person he turned into while grieving."

There is a silence between the two of us.

"We don't know why you killed Avon." Tasar chokes out the words. "But, we do know that there must be a good reason behind it." I watch his throat bob up and down. "We are scared. But we know that you aren't a monster. You don't kill someone for sport. Let alone someone that you love so dearly who loved you a thousand times over."

My eyes feel as if they are piercing. "I had to…I had to because Caolan needed Avon. And if Avon is with Caolan then he is with my son. With them together, they will build us an army so we can defeat our enemy and finally live in peace."

Tasar pulls me into his embrace. "We all will follow our Queen to the very end."

Chapter 17

"No! Your hands go here." Tasar flops his hands heavily against the keys of the piano. Luthias chuckles from his stool as he sits in front of the canvas. Earlier, I had encouraged him to paint again.

I blink past the morning light that now shines through the open windows and balcony doors. The summer air is floating freely in and it makes the room stuffy with heat. Tasar's hands stumble across the keys and he quickly places them in his lap.

"Your hands are dancing. Now, follow my lead. Lightly!" I remind him as I place my own fingers against the higher toned keys. I play a three note tune and he does the same on the deeper notes on the piano. I repeat the tune and each time it becomes longer and longer and then finally into a song.

Tasar memorizes it rather quickly and I begin to play the partner side of the song. "There! You got it!" It is nice to have these small uplifting moments to take my mind off of my guilt. I have tried to focus my thoughts on happy memories instead of dwelling on all my wrongs.

I close my eyes as my hands glide across the keys. Avon used to sit in the study and watch as my fingers prances across the black and white ivory. He would laugh and smile at my made-up tunes but grow serious when I showed him something on the sweeter and serious side.

Always, he would be smiling. And sometimes he would sit by my side, perhaps to catch a closer glimpse of my smirk.

Luthias' chuckle pulls me out of my thoughts. I turn to look at Tasar's face as he sticks his tongue out in concentration. He soon begins to grin as the tune becomes easier and easier for him to play.

I pause to allow Tasar to play on his own. I look past Luthias and out of the balcony doors. I can imagine Avon leaning against the railing as he much rather liked being alone then joining in group activities.

My eyes then focus on Luthias' painting. I rise to my feet to stand behind him. While leaning my chin on his shoulder, he pulls his paintbrush away from the canvas. He is painting a skyline of the kingdom. I see that he has put a lot of work into the stone walls, but now he seems to focus more on the mountains.

I sit myself onto his knee while taking the paint brush within my hand. "What if I added a little something here?" I mess around by putting the paintbrush dangerously close to Luthias' canvas.

He knows how awful I am at painting so he tries to take the paintbrush from my hand.

"Don't you dare." He growls.

I spin around quickly enough to smear the remaining paint of the brush across his freckled cheek. My husband turns his face to the side.

Luthias plants his hand into his paint palette. "You asked for it."

The paint is spread across my face and I go to wipe it from my cheeks. But when I place my hands back into the view of my eyes, my world begins to fall apart once more.

It is a brighter red than Avon's blood, but it still resembles what clung to me on that day. I shake while brushing my hands onto the lavender silk of my dress.

"I'm sorry." Luthias' brow furrows as he attempts to clean my hands and face with his own shirt.

I turn away from him. "It's fine. I'll just go wash up myself."

I expect my friends to just let me descend down the stairs, but they both grab at my arms.

Luthias steps in front of me and motions for me to jump onto his back. He wraps his arms around my legs as I wrap my own arms around his neck.

I need my family, but I have just been scared to ask for that sort of help. How do I even make them understand the reason why I have done what I have? They will never quite understand. And I can't quite seem to put it into words of what I need exactly.

How do I mourn when I was the one that caused my best friend's death? I wrap myself tighter around Luthias.

"You know, we haven't really gotten the chance to explore yet. Maybe, once you get washed up we can find our way to the library."

"Maybe." I shrug my shoulders slightly. I don't understand why they want me to go there knowing that is where I brought an end to my best friend.

"I am sure that it is much bigger than Ambrose's and Lithien's collection."

Bribing me with new, unknown books probably sounds like a good idea, but imaging where Avon's blood seeps into the floor makes my heart skip.

The last rays of sun shine through the windows as I look up towards the ceiling. Luthias and Tasar have luckily avoided the section of the library where I committed the greatest sin, but my gut still tumbles into knots at the reminder.

I turn my mind to the rows of books that don't just have a ladder to the upper levels. They have staircases. But, a large book upon the pedestal in the middle of the library catches my eyes and draws me closer.

My hands run over the yellowed pages with curiosity. I turn back towards Luthias. His own blue eyes scan over the text.

Lenair was once great and plentiful when it came into existence. It was a place of peace and Aquitaine fought for Elves below the Electa to have a safe place to live and prosper. Only the worthy were allowed the right to enter the Hidden Kingdom. Its twelve gates protected the city from those who were dangerous to the existence of the kingdom.

The King, Greythore, ruled over this land with a kind heart. His people loved him and cared for him, and he did so in return. His wife bore him twelve children. Six boys and six girls.

His children grew up not knowing what war or destruction was like. They were innocent to the outside world. They did not know what took place outside of those grand, marble walls. *Not a single one seemed the slightest bit curious until a stranger entered their gates.*

"This is about Doran." I turn to Luthias.
"Keep reading." He seems too intrigued for me to stop.

They greeted every stranger with kindness and offered them a home, so they did the same for this strange man. They suspected nothing evil from this stranger even though his demeanor was dark. His eyes held kindness and the children caught a liking to him very quickly.

The stranger went by the name of Doran. He told many stories of dragons, wars, and the daring rescues of princesses and Queens. He had most of the royal children begging at his feet for more stories of far off kingdoms and distant lands.

Only the eldest children were distraught by Doran. Whenever Doran spoke of those wonderful stories, Aslan, the eldest, would cross his arms and wait patiently behind his siblings. His eyes would watch Doran carefully, but the storyteller watched Aslan back with keen eyes.

I slam the book closed as the room begins to fill with a chill air. I turn my gaze behind me. Can this place really be my home? It has been tainted with so much death. I am not sure if I will survive the guilt I have placed within this beautiful kingdom.

"We forgot something." I turn to Luthias. "We forgot that Avon had the stone."

"I didn't forget." He pulls it from his pocket. "I didn't want you to have to worry about it while going through this situation."

I move back towards the book's perch with the stone in my hand. Around the podium runes are carved into the wood. *There are many pages, so ask and you shall find.*

"The Saryniti." The pages begin to flip by themselves until the book lays flat again.

The Stones of the Electa: The Saryniti

Maglanor, a great craftsman of the first age, was brought before the Electa. He offered each of them his greatest works as gifts. But he gave four of the Electa far greater things. Maglanor gave Elbonare, Caolan, Lyraesel, and Sybilla each a stone that fit into the palm of their hands.

But the other members of the Electa, being angered that they were not given such powerful gifts, planned to rebel and to split the stones into equal parts. Navain, son of Caolan, stole the stones from their masters and hid them within the Earth. Elbonare took charge and banished Navain from their homes.

Navain's powers were taken away, as well as his knowledge of where the stones were hidden. The Electa continues in search of the missing stones, but they are yet to be found, their power missing from the Electa.

*But one was found by an Elven Princess of Thia. Lauralaethee had one day reached into the ocean and found the first Saryniti. But when she died, Lauralaethee tossed it back into the sea in order to keep it safe.

Soon, Avon Halhen Orthien was shown the location of the first stone and kept it with him until death.

My heart flutters within my chest as I turn back to Luthias and Tasar. I step further away from the book. My center of gravity seems pulled to the floor and the next thing I know, I am looking up at the ceiling. My head spins with too much information and thoughts and my heart suddenly feels much heavier that it already has been feeling.

"There is a fourth stone." Luthias and Tasar stare down at me. *A fourth stone.* I feel as if this sets up back ages, but in reality it doesn't. We are already at that point. We have no other information other than that we must find the Saryniti.

My heart drops further in my chest at the fact that Avon is no longer in the living world to help us. When I was younger we would enjoy figuring out those difficult and challenging puzzles. But, perhaps he will help me like how I helped him find the stone we currently have.

It reassures me to think that Avon is watching over me the same way I watched over him.

"I am going to go process everything." I let Luthias and Tasar know. They know I need a lot of time to myself.

Once I disappear from their sight, I sprint down the hallway. I don't know where I am going, but I am sure there will be an empty room somewhere. I swing open the first door I see and I enter the servant's passages. I lean my head back as I stare up at the winding staircase. My hands reach down to feel every step as I finally reach for the railing.

I sit in the first window and I pull my knees to my chest. While leaning my head on my knees I push open a pane of the window. The sweet smells of the garden loft in as I breathe in deeply. I pluck a flower from the vines that grow on the outside of the tower wall. The tears no longer fall and I don't think of anything but the view in front of me. *Think of only this.*

Think of dancing in the ballroom. Think of parties. Avon's voice seems to echo in my mind. *Think of the excitement of having a home. Think of everything you can finally do. Think of being Queen. Think of being free.* My eyes shoot open as the sound of a horn enters through the window and rings up the stairwell.

The memories of Avon well up in my mind and I rise to my feet a little too quickly. I fall back onto the steps and my shoe tumbles down the staircase. My shoes slip my mind as I hear familiar voices from the courtyard. *My family.*

With one hand on the railing and the other holding my dress, I fly down the stairs as quick as I possibly can. I run right past Luthias and Tasar and right into my brother, Eldar's arms. He smells of home and I sink into his arms as he holds me tighter. *Am I homesick? Homesick for Ambrose?* The smell of parchment paper and cinnamon fills my nose as I lift my legs up from the ground.

"Don't squeeze too hard." Eldar whines as he sets me back down onto the ground.

"It is nice to see you. Been awhile." Eldrin speaks from upon his grey mare.

I look up to him. "One hundred years is an awfully long time."

Eldrin, who is now paralyzed, but unbelievably still able to ride a horse, will never run again. He will be bedridden and stuck to the confinements of a chair. I see that it grieves Eldrin very much. He doesn't have that same playful smile that he once had. I can see the sadness in both of the twin's eyes.

Elora runs up to Eldrin with Silevel at her side. Silevel smiles at me. *Her father's smile.* She stares at me with bright, crystal eyes as Elora dotes on Eldrin.

"I left for five minutes. Five minutes! And you just think you can run off like that?"

"Elora," Eldrin speaks calmly to her. "I can't run."

She sighs, letting her shoulders relax. "I didn't mean it that way."

"I know you didn't."

"Come on," Elora motions with her head. "We need to get you down from there."

"Elora. Let me see my sister first."

Elora turns around quickly and her mouth gaps open. "LaRue!" As I expected, her hug comes quickly and she wraps her arms around my neck. "We all thought you were dead, but then we got news that you were alive and then you left!" She speaks rather quickly while hugging me tighter in the process.

"Mother," Silevel cries. "I think you are squeezing her too hard."

She releases me and turns towards her daughter. "Silevel, I would like you to meet a great friend of mine."

"I know who she is, mother."

"And I know who you are Silevel. But I only saw you when you were about this big." I measure the length with my hands.

Elora places her hand on the back of her daughter and leads her inside of the palace. Eldrin leans down to whisper in my ear. "Elora is a bit protective."

"I can see that." I smirk.

"It drives me crazy. She's constantly by my side. You know I don't mind, but I just feel so helpless." I can see that he is really struggling to stay on his horse. "Plus, what would I be able to do in a situation if Elora or Silevel were in danger."

I take the reins, leading Eldrin to the front steps of the palace. "We can find a better place to talk. It looks like it's going to rain." I look up at the clouds. They're dark and gloomy, blocking the warmth of the setting sun.

Eldar reaches to lift Eldrin up off of his horse. Neither of them seem happy. I lead them into a sitting room with a roaring fireplace. Eldar lays Eldrin onto the couch and he sighs.

"We've been trying to find a way to fix all of this." Eldar turns towards me. "But there seems to be no cure. We even had the healers attempt to summon Lyraesel."

"I'll look in the library the next chance I get. There is bound to be something in there."

"LaRue, there's no need to do that." Eldrin speaks softly. "I know that you are going to be very busy."

"Family means more to me Eldrin, not how I'm going to run a kingdom."

"What about how you are going to kill Malien? Or how you are going to find the stones." Dehlin must have filled my court in on all that has happened.

"We are going to have to put everything aside in order to find the stones as soon as possible."

"Everything will fall into place at the right time."

Luthias is laughing with Amar as the two of them enter the room. He walks up to me, whispering in my ear. "How are you feeling?" His grip tightens on my shoulder.

I know he is worried that my court will bring up Avon's death and I'll shatter before them. "I'm okay."

The doors to the sitting room open and Elves begin to pour into the room. A lot of them take up the space at the table and I move to sit down into a cushioned chair.

Tasar walks in and plops down into the chair next to me. He winks as he takes a bite out of the apple in his hand.

"You know I think they were expecting the Queen to look more presentable." He looks down at my bare feet.

"Shut up." I had abandoned my shoes in the servant's staircase.

I pull my legs to my chest, leaning my head onto my knees. I close my eyes as I let a vision take over and change the room into the walls of Lenair.

The platform used for executions in the First Age is before me. This is where prisoners were thrown off the cliff and killed. But I lay at its edge with my arm dangling over the cliff and a silver circlet in my hand.

Dehlin has magically appeared at my side and he places his hand on my shoulder. He smiles, his ice blue eyes bringing warmth to my heart. "I don't think there is much to discuss at the moment since you are most likely beyond tired. But I do want to alert you all that we know of Malien's location and that he does have an army. They are travelling here as we speak. Our scouts are behind them."

"When will they arrive?" I ask. I want revenge on Malien for killing me. Maybe that will somewhat calm the outrage in my heart for killing me and putting my family through the heartbreak.

"We have estimated two days. But it will be hard to tell."

"Will our troops be ready by then?" A full out battle is far from what we need at this moment. But I know that I can be reassured by Dehlin's efforts. While under my father's rule, he always made sure that Ambrose was prepared for the worst.

What will my father do if Dehlin stays here and Avon is gone?

"They are ready now. I have already dispatched them around the border of the wall, gates, and inside the city. My most trusted soldiers are inside the palace." Chalsarda enters the room. "Speaking of."

A silver arm band is around her right arm, signifying that she had been promoted to captain of the Ambrosian guard. I see that her efforts with the blind Elf, Allister proved worthy.

She passes by me, smiling shyly as she sits down onto the couch closest to the fireplace with Amar.

I haven't seen most of these people since my passing. I am proud to see what they are doing with their immortality. I smile lightly at the thought that I wouldn't want anyone else within my court.

I have the most renowned warriors surrounding me. Healers that are worthy enough to stand at my father's side. And the softest, yet strongest and bravest people I have ever met.

I close my eyes to envision the important people who are missing in this picture that I see before me.

I am sure that Caldon would be protectively standing at Avon's side as they stand at the edge of this picture. Avon's soft smile would gleam partially with embarrassment as he crosses his arms to hide the fact that he is happy to be included.

Silvyr, who would be inches away from Elora, would have his daughter in his lap. Bright smiles would be escaping that happy family.

Tasar and my twin brothers would be embracing Vestan and leaning on his shoulders to see how much weight he might be able to hold up. Amar would be near them with Chalsarda locked at his hip.

Dehlin, golden with sunshine, would be fixing his hair at the last minute with a soft arm around Tolendeil. I even imagine Luthias' brother gripping his little brother's shoulders. Luthias and I would be sitting in the middle of the group. Our son sits between the two of us in a fury of bright red hair and gleaming eyes.

"I want all of you to get enough rest. We don't know what tomorrow will bring. I want you all to be on your toes." Dehlin urges my court to leave the sitting room and get any sort of rest that is possible.

They begin to leave the room with soft smiles in my direction. I know that they are waiting for the perfect time to talk to me about all that has happened.

Dehlin turns to me once the last of them leave. "That means you too."

"I think I will have a look at that army you are talking about." I wink at him. I have no doubts that this kingdom is beyond safe tonight.

When I step outside the air is damp and cool. The fog sits low to the ground and I can't even see two feet in front of me. I walk up the stairs of the wall, slipping from the moisture left from the fog and rain over the past few hours.

I push myself up from the steps before making my way to the edge of the great wall. I dangle my feet from the wall, the fog makes a canopy of grayness over Lenair. I listen to the steady beat of soldiers walking.

An arrow whizzes blindly past my head and skids to a stop on the marble walkway. *It is not our own weaponry.*

I rise quickly to alert Dehlin, but my feet slip out from under me. I grab the side of the wall as I attempt to pull myself back up. I look down, but the fog forbids me to see the bottom.

My hands slip slightly and I struggle to get a better grip. "Help!" My voice echoes lonely through the damp air.

Another arrow is blindly shot and I tuck my head under my arms to shield from anymore. My hands slip more and my fingertips strain as I grip the marble wall tighter.

A familiar hand shoots out from the fog and then pulls me up and over the wall.

"Malien's army is here." I tell Luthias as I rub the ache out of my hands.

He rolls his eyes and scoffs. "You don't think I know that."

We rush down the stairs, taking our separate ways. Luthias heads to the armory and I head up to our room. I run up stairs, tripping up every other one as my breath burns my lungs. I throw open the door to our room. I shove open the wardrobe, revealing the violet and silver armor. I quickly slip it on, grabbing my weapons and making my way back down the never ending stairs. *This is my chance to finally gain revenge for the wrongs that Malien has committed his entire life. Avon could have had an entirely different life if it wasn't for Malien.*

Chapter 18

The gates fling open with a crack of splinted, worn wood. The fog spills from the opening as Malien's men rush through the gate. I bump into some of my own soldiers and end up hitting one of Malien's men with my shoulder. He tries to shove me to the ground, but my dagger quickly finds his neck.

I continue to run through the thick haze in search of Malien. If he is to die, I shall be the one to do so. Figures rush by me and I try to look beyond the fog. I find myself near the entrance to the open platform of the wall.

This is a dangerous place in general, but the mist makes it ten times worse. Just one wrong step and I will be falling to my death. This place was used for executions once. Let's hope it won't be for mine.

The moon shines through the clouds for just a second allowing me to see Malien leading Tolendeil towards the edge of the platform. I can hear them speaking as Malien places his hand onto her back.

"Tolendeil!" I call. My heart drops as the meaning of my vision becomes clear.

"I know what you did, LaRue. You killed Avon." Her face turns up into a wicked sneer. "I have no desire to live, if I have to live under your rule. *The killer of innocence.*" She growls the last words.

Malien disappears as I walk closer to Tolendeil. Her white hair sticks out in every direction from the summer humidity. "Please. Don't take another step Tolendeil. We can talk this through."

She looks down at the cliff, then back over to me. Just one step and she's dead.

I step forward while reaching out my hand. I hope she can see how my eyes are pleading, because I can't make a single word escape my mouth.

I try to reach out for her again but Malien finishes off the deed by shoving her back, leaving me to only grab her silver circlet and a hand full of white hair.

I dare not look down at the bottom of the cliff, even though I know that the fog has stopped me to see anything.

I lay there, unable to move as I stare at the circlet in my hand. I toss it to the ground as I rise to my feet to meet Malien who now stands in front of me.

I unsheathe my sword. It seems like years since I last felt its familiar weight in my hand. I stare down at the blade, bright from lack of use, yet still very sharp. *I killed Avon with this sword.*

"You have ruined too many lives Malien. And if I am to die, you are going to the depths of Hell with me."

"I killed you once, I can kill you again." His eyes are like coal, unlike his sons, bright blue orbs. I notice the gleam of a silver amulet wrapped around his neck. "It was a shame for her to fall. A pretty once she was."

My skin crawls as I raise my sword higher. Lightning illuminates the sky as the clouds begin to cry. Thunder pounds through the rock walls. I await Malien's first move.

I bend backwards, avoiding both of Malien's blades. I swish my own blade towards his legs, cutting his ankle. He punches my lip with the pommel of his sword.

My sword begins to slip from my hands a little bit at a time from the dampness in the air. After a few moves, it comes dangerously close to slipping from my hands.

The sword-edge bites a part of his black robes, causing it to rip right across his chest to reveal a large scar.

He stands in shock for just a moment before a wave of anger washes over him. I stand in place as he rushes towards me. My mind churns and churns. *He has been killed once before.*

Two guards enter from the thinning fog with Luthias behind them, barking orders to capture Avon's father.

"I don't care if you kill me. Elbonare will only make me stronger in the next life." He screams, laughing with hysteria.

"I can't kill you Malien. You deserve to suffer with your thoughts."

He screams vicious words all the way to the dungeon. He seems to have gone mad in power; a power that Elbonare should never have been able to give him.

I kneel onto the execution platform as I pick Tolendeil's circlet off of the ground. I pull it to my chest as the overwhelming pain of grief sits in the pit of my stomach.

This kingdom should execute me for all the innocent lives I have brought an end to. I don't know how anyone thinks I am fit enough to rule this kingdom.

A hand shoots into my perspective. I allow the circlet to drop into my lap as I take the hand. Luthias doesn't attempt to raise me to my feet, but rather kneels down beside me.

"It's over."

"It is far from over." I whisper.

"Well," Luthias clasps both of my hands between his. "We won't have to worry about Malien."

"I think we have a lot to worry about. He's Elbonare's servant, I know it. I am sure that the God of Wind won't be happy that his loyal subject is imprisoned within Lenair."

"Will the Electa ever be happy with us?"

🌿

The path down the gardens is paved in starlight. The clouds have parted and the warm summer air seems to seep from the stars above me. I place myself onto a bench inside of a pavilion. I unclasp each piece of armor and it drops onto the wooden floor with a clunk. I unsheathe my sword from my belt and it joins the pile of metal.

I don't ever want to feel it in my hands again. *I vow to never hold a sword.*

I rise to my feet to throw my daggers across the garden while aiming my spear at an oak tree to my right. The leaves scatter down in a fury of anger. I leave the pavilion and everything in it behind me. Maybe somebody will find my things and use them far better than I ever did.

I sneak back into the palace, not wanting to be dragged into the current celebration for the victorious battle won today. I walk up the many stairs until I know that no one will make the trek up this far.

The servant's tower seems to be my only escape. Only my feet echoing off the stair's walls provides me with company. Step after step, I begin to lose that never ending voice in the back of my mind. Each click of my boots sends the phrase, *the killer of innocence,* to the far depths of my mind.

The window provides more solace as it shows me a view not overcrowded with people and their many questions on my reasoning behind the things that I did. There is no one here to bother me. No one, but myself.

The door clicks open at the bottom of the turret and my eyes shoot down towards the noise. I would much rather be alone right now, but I know that Luthias can't help but to check up on me.

"LaRue?" Luthias calls from the bottom. I don't answer, but I hear him come up the stairs. I swear he can always hear my silence.

He sits a step lower than my own dressed in his pants and a white night shirt. "I brought you something to eat." My husband places the pastry wrapped delicately in a violet napkin into my hands.

"I don't have much of an appetite."

"It's filled with strawberries. Please don't waste it or I will have to eat it and I have already had five."

I attempt a smile as I force myself to take a bite so it will please him. I watch as the crumbs fall into my lap. I don't have the energy or care to brush them away.

"Your father would probably have a fit if he saw the mess you have made." Luthias wipes the crumbs from my dress. He seems to shift in uncomfortableness, but he places his hand on top of mine. "I know that things have been tough," his grip on my hand tightens. "But you are strong-"

"I see that you are still taking cliché cues from your brother. He would be proud of you." I smirk slightly.

A bell chimes, making us both jump. It rings twelve times, marking the time of midnight.

"Let's get out of this tower. It has been a long day."

I have no desire to fight against it. He wraps his arms around my back and under my legs, picking me up into his arms. I lean my head against his chest, feeling his heartbeat. I wrap my arms around his neck, never wanting to let go.

My husband kisses my forehead and then pushes the door to our room open. The room is a mess.

When Dehlin returned to Lenair, he didn't only bring soldiers, but all of our belongings. Everything is packed into traveling chests and it looks like Luthias attempted to go through some of it. He sets me down onto the bed and I wrap the blankets over me. Luthias moves to open the window.

"I'm going to cut my hair."

I sit up in bed. "You are going to what?"

"For Avon." He grabs the scissors off of the bed side table. "Will you help me?"

I take the scissors into my hands.

"All the other males cut their hair when you died. It is a Lithien tradition and even Avon followed it. He was reluctant though."

"And did Dehlin cut his hair?"

Luthias simply chuckles. "No. He would never."

Chapter 19

Yellow blankets adorn the bed in a messy heap, as I roll over to face Luthias. His freshly cut hair is sprawled out in every direction along with his arms and legs. It has to be midday by now and he is still fast asleep. I woke up an hour or so ago, but I have no inclination to leave the comfort of the many blankets and my handsome husband beside me.

I caress his freckled face that is warmed by the sun currently shining through the open balcony doors. He stirs slightly as I prop my head up with my hand. Soft, tired eyes, still lost in sleep, meet mine. "Good morning, my beautiful wife." Luthias grins as he squints his eyes closed and stretches his arms out behind him.

"Good afternoon." I giggle into the sheets near his face.

"Afternoon? I really slept that long?"

I roll closer to him as he snuggles his face into my hair. His arms wrap around my waist as he breathes in deeply. I turn to my other side to face him.

"I like your hair like this." I smile as my hands run over the top of his head and through the short length left to his red hair.

"The last time I cut it, I left it a bit longer and the style didn't suit me."

"I appreciate you feeling that Avon is important enough for this tradition. I know that you two had your differences."

I wrap the yellow blanket around my shoulders as I crawl out of bed and onto the floor. I look over my shoulder as Luthias reaches towards the bedside table for the cup of tea. He grips the painted cup with lavender flowers around its base with a light touch. He coughs slightly as he fights the urge to spit it back up.

"It's cold!"

"What? Did you expect warm tea in the afternoon from your wife? That's from yesterday."

Luthias huffs in frustration as he too finds himself on the floor next to me. I open the chest in front of me. My husband wraps his arms around my neck as he kisses my cheek. The warmth from his shirtless body fills me with a unique kind of happiness.

I unwrap the first object from the chest. Based on the carvings on the front of the traveling chest, I assume that it is our hope chest. A place where Luthias and I could put momentums from our past and future.

Loose petals fall onto the floor as I find what is left of my wedding bouquet. Someone had managed to find daffodils in the winter and I never knew who to thank that day. It's a miracle that it's not completely dust after being trapped in this chest for over a hundred years.

I run my hand over the hope chest. Carved words line the bottom of the box. *When I am lost, your hope shall find me.* Under where my bouquet sat, my wedding dress lays. There is a slight vintage tint to the fabric.

I continue to take things out of the box. A box of letters that belongs to Luthias now sits in his lap. Hundreds of notes just from his mother overflow the box they reside in. There are also drawings of his family. All four of them are smiling, innocent from the world full of darkness and death. I know that all changed after Laura was killed in battle.

Luthias quickly sets down the picture and pulls out a small wooden arrow. His smirk grows and he looks at me. "This is the first arrow that I shot a bullseye with. That must mean my bow must be in here somewhere." He rummages through the chest until he reaches the bottom and carefully pulls out his first bow.

The comparison between the war bow he uses in battle and this, tiny thing, is comical to me. It is hard to imagine that he was once so little.

Luthias places a kiss on each side of my face before he reaches for his shirt draped over the chair. He goes to open the door and speaks a few unheard words to the guard outside. I don't quite like the idea of being guarded this closely, but Dehlin's orders are for the safety of everyone here.

The door opens once again and a woman comes rushing into my arms. She lifts me off the ground, embracing me in a tight hug. I giggle as she sets me down. She pushes a loose hair away from my face and behind my pointed ear.

"Everyone has been so worried about you." Etta rushes through her words, out of breath as she embraces me once more. "I missed you so much."

"I missed you too, Etta."

She quickly places her hands on her hips. I can tell that she is already preparing to fix me and my tangled hair. "Now, what have you done with yourself?" She lifts up my arm, shaking it. "You're paler than your sister."

"I've always been paler than Eryn." I pause for a moment. "How is she?"

"Wiser, more beautiful, and mother to more children."

"How many children did they have?"

"Four in total. Three girls and one son. Their poor son, he is constantly followed by them. They really do look up to your sister's son." She walks to the closet, opening the doors to look amongst my array of gowns. Etta begins to rummage through the clothing and I watch as she stops to put up her dark hair. With a fluid twist, she sticks a thin piece of decorated ivory into her hair to hold it all together. She takes a wine red gown from the closet.

"Please not red. Anything but red." Red reminds me of the stained clothing after Avon's death. Luthias is prepared to step in, but I raise my hand to both him and Etta. I then look to Luthias as I lower my head, giving him the signal that I would like to speak with Etta alone.

"Yes, darling?"

"Am I doing something right?"

"Something right? What do you mean?" She takes a seat in the tufted chair. She seems confused by my meaning.

"I mean, am I doing the right thing with becoming Queen and all? I feel like I am too weak to do this. I am not strong enough. That I don't have the right sword for the right battle."

"Every sword is sharpened the same, it's the hand in which wields it that you should be scared of." She shakes her head and mocks me. "Am I doing something right?" She laughs as she rolls her eyes. "You are doing everything right. You are a force to be reckoned with. And your arm with a sword, everyone should be frightened."

I pull another gown from the closet. One of a yellow color instead of the blood red.

"Now, one more thing LaRue."

"Yes, Etta?"

"Smile."

I smile just for her, but I am not sure if it's going to last the walk down to the dining room for lunch this afternoon. I exit my room and Luthias quickly takes my hand.

We descend down a different staircase, one that doesn't lead to the dining hall. "Are you lost?"

"No, but I have been told that everyone is having lunch in the gardens. It's too nice of a day to spend inside anyways."

The two of us exit a passageway leading outside. Food is set out on a few tables and my court is sitting on the bright green grass.

They all turn to me, smiling. I sit down next to Tasar and I notice that they are all still wearing the necklaces from the oath we took many years ago. *Had they felt all the pain I was in? Even when I died or when Avon died?*

It seems that I get a hug, after a hug, after a hug. *Do they know that they are embracing a murderer?* Tolendeil's words echo through my mind. *The killer of innocence.* The world, *children,* brings me out of my thoughts.

"What?"

"We were just discussing how there is a lack of full Elven children." Elora explains, while braiding her daughter's silver hair. "We are wondering when there might be a new Prince or Princess." She smiles.

"I refuse to have children until the evil we are fighting is gone from this world. I am not bringing a child into this world while it still lives." *I will only make that mistake once.*

Eldrin reaches over to grab an apple for me. It saddens me that he can't move his legs anymore, but his upper body is perfectly functional. My brother tosses the apple to me and I catch it, placing it in my lap. He grins.

"What exactly happened?"

"I fell off a cliff, broke my legs, passed out, and then I couldn't move."

"I meant the specifics. Like how you feel off of the cliff in the first place."

He clears his throat. "I was being chased out of the Lithien borders by Elbonare's servants. I assume they are a part of Malien's men. It seems that they are seeking out swords. It's an odd thing to look for, but Mim did the same with rings. So, I refused to give them my sword and they decided to try and kill me. I ran and they ran me right off of the cliff to what I thought was my death."

Chalsarda pipes in. I smile as I hear her voice. "A few names of swords have been mentioned in the black market. It seems like they are all weapons from the Oath takers."

"And why were you roaming around the black market?" I widen my eyes. I know that only the highest trained Elves are sent there secretly. That was how they found copies of my prophecy.

"I have been promoted." She points at the arm band that sits above her elbow. "Amar and I have been in charge of going undercover in the black market. They have been becoming more and more popular these past years."

"We come back with all sorts of information. The price on all of our heads is a common one. It is always changing, always rising. Even though you were dead, there were rumors that you were roaming the wilderness like an ancient sprite." Amar butts in.

"Or seeking revenge for those who did you wrong."

"When we interrogated people we would warn them that LaRue was watching their every move."

Luthias chuckles. "I like the idea of you as a sprite. Whoever came up with that ridiculous idea?"

"I mean, she did just wake up and walked away." Tasar speaks with his mouth full. "We didn't believe the guards when they said that your body had just walked away from your resting place."

I smirk. "It does sound a bit crazy. If anyone decides to write a novel about me, they might think of changing that part up. I do like the sprite idea."

"I like to think that father was behind the sprite idea." Eldar sits closely to his brother. "He used to call you that when you were younger, right?"

"Very often. When he wasn't calling me by my full name when I was in trouble."

"Sprites are troublemakers."

My heart seems to clench inside of my chest. I would assume that Avon would have made that comment if he was here, but it comes from Dehlin instead.

Dehlin smirks. "Avon would joke with your father that you were secretly a sprite that Elender had found one day and decided to keep."

"Back on this sword topic. I did place your armor and such in the throne room." Amar keeps his eyes on his plate. "It is not the best of ideas to leave it out on the pavilion floor."

I nod my head in thanks. My friends spend too much time watching out for me. How can I ever repay them for practically babysitting me my whole life?

"You've gotten yourself into a lot of odd situations that I don't think the Electa had planned."

"I think they just say the Electa plans out paths, so we will be more conscious about our own decisions and how the Gods are the ones with all the credit."

Elora's daughter catches my eye. "Mother used to tell me about your glorious, golden armor, why didn't you wear that into the recent battle?"

"It was originally my mothers. So, I felt that I needed something of my own."

"You don't know much about her, do you?" Elora attempts to shush her daughter's interest, but I don't mind. Talk of Andwin is socially forbidden in Lindalin.

But nonetheless, my shoulders tense up. "I don't know a thing other than her name was Andwin. I know my grandparents, but they don't speak of her either."

I look to Eldrin and Eldar hoping that they might provide a little more information for the curious Silevel.

"What of her death? Do you know how she died?"

"No." I look to the floor. "I don't. I imagine it would be in a morbid way if no one talks about it."

Silevel's curiosity seems to be filled as she has no more questions about my mother. Dehlin places his hand on my shoulder.

I am pushed backwards into an empty seat as Dehlin drops a stack of papers onto the table and ink beside them. "Some rules need to be set up. I don't expect you to go through all of them." The Golden Lord lifts the top page from the stack, but I am too busy admiring the view from the window. "This is the original set of rules from King Greythore's reign."

I loom over the first page. Water damage has taken its toll and some of the words are difficult to read. No wonder why my father spends so much time rewriting damaged documents.

Rules of Lenair: The First Age

"I can already tell this is going to be boring." I tell the two males in front of me.

1. Everyone who enters the kingdom of Lenair must be sworn into secrecy of its location. If this rule is broken, they will either be imprisoned or executed, depending on the severity of the matter.
2. Access outside of the gates must be granted from King Greythore himself or the royal court of Lenair.
3. Guards are required to protect the King and his heirs at all times. Even when off duty, they shall be prepared for any sort of danger or attack on the kingdom.
4. All seven gates will be locked at dusk and will be reopened at dawn.
5. Violence is not tolerated.
6. Beggars who sit in the streets will be brought to King Greythore's council.
7. Marriage, birth, and death is to be documented in the library hall.

8. *The Lords of the Twelve Houses and that of the Healing Houses must be on duty at all times, unless leave is given to them.*

"I agree with most of it." I make a few scribbles, crossing out execution mostly. Along with replacing King Greythore's name for mine and Lu's. *Lu; the little, bright red haired boy with freckles littered across his cheeks.* Luvon and I would call Luthias that all the time. "I think we should plan the coronation to be on Ellatae."

"The summer celebration." Luthias chimes.

"Or in other words, The Fall of Lenair." Dehlin's crystal eyes look past me.

I place my hand onto his arm. "No. The Rebirth of Lenair." Dehlin disappears with a smile and a nod of his head. I meet Luthias' glance. "What are we going to do about Malien? Because I think we should have a council. A judgement of his manner."

"I am leaving that up to you. You have certain personal feelings about the decision and I think you should be the one to decide what should happen to Malien." Luthias plants a kiss on my cheek. "I'm going to spar with Tasar. If you need anything, you can find us near the armory."

Luthias turns towards the door and leaves. I am left alone for a moment, but I leave before I can get annoyed by the silence. I walk past two guards at my door and they follow me down the hall, a flight of stairs, and into the dungeon. I turn the corners until I reach the only occupied cell.

"Oh, look. The bitch Queen came to visit me. How nice of her." Malien purses his lips and the guards behind me stand at attention at Malien's comment. Their hands rest on the hilt of their swords.

"Malien, I am tired of your attitude."

"I am already tired of yours." He rests his head against the bars of his cell.

I quickly change the subject. "I must ask you some questions."

"Aren't you supposed to hold a trial and ask me questions there?"

"These are more on a personal level. They're about Avon."

"Oh, so, after you kill him you want to get to know him. Will that make your grief and guilt fade away into nothing if you at least know something about him?"

"I knew him for much longer than you ever did." I growl through my teeth as I clench my fists. "I want to know about his mother."

He pauses for a moment and then pulls something from his pocket. He holds it out to me from between the bars. The silver locket is engraved with a cursive *A*. Avon had a similar one when he came to Ambrose.

I open the locket revealing two drawn portraits. One drawing is of a young Avon and who I suppose is his mother. The other is of Malien and his wife, smiling at each other. They seem so happy. *Avon seems so happy.*

"He never told you, did he?" Malien asks. "Why we sent him to Ambrose."

"No. I don't think he knew."

"He knew I was Elbonare's servant. My family line has an oath with the God of Wind that a son must at all times be by Elbonare's side. It was dangerous for Avon and we didn't feel that we could protect him. Aneirin died in the forest of Ambrose, but Avon was safe and that was all that mattered."

"She died. She is buried in Ambrose." There is silence between us. "Why did you wait so long to come back for Avon if you knew he was in danger?"

"Because Elbonare is scared to lose another servant. He wants someone as a backup for me. That is why Avon is better off dead. No one but Caolan can touch him there."

I shove my hand through the gap in the cell doors to hand Malien back the amulet. He pushes it away. "Keep the amulet. To remember the two of them."

I give a nod of thanks before leaving the dungeon.

Luthias steps out into the hallway with his travelling gear over his shoulder.

"Where are you going?" I am puzzled.

"The cabin. Or what is left of it." He shifts nervously on his feet.

"The cabin? Why would you go to the cabin?"

Luthias drops his bags onto the floor. "I need to see where you died. I am struggling with it and I need to just see it and be there." He grabs my face and kisses me softly. "I will be back in a few days."

"I need exact time." My voice becomes stern.

"Four days, possibly five. So expect me on the fifth. My father will be here in two days so he will be glad to see you."

"He will also be glad to see you. Which is another reason why you should stay." I cross my arms over my chest.

"LaRue. This is something I need to do for myself. And I think you understand that very well. We all go through things differently."

"If you must."

"Thank you." He reaches up for me to spin me around in a circle and then to finally set me down safely onto the floor. He places his hands on my shoulders and kisses my head. "I love you."

"I love you too." He turns to leave. "Luthias!"

"Yes?"

"Don't die."

He smirks. And as he leaves it is like everything falls apart. I sit down onto the stairs, propping my head up on my hands.

"LaRue!" Etta hollers. I sigh, covering my face, thinking that maybe, just maybe she won't be able to see me. I hear Dehlin walk down two steps and he places his hand on my shoulder as if protecting me from whatever Etta has planned. *Probably experimenting with my hair.*

"I need LaRue for the next few hours."

"She is relieved from all duties today."

Etta doesn't disagree with Dehlin because she knows this is a fight she can't win. Dehlin always overruled her decisions when it came to me. *The battle between a trainer and a nursemaid is terrifying.*

"When do you want to hold trial for Malien's crimes?"

I just want to get it over and done with. "Today."

"Today? Are you sure you are in the right mindset to do so?" Dehlin sighs, letting his broad shoulders drop. "Wear something that will make you look powerful and superior above all others. Make an impression that you are strong."

Without giving him another word, I begin to ascend the many stairs. Why are there so many stairs? The palace is filled with turrets and towers, secret rooms and hundreds of doors and windows. It's like a maze, a game of strategy to get to where you are going.

I pretty much have the path to my room figured out. I occasionally wander outside to admire the flowers or to see what Luthias is doing outside.

I open the door to the room and it is quiet. I hate this silence, hate knowing that he isn't here anymore.

Luthias will be back in a few days, but I can't help but feel like he will never come back. That I will never see the color of his eyes or the smile on his face.

While shoving open the wardrobe, I shuffle through coats and dresses. It seems that Luthias or Etta has just shoved all my old clothes into this one closet. I pull the violet gown that I had worn once for a celebration in Lithien off of its hanger. It goes well with the palace's white, marble walls and tiled floor.

I slip the dress over my head, tightening the corset back. I then shuffle through the hope chest to find the jeweled necklace. I clasp it around my neck. *Elbonare's prize.*

I stare into the mirror. I am not expecting another person to stare back. This isn't me, this is a different version of me. I look so skinny that if someone was to grab my arm it would break in half. And my hair seems to be a rusted color compared to its once golden hue.

And my eyes. They have no light to them. The dress even bulks up in the back and I notice how tightly I have to tie up the corset.

This is not me.

This is a fragile being, which is being killed by her conscious.

Avon's death is tearing me apart.

I shove the mirror towards the floor. It shatters to the ground and each piece falls onto the ground with a crash. I stare at the broken shards, shattered and unable to be put back together, just like me. The door swings open and Dehlin freezes in the doorway.

"Are you alright?" He asks while taking slow steps towards me.

"I'm fine."

He takes my hand, pulling me away from the shattered piece of the mirror. "Come on." He looks at me. "Are you sure you want to do this? Are you sure you are okay?"

"I'll be fine."

He fixes a piece of my hair before we enter the throne room. He enters first to announce my presence. I step into the throne room, walking up the hall. People look at me, smiling, but I meet the eyes of a young woman dressed in a red gown. Her blood red gown makes me avert my eyes to the floor. But the floor is carpeted in red. I look straight ahead at Tasar, keeping my eyes away from Chalsarda's red hair or the ruby jewels in Dehlin's sword. It all reminds me of Avon's blood. Vestan's blood. Caldon, Silvyr, all the others that I have killed and that have died under my watch.

I turn, slowly sitting down into my throne. I clasp my hands together trying not to think about the blood that was on my hands. No matter how many times I have washed my hands, I still feel like I can feel the blood on them.

I scratch at my knuckles and palms. *The feeling won't go away.*

"Now enters Malien, son of Doran who has been convicted for the murder of Tolendeil, daughter of Tervaughn, Avon, son of Malien…Laerune, daughter of Elender." The names seem to go on forever. He wasn't even the one to kill some of these people. I was. "He has been convicted of treason in Lenair, Lithien, Ambrose, Lindalin, and in Everford. He is suspected to be part of a greater evil and will be convicted on the crimes of harming the Queen. The final decision of his punishment will be granted by the Queen herself."

They shove Malien in with his hands tied in front of him. Two guards shove him into a chair a little farther from mine. "Malien do you agree that you are guilty of these crimes."

"No." The room is silent. I look up to him, almost begging him not to tell them that I was the one to kill Avon. I have yet to tell everyone the murder I have committed. "You think I killed all those people?" He points a chained hand towards his chest. "Trust me, I had help. I had lots of help from this bitch." Swords are pulled from their sheaths and my council stands a little bit closer to me, but I just sit up in my chair ready to embrace it all.

"Tolendeil killed herself, I just gave her a little extra push. Deulara and Daralien were killed under her and her council's swords. And for Avon. I think we all know what happened there. She drove her sword right through his stomach."

I force the tears back as I sit up straighter. Gasps escape from the crowd's mouths.

I grip the arm rest of my chair as I force myself to my feet. I pull the sword from the armor stand next to me.

"LaRue, this might not be the best place to kill him." Tasar whispers to me, but makes no move to restrain me. The walk to Malien seems long and his face looks as daunting as his fate.

I raise the sword over my head, ready to end Malien and the disaster he has created. The room is silent as everyone prepares for what I am going to do.

Chapter 20

I throw down my sword, cutting the chains that bind his hands. He lets out a breath. I then hand him the handle of my sword and he carefully takes it from my hands. His blue eyes, just like Avon's, blur in confusion. His brows furrow together.

"If you think it's just, then kill me." I whisper to him. "If you think that the darkness of my heart caused me to kill Avon, then end me."

The sword clatters to the carpeted rug. "It wasn't your fault."

"Malien, son of Doran, you shall be spared from any and all punishment. But, if I find that you are working with the enemy I won't think twice about making your life a miserable hell." I turn towards the guards. "Release him."

My choice doesn't go over well with the crowd and angry voices are like an encore as I leave the throne room.

Sentier meets me head on down the hallway. No hug is there to greet me. Just a simple question. "What is going on in there?"

"I've upset them for sparing a life."

He raises a dark eyebrow.

The King of Lithien, who I often find as my second father figure, places a hand on my shoulder. The gesture would seem small to others, but I have seen how he uses simple touch towards Luthias. *A gesture of proudness.*

I find myself nodding my head in understanding to him.

Sentier clears his throat as he returns his hands to his sides.

"I see that you decided to dress in Lenair's colors." I point at his violet tunic lined with yellow thread around the collar.

He pulls at the bottom of it. "I think I have been wearing blue for far too long. I am happy to support your kingdom." My father-in-law steps closer to me and leans towards my pointed ear. His words are quiet as a crowd of people begin to file through the doors of the throne room. "There are rumors?" I know what he is talking about already and my grin dissipates. "Are they true?"

189

This is my first meeting with Sentier since my death and I never imagined that we would be discussing rumors. My breath rattles deep inside of me or perhaps it is my broken spirit rattling within me. "They are true."

Without asking for the King of Lenair's help, he pulls me away from the hall as it becomes crowded with angry Elves. He locks the door of an empty sitting room and begins to open the curtains of the windows. Bright sunshine enters the room, casting warmth against my face. I take in the rays as if it would perk me up like a wilted flower.

"Elender sent me a letter telling me about the rumors."

"That should have been your first guess that it wasn't a rumor. He sees everything."

Sentier grins slightly. "He was the first to see the Great Laerune alive and back on her feet." He keeps a steady gaze on me. "I am sure he knew how everything would play out."

My grief suddenly turns into anger as I lower myself onto the tufted chair. "My father probably knew that the moment that he brought Avon into Ambrose, that I was going to kill him." My words rattle with hurt. "He knew I was going to die too."

Sentier keeps his straight backed posture near the window.

"What good can come from Avon's death? I've made a mistake and I feel tricked."

Sentier seems to ignore my comment. "Your father didn't tell you because he didn't want you to be afraid."

"Be afraid? I think I would have been stronger if I knew that I was going to die and come back."

"I don't think your father knew if you were coming back or not." The subject changes. "Where is my son?"

"Heading towards the Erutan Mountains as we speak."

Sentier looks puzzled.

"He wanted to see where I died. I guess to have some sort of...ugh...I don't know the word. Resolution? Conclusion? Closure!" I finally come up with the right word. "But I disagree." I swallow my words as I fight to find the more civil set of words. "I am here. I am not gone. I don't understand why he needs closure when I came back. I understand seeking this out when I was still gone. But why now of all times?"

"Everyone goes through things a little different LaRue, maybe this is just his way of realizing that you are still here and with him. Maybe he is taking this time to better himself with the situation with you and Avon. You do know that Avon was there when you died. Maybe he is asking himself questions about what your motivations were?"

I cross my arms across my chest.

"Why don't you just ask him when he comes back? When was the last time the two of you actually sat down and talked about what happened?"

"We haven't talked about it."

"Communication." I lean back into my chair as Sentier looks for a comfortable place to sit, but he seems undecided and remains standing.

"When did he say he was coming back?"

"He said he would be back in five days. But I suspect that it will take him longer if he is taking time to reflect."

Sentier sighs as he gazes out the window. "Lenair is so large compared to Lithien. I have heard stories when I was a child, but I never expected that it would be so vast."

"You heard the stories when you were a child?"

He turns to me with some sort of elegance written across his face. "I don't think you realize how old Lenair is. The Electa once resided here when there was a change in rulers. This was once Aquitaine's kingdom just like Ambrose was once Lyraesel's."

Sentier continues with his history lesson. He gets a certain kind of kingly tone to him, just like how my scholarly father sounds every day.

"But the Gods gave their kingdom to their servants and their servants then passed them to their disciples. They grew tired of this lowly world." He takes a deep breath. "Your father, unlike I, was the first generation of Ambrose. Tervaughn renounced his lordship to Elender in the First Age. And that is when your father met your mother."

The topic of my mother perks my interests. "Did you ever meet her, my mother?"

Sentier steps behind my chair and reaches for my golden hair. His soft hands run through my curls. "Yes. She was both terrifying and beautiful. Just like you." He chuckles. "And she was a far greater healer than your father."

I tilt my head as he continues to play with my tresses. "That's hard to believe. I watched my father heal even the deepest of wounds."

"But yet, he could not heal you when you were sick."

"I like to think that he knew I could do it by myself." I sit up straighter as I turn around in my chair to face him. When I was much younger, I contracted a horrible sickness that nearly killed me.

"Maybe that has been what he has been trying to tell you all of these years. That you," he points to my heart. "Are strong enough to face things on your own."

"There was a lesson in that, wasn't there?" I roll my eyes.

Sentier pats my shoulders. "You should listen to your peers. There are many lessons to learn from them."

I turn to face him. "When will my father be visiting?"

"Not any time soon."

I sink lower into my chair. I will resist any type of council about Avon until my father arrives. He will know what to do with my situation and how to explain it to everyone.

I have been keeping the thought of Avon to the back of my mind. But the grief is ever constant. If he was still here, I know he would be right by my side through everything. But everything that is now, is because I killed Avon. Trying not to overthink is my main focus. I just have to keep a smile on my face.

I hop up from my chair as I wrap my arm around Sentier's. "Come on. Let's get a drink."

🖋

Tea and drinks are far from the least of my worries. And I am able to give a sigh of relief as Sentier disappears to start on other business. I am sure he is stressed like the rest of us.

There is no heir to his kingdom anymore. Luthias is now King of Lenair and Lithien is left with nothing but Sentier and a few of his distant cousins. There is no one to carry the line of Lithien Elves if Sentier were to fall.

For once, I am able to avoid everyone.

I pull my knees up to my chest as I sit at the edge of Avon's resting place. I find myself talking and my voice echoes off the quiet walls.

"I have pushed Tolendeil's death to the back of my head and I feel guilty for it. They carried her body into the palace to prepare for burial, but I couldn't bring myself to leave the gardens that day. She is another person I have let down, and I couldn't even kill her murderer in fears of Elbonare turning him into a stronger version in his next life."

I wipe my eye with my sleeve. I can imagine Avon speaking back.

"You should really start to carry a handkerchief, you know?" Avon would tell me. *"You will ruin your dress sleeves."*

"I keep myself locked up in the upper levels of the palace. There are too many fears that might consume me on the lower levels of the palace. Speeches, confrontation, what to do with Malien, and of course the idea of having a coronation anytime soon."

I wrap my arms around the tulle of my dress. I can't help but feel furious.

Footsteps echo up the stairs and I dread the fact of anyone trying to talk to me.

"Go away. No one is welcome here."

"Is Death welcome?"

"No." My voice comes out cold. "Why are you here?"

Caolan kneels down beside me. I refuse to look at his pale, composed face. "To warn you."

"Of what?"

"Elbonare. He has found out that I lead you to the first stone. I am currently hiding in your realm. Elbonare is beyond upset and has the Electa's servants searching for me, you, and

193

your oath takers. I suggest you hasten your search and bring your court together. He knows you are here."

"Are you suggesting that I leave this kingdom without a King or Queen during its ascent?"

"Dehlin is more than capable of taking care of this kingdom while you are gone."

I bury my face into the fabric of my dress's sleeves, "Why should I trust you?"

Death sighs and rises. His knees crack as he stands. "We have gone over this Laerune. Elbonare fears you. If you have a higher title and rank, then you are closer to him. And if you have the stones, then he shall be terrified of your power."

"I don't think a mighty God like Elbonare could be terrified of me."

"I wouldn't doubt yourself so quickly. He sees you as a threat." Caolan reaches his hand out for mine. "I know it's difficult to trust during these hard times, but please. I am trying to help you like I always have."

I let a deep breath out as my hand clasps around his. "I hope that this will all make sense in the end."

"In time." His grey eyes hold a steady gaze with mine.

Chapter 21

Four days exactly pass when Luthias finally arrives back home. I feel that a part of me has been struggling these last few weeks due to the fact that so much misery has come from the empty halls of this place.

I have found myself hiding from my people, but with Luthias back, I feel more confident in escaping from the prison I call my room.

Amar knocks on my door to announce Luthias' arrival, but I have been watching the window since this morning. "Your red-haired prince is back."

While placing a delicate hand on Amar's shoulder, I smirk. "Red-haired King." I speak sarcastically.

"Not yet! A coronation is still in order."

"Then soon!"

I pull my golden cloak from the chair as I sweep it over my shoulders. The shimmering fabric glistens in the lowering sun as I descend the stairs with Amar at my side.

I have been hiding from most of my court these past few days. I fear that they did not agree with my choice on sparing Malien's life.

The castle doors glide open and a grinning Luthias rushes into my arms. My hands find his short, red hair and I pull him closer.

I shut my eyes as he places kisses across my cheeks and forehead as he finally finds my lips. A few seconds pass before he steps back to see my face. "You look better. More bright."

"Brighter? I've barely been outside."

"You know what I mean."

He grins at Amar, but suddenly becomes straight back as a door slams shut. We all become silent and still as Sentier's voice booms through the hall. "What did you do?"

My eyes widen as Sentier pulls on Luthias' now short hair.

"Tradition, father. In honor of Avon."

The King of Lithien makes no sound as he doesn't quite know how to process the image of his son with cropped hair once again. "You two have lost so much. You shouldn't have to be doing these things this often."

"What was it like? At the cabin?" Luthias and I sit cross-legged in the window seat.

"Burned. I never realized that it was completely destroyed. I thought perhaps there would be something left."

I avert my eyes away from Luthias and to the stars shining outside of the window. "Did you find what you were looking for?"

"Answers? No. This? Yes." Luthias dangles a chain in front of me.

I grab for it like a child with sticky paws. I roll the ring around my fingers. I had thought that my father had made Avon a ring that held a ruby stone to signify Avon's importance to Ambrose, but Avon had simply bought it from a blackmarket when we were younger.

"Your father said it would be there and if I got the chance to go and find it then I should." Luthias places the ruby ring onto my right hand. The ring was once my engagement ring from Avon. "You have a piece of both of us now."

Chapter 22

Days pass and Luthias' and I's coronation has arrived. I dread the thought that the coronation is today. I mostly dread the thought of getting ready for it. So, I give myself a head start hiding from the maids.

The sun shines into the courtyard and the white walls of Lenair make it even brighter. I sit down on the edge of a fountain, admiring the sunrise. The wind whips the flags above me. The purple and yellow fabric shimmers in the dawn sunshine.

This is the first step to becoming myself again. I sigh, wondering where Etta is at the moment. I don't want to spend all day putting on dresses and having my hair pulled for hours on end.

"LaRue, they're all looking for you." Luthias says, sitting down next to me. "You have Etta in a rampage."

"Well, they certainly aren't looking very well."

Luthias lowers his head. "She is worried that you are…well…speaking to Avon. And she doesn't want to bother you during that time."

I smile at Etta's consideration of my time alone. Avon should be here. He always talked about me becoming a Queen someday and that he would be by my side to place that crown upon my head.

Etta enters the balcony's courtyard and she stomps towards me with an angry smirk across her face. "I have been looking everywhere for you." She grabs my hand and pulls me away from the fountain. I am led into a dressing room that only contains a closet, a vanity, and a large stand up mirror.

"It seems that you have it very easy today."

"Why is that?" I sit down into the nearest chair.

"Because, while you were taking 'you' time, Luthias had picked out everything for your extra special day."

I look over to the privacy screen and at the beautiful lavender gown that hangs upon it. Etta begins to play with my hair and then tells me to go and put on my dress. She holds open the skirt as I step in. The fabric is soft against my legs as she pulls it up and begins lacing up the back.

The little pink flowers around the skirt make the dress seem delicate and innocent. It makes me look beautiful. Soft. Kind. *Innocent.*

Etta has me sit back down and she begins to work her magic on me. I expect her to pull my hair into elaborate braids, but she only pulls some of it back, leaving the rest in a cascade of curls. She begins to place pink and purple flowers in my hair.

My nursemaid releases me from her tight grip as soon as she finishes my hair. I leave in search of Luthias. His maids had also taken him away and all three of them are fussing over what tunic he should wear. But, I think it is just an excuse to see their future King shirtless.

They seem to stop bickering as I close the door behind me. Luthias gives me a look, asking for help. "You may leave." I tell the three girls. They bow their heads and scatter away with giggles.

"You look absolutely stunning." Luthias smiles.

"Thank you." I begin to search through the different shades of purple, pink, and yellow tunics. The maids have really made a mess out of the pile. But after a few minutes, I pick one out. Luthias doesn't complain as he looks into the mirror at the lavender shirt. I make him stand so we can both admire ourselves in the mirror. I rest my head on his shoulders as he smiles.

Sentier enters the room with a box within his hands. "This was left in Lithien. Your mother would have wanted you to wear this before the weight of a larger crown sits upon that pretty head of yours." He opens the box to reveal my mother's crown. He places it into my hands. The silver metal and violet jewels shimmer. "Your parents are proud of you. Remember that." I close my eyes as the crown is placed upon my head. It sits heavily.

"Are you ready?"

I desperately want to say no, but I run my hand over Avon's ring that I have placed on my right hand. I wear it as a reminder of my first home and of Avon and everything I owe to him.

"Yes."

We wait for the grand doors to open. Luthias takes my hand in his as we both take a deep breath. The hall is quiet and I pace back and forth; the only sound is my heels clinking against the stone floor.

"I don't know why I am so nervous." My husband tells me. The Prince of Lithien is hardly nervous.

The doors open and there is a bigger crowd than I thought there would be. But, I stay calm as I look at the love of my life by my side. He looks at my eyes, grinning. We reach the two thrones and we stand before them. We kneel down to announce our oath. Dehlin stands before us.

"I here present unto you, Laerune and Luthias, your undoubted Queen and King. Wherefore all you who have come to this day to do your homage and service, are you willing to do the same?"

I look to Luthias as Dehlin continues. "Will you solemnly promise and swear that you will protect this kingdom of Lenair and your possessions and territories as well as your people?"

"I solemnly promise to do so."

Luthias and I rise as we ascend the steps of the dais and find out spots in the stone thrones. Amar and Tasar each place a crown onto our heads, replacing the ones we originally wore into the throne room. Avon should be here placing this crown upon my head.

"All hail King Luthias and Queen Laerune."

There is a celebration of sorts outside, but I find myself wandering the halls to the observatory. The wind brushes through my hair, sending the flowers drifting into the breeze. I lean up against the balcony. The fall to the bottom seems like miles away. Lights soon drift up into the air, filling the sky like stars. The desperate need to share this view with the ones I have lost is overwhelming.

Luthias walks in with his shirt off as he replaces it with a comfier tunic. I walk over to him, slipping into his arms that welcome me with a warm embrace.

A horn echoes from below the tower and Luthias and I both look to each other with a worried look. *What could it be this time?*

Please be nothing bad. Please.

A guard rushes in and I close my eyes, preparing myself for the awful news. I find the closest chair to seat myself into.

He bows before us, addressing us as King and Queen. "An Elf has entered the gates."

"Well that certainly isn't much news."

"You will understand when you see him for yourself."

We follow after the guard. My curiosity is rising. Who would be so important that we need to be there so quickly?

We stop at the gate in shock as we notice Dehlin embracing an Elf tightly.

"You were dead. They told me you died!"

"I watched as you were pulled down by our enemy."

"It doesn't matter how or what happened. All that matters is that you are alive and here, Flavel."

Flavel. Lord of the House of the River. The slayer of Ender the dragon. In books it is said that he had the most beautiful voice and the most musical talent with a flute. And now, he has returned from the dead. *He has been reincarnated.* Death continues to hold his promise of returning Elves to the living world.

Dehlin turns towards me, releasing his tight embrace on Flavel.

Flavel bows to me, a silver flute in his hand. "You are LaRue?" He pronounces my name with a slight accent. "It is an honor to meet you. There is much talk of you in the Halls of Caolan. It is said that you had arrived there and then decided yourself that you wanted to come back. But I am not sure if the rumors were true." The Elf bows.

"Something like that." It is an odd feeling to be both popular in the living world as well as the halls of the dead.

Flavel bows again, his long dark hair covers his face. He brushes it away and then takes my hand in his free one. "May we speak alone?"

We walk quite a ways from where we started. He holds my hand tighter, his flute in his other palm. "Your hands are warm." He confesses. "It is different for me."

"How so?"

"When you are dead for so long, everything starts to feel cold." He sighs, letting go of my hand. "I've been dead since the First Age. I feel like I have to relearn everything now."

"Why are you here, Flavel?"

He glides over to the balcony overlooking the city of Lenair. His eyes wander over the kingdom. "I have many reasons." The tall Elf turns towards me. "I've come to speak with you. To speak to the Queen of my home. To give her a message. To help her. I've come to find my best friend. But most of all, I've come to live my life. To live, not exist as a memory."

"I know how it feels."

"Of course you do. Not many people can understand how it feels to watch your life fade away and how hard it is to turn away from the riches that Caolan has to offer."

"But then we return and the world is different. People are different. They don't want to believe in you anymore."

Flavel kneels down, taking my hands in his. "The Electa wants to imprison you. They want to use the Angale to hold you in their land." I look down at the floor. "I am here to help you LaRue."

"The Angale is supposed to be for the highest dangers in Laquilasse. Not for me. I haven't done anything wrong. Well, not at least anything endangering this world."

"We know this LaRue. I was offered the chance to sit in on one of the Electa's meetings. They are planning things."

"Imprison me? Why don't they just kill me?" The Angale is a chain of sorts and is used to hold prisoners accused of the worst crimes. I have read that it will cause excruciating pain to the one who is locked in it.

Flavel sighs, rising to his feet. "Too many people love you. It would cause an uprising if they killed you. They are sending out information to betray you. Plus, Caolan would bring you back to life in an instant. If you aren't dead, the God of Death can't have any power over you."

"But that would never happen."

Flavel turns back to look at the city.

"You said you have a message for me?"

"It seems that they want to deliver the message themselves."

"Who is sending a message?"

"They will speak to you later tonight."

He sighs while setting his flute in his cloak pocket. Flavel begins to sing. His voice stops me in my tracks. It calms me. Its sweet sound is the most enchanting I have ever heard.

> *The clean valley air,*
> *The golden leaves*
> *Falling from the tall trees.*
> *The rushing sound of waterfalls*
> *And the hymns of the singers.*
> *Where there is playful laughter*
> *And peaceful stories of adventure.*
> *Where time stands still,*
> *And illness can't reach its borders.*
> *With ivy covered slopes*
> *And hills of lilies that*
> *Perfume the air.*
> *Where the sun shines*
> *The brightest,*
> *Where the Elves yet dwell*
> *In Ambrose.*

"You miss home LaRue, don't you?" He turns towards me. "You miss what your life was like. You miss Avon. You miss your father, your sister. You miss your home kingdom."

"Always."

"Home will always be there for you."

I sigh. "I'm afraid that if I don't finish the task that is ahead of me, then there will be nowhere for me to call home."

"Don't think like that. You doubt yourself."

"But the Electa. How will I do anything if the Electa are going to be against it?"

"Just push them off their high pedestal. Nadalahine, the all mighty God of the First Age, wouldn't have wanted them to be this way anyways. All they care about is popularity and power."

I return to the observatory. The golden telescope points towards the sky. I place my eye to the lens to gain a closer look at the stars. I gaze up at the brightest, the light shining with a million different colors.

I then walk around the telescope and to the railing of the balcony. It's as if I could reach up and take the star for myself.

"Laerune Aduial." A silk like voice speaks from behind me.

She is clothed in purple starlight with the light of a thousand stars strung upon her hair. White markings crossed over her face are in the shape of constellations and she smiles, almost laughing. It was as if her eyes were the galaxies themselves. They are onyx and they too have stars within them.

She walks closer to me, reaching her hands out for mine. "I am Sibylla-"

"The Goddess of Stars. I could tell by your eyes." I speak.

"You are just how they depicted you. Well, not the evil part." The constellations in her eyes change as if the sky above was changing its star patterns for the season. "They depicted you as a villain, the one who would destroy us all." She walks around me, her train of stars wrapping around my legs. "I didn't believe them though. I can see the kindness in your eyes."

She doesn't exactly focus on me, but beyond me. "Are you blind?"

"Blind to some things. Not all." Sibylla looks up at the stars above her. "I can see what the stars reflect. You have stars in your eyes, that's how I can see you." She caresses a pale hand over my cheek. "You are kind. You have a star in your heart."

"Why have you come here?"

Sibylla lowers herself down to the bench. Her gown seems to liquefy, bleeding into the night sky as she creates her unique constellations. "I wanted to see you for myself. And to help you of course." She offers me a seat next to her. "Caolan sent me to you. But we must be mindful, for Elbonare could be listening through the wind."

Sibylla then takes my hands in hers. They are cold, just how you would imagine starlight to feel. Cold, yet comforting. She traces a finger over my hand, forming freckles upon my skin. "You are now part of the stars Laerune." She places her hand under my chin to show me where to look up at the night sky. The same pattern she drew upon my hand is now reflected in the heavens.

"Remember that pattern at all times." Sibylla reminds me. The brightest star shown right in the middle of the constellation. "You will need it in time."

"Is it one of the stones?"

Sibylla rises to her feet. She is silent, yet her smile says more than I can understand. "There are some of us still on your side Laerune. Do not give up hope on all of the Electa."

She seems to fade away into the sky itself. Now the area around me is nothing but cold, shining stars wrapped in darkness. And I am alone.

I run a hand over the backside of my palm. The pattern does not rub away nor fade from my skin. It is permanently there forever. I shiver as the wind brushes by.

Is Elbonare listening?

Who is on his side?

The festivities down below me roar. The music is so loud that it causes me to smile as I look over the balcony. I wonder if Luthias is down there.

I descend the stairs in a rush as I wish to be joining the festivities with the others. I smile as the crowd who was just dancing bows to me. Smiles shine upon their faces and they know that my position as their Queen is just. I feel confident and my heart pounds with excitement.

Luthias appears at my side with a different outfit on. *Oka.* I had died when she was only a pup but one hundred years later is a long time for a dog.

I notice Elora with Oka beside her. Before I had died I had found out that my pet was in fact a Wolf God.

Her giant paws thunder through the crowd as she strolls to where I stand. Her large head reaches my shoulder. Oka simply lowers her head in respect. A growl rumbles from her jaws as she sits at my feet, pushing her nose into my hand.

My loyal protector. None will dare harm me while this great, Wolf God was near me. She shows her teeth in dominance as she lowers to lay her stomach against the grass. Another rumble echoes through her.

"Oka has grown aggressive and hard hearted in the long years while you were gone." Her eyes flash to the different people in the crowd as a warning. When she growls it seems like she was telling them not to bring any harm to her master.

I am handed a glass of wine as the crowd around me begins to quiet down.

"I am glad to announce that with our new titles of King and Queen," I turn to look at Luthias, "That we will need to officially appoint a court."

"Our court will play different parts, but they all shall be Princesses and Princes of Lenair."

Amar and Chalsarda walk through the crowd with crowns of silver upon their red hair. Eldar and Eldrin walk through the crowd dressed in light purple robes. Eldrin is being pushed in a wheeled chair.

Elora and Tasar walk together with Silevel in tow. Elora's hair is adorned with violets.

Dehlin enters, not in purple, but in shining gold. The golden Lord of Lenair is finally home. I raise my glass to all of them. To my family, my binding oath takers. *They shall feel my pain as I feel theirs.*

I imagine what we must look like to everyone else. "We are now a united court. Yet few are missing. My heart yearns for them to be here with us today. So I ask each of you, to raise your glass to the fallen." We have all lost someone so there is no need to explain.

The glasses are raised. "To the fallen."

I whisper all of their names under my breath. *Avon. Tolendeil. Caldon. Silvyr. Vestan. Lorindel.* But yet my heart is calm. Caolan has seemed to calm my heart and their death.

I look up to see a raven and a nightingale sitting on a branch together. I grin as they ruffle their wings. *Some of the Electa are on my side.* They bow their heads in greeting or perhaps in proudness.

I smile at my court.

"We have healers looking for a cure."

"Too bad that we can't get Lyraesel to just appear and fix all of this."

I place my hand onto Eldrin's back. "I promise things will get better."

He grins widely. "You never want to give up, do you?"

"Not when it comes to all of you. You never gave up on me." I pull Eldar into a hug as well and the rest of my court joins us. "I am so glad that all of you are my family."

"We couldn't ask for a better King and Queen." Tasar tells us, the rest agreeing to his comment.

For a single moment, everything seems perfect. It seems just the way it should be. There is no war and death for just this single moment. But I know that it will change in a matter of days. After this celebration we will continue the search for the remaining stones of the Electa.

Dehlin approaches me. "There is someone waiting for you in the observatory."

🖋

I shudder at the thought of being transported elsewhere. Because elsewhere is exactly where I am. Caolan's halls have appeared to me.

Before words can escape my mouth, those familiar arms wrap around me, filling me with warmth and love. The smell of peppermint reaches my nose and I laugh.

"I feel like I've walked a thousand miles to just find you, LaRue!" He picks me up and begins to spin me around the black halls that surround us.

His eyes shine the brightest blue they have ever been. I run a hand over his raven black hair and then his pale cheek as I bury my face into his neck.

"Avon, I am so sorry."

"Don't be." His eyes become filled with understanding, as he too runs his palm over my cheek. "I knew why you had to do it, so don't worry yourself." His grin widens. "And you are here, even if it is for a short while." Avon then looks down at my gown. "Some grand celebration?" Although Avon questions the celebration, I know that he already knows.

"Coronation."

His eyes light up as he bows. "My Queen."

"Oh, stop it." I slap his shoulder.

"Is that my ring?" He points at my hand.

"Luthias found it at the cabin."

He chuckles, taking my hand in his. "I knew he would." Avon walks with a leap in his step. "I want to show you my favorite place. I go here often when I miss you."

As if I was walking through his dream, the black halls turn into the rolling waves of the ocean.

Avon sits upon the sand of the beach, crossing his legs. "We would always dream about going to the ocean together. The ocean reminds me of what we dreamed of adventuring." He walks closer to those glistening waves.

"I can walk the endless halls of Lithien, read in the trees of Lindalin, or even watch the Dwarves mine in Makya. Of course when Caolan doesn't need me for whatever business." He sees the sadness in my eyes. "What's wrong?"

"I want you back in the real world. Not walking through it like a ghost."

"You will see me one day. Caolan is using a lot of his power, which is why he needs your son here. If the God of Death's full soul isn't present, then Elbonare will think he is up to something. But if Lorindel's strong soul is in Caolan's spot, than Elbonare doesn't know the difference."

"We just need to find the rest of those stones."

"*You* need to find those stones."

I shake my head. "I know. I know."

"Time is running out."

At first I think that Avon means the time to find the stones, but the air begins to feel as if it is slipping away. Avon places his hands onto my face.

"We will be reunited soon."

"I love you. Don't forget about me." I beg.

"How could I forget about the great Laerune?"

The world returns and Avon is no longer with me.

Chapter 23

We all enter the sitting room, the fire in the fireplace blazing. We take our seats. Some of us in cushioned chairs, others upon couches.

"Caolan is resurrecting the dead as an army. He is emptying his halls, sending back the ones that deserve to live."

Luthias' eyes gloss and I know that he is thinking about not only his mother, but his brother as well. All of the members of my court think back to family and friends that they have lost. I am sure of that. The more news we hear about it, the more real it feels.

"If we have Caolan on our side, who else is on his?" Amar questions.

"Lyraesel. Sibylla. There may be others, but I am not sure."

"What of Aquitaine?" Sentier enters the room. "Isn't she the lover of Caolan?"

"She is. But she is trapped in Elbonare's halls. I doubt she even has the ability to help."

Everyone stares at me. "Are they going to return?" I have never heard such a small voice come from Chalsarda. Elora nods her head in agreement. I know who they mean. I know who we have lost.

What will we do if they return? What will happen between Elora and Eldrin if Silvyr comes back?

I have seen how their relationship grows. Will that relationship end in conflict?

I look at Elora's daughter, asleep in her chair. A girl who was born to only a mother, her father had been taken away. But my brothers, especially Eldrin, have become father figures to her.

A bell chimes twice. "It is two hours past midnight. You all should rest."

"We still have much to discuss." Tasar growls. "How do we speak to Caolan?"

"We don't. We just have to wait for him to come to us."

Sentier searches the room for a glass and a bottle of wine. "Does he come to you often?"

"Occasionally." I open the cabinet, handing him the whole bottle. "Elbonare wishes to imprison me." I take the bottle away from him, taking a swig before sitting back down into my chair. "He wishes to chain me in his halls with the Angale."

Half of my court swears colorfully. "Why?" The question echoes through the sitting room.

"They wish to use the stones to become more powerful. They wish to destroy this world and become its highest superiors. I am a threat in Elbonare's way."

Luthias takes my hand. "We aren't going to let that happen."

"Maybe it needs to happen. Then they would be distracted by me and you can leave in search of the stones."

"That's not going to happen Laerune." The rest of my court chimes in. "We wouldn't give you up to Elbonare for all the jewels in Laquilasse."

I lean back in my seat. I sit on my hands in an attempt to not reach for the bottle of wine that now sits in front of me.

"It's late. We should discuss this in the morning." I get nods in agreement. "Dehlin, Tasar, can you please work together to prepare for our leave taking?"

"Some of you must stay because the kingdom needs a protector."

"I will stay." Dehlin volunteers. "I know how this kingdom works."

"I will stay behind as well." Both of my brothers chime in together.

"Will you be able to take care of my daughter?" Elora seems almost hesitant.

Eldrin attempts to sit up straighter. "With my life."

With a nod of my head, I dismiss them. Luthias follows closely behind me. "We travel to the mountains." I call behind me as I make my way down the hall. "We leave the day after tomorrow." I attempt a smile.

I slam the door shut as Luthias enters the room and pushes me towards the wall. "No more secrets, okay."

"What do you mean?"

"You can't just spring these plans on us."

"But they come to mind when I'm just sitting there. They spring up on me too."

Luthias shakes his head. "Why didn't you tell me?"

"That the Electa wants to hold me prisoner with the Angale?"

He nods his head.

"Because I don't want to believe it. I'm scared. The Electa are our high beings, our rulers. If they do capture me, I don't think I would be able to escape."

"They aren't even going to see you Laerune. I…Our court, will protect you and make sure that none of this ever happens." Luthias kisses my forehead. "You must be exhausted. This gown looks like it weighs a ton." His sideways smirk shines mysteriously.

🪶

The gown is neatly hung up in the wardrobe when the bell chimes thrice. "I saw him tonight."

Luthias raises an eyebrow.

"Avon." I swallow the pain that comes with his name.

"He wouldn't miss it for the world." Luthias smirks.

There is a knock on the doorframe, but when I open the door, no one is there. Luthias and I enter the hall. A shadow disappears around the corner. I rush down the hall with Luthias in tow behind me.

The shadow seems to be teasing us.

We run down the last turn, knowing that it will be stuck in the dead end of the hall. But nothing is there. Only a mirror reflecting ourselves and a raven feather on the marble floor.

"That wasn't just our imaginations." Luthias growls.

"No. It wasn't." I walk closer to the mirror to place my hand upon it. The edges are decorated in silver vines and violet flowers. At the top a dragon is perched with its wings spread and its tail twisting around the right side. At the base it is covered in jewels of every color.

Walk through.

"Are you coming?"

"Where?"

"Into the mirror."

My hand slips through the reflective glass. I step over the frame while grabbing for Luthias' hand to pull him in with me. The air is warm, but a cool breeze whispers through our hair. The sweet smell of parchment and lavender reach my nose and I smirk. *Ambrose.*

As our eyes adjust we find ourselves in my childhood room. I look behind us, my mirror the same mirror it always has been.

"Are we in Ambrose?"

"I was thinking of my father when I entered the mirror."

"Can we go anywhere with that mirror in Lenair?"

"I would think so."

"What was that shadow?"

I smile at Luthias. "Caolan."

A horn bellows and I run from the room. Luthias and I run towards the docks. The lake connects to a river that runs from the sea.

The boat that enters into the docks has a large sail. It looks like a cloud amongst our small fishing boats. Rows of men use large oars to paddle the boat forward. Women sing upon the ship as drums beat and horns bellow. At the front of the ship, a woman clad in rose pink, stands. Her posture is strong and she seems spirited.

Luthias looks to me and then to the symbol on their sails. A tree adorned with flowers; the roses stand out the most.

"Thia."

Thia's crest was once originally just a rose surrounded by thorns. But after the unity of Thia and Lithien with Sentier and Laura's marriage, the symbol was combined with the tree of Lithien.

They were sharp like thorns, but delicate like roses.

My father and his court stand beside us on the docks. "When did you arrive?" He questions. His red and gold robes glisten. Not even the look of shock is plastered on his calm face. *He knew I was coming. Or he knew about the mirror.*

"Just a few minutes ago actually." I point towards the ship. "I thought Thia was extinct."

"It was."

I find Luthias climbing to the upper level of the docks to get a closer look.

He nods his head. "Congratulations on your newest title."

"Thank you, father." I take his hand.

A sound escapes from Luthias above us. The sails drop on the ship and ropes are thrown from the docks to pull in their boat. A wooden step bridge is shoved against the boat to allow the passengers to step off.

Luthias rushes down the steps as the first passenger exits the boat. Her eyes meet with my father's. "Elender, we meet once more." Her voice is as soft as rose petals; a voice that I have only heard in visions.

"Mother!" Luthias almost runs to her with open arms to embrace her, but he creates a calm attitude when he stands in front of her. Her face is serious at first, but then turns into the widest smile I have ever seen.

They embrace, her pale, golden hair falling over her shoulders.

Another passenger exits the ship. "I'm surprised you're not rambling, brother. Have you grown out of that shy stage yet?"

"Luvon!" Luthias moves away from his mother to his brother. "I thought I would never see you again."

Laura turns towards me. "I'm sorry for the pain you have suffered. You are a great hero in my eyes. I am sorry that there wasn't more that I could do in your time of need when you were in Makya."

I bow my head. "You kept me calm. You kept me strong." I think back to the kind words she said to me when I was imprisoned in Makya.

She embraces me in her arms, kissing my cheek. "I've always wanted a daughter."

"You grew to be a pretty one." Luvon jokes. "My brother picks good ladies." Luthias shoves Luvon's shoulder at the remark.

"Is Sentier in Lithien?"

"No. He is in Lenair."

Laura becomes saddened. "That will take a week to get there."

"Luthias and I have a faster way." I wink.

🪶

I take a few minutes alone to explore my old room and if there is anything left to bring back to Lenair.

I glare at the gift sitting in the bottom of my wardrobe. My brows furrow at its perfectness. Neatly, it is tied with a cerulean ribbon.

Curiosity itches within me. I had received the gift the night before Avon and I were to be married. It seems like a cruel joke that my father got rid of all those wedding gifts but this one. Perhaps, he too, was curious.

My sticky paws grab at the gift as if I was a greedy child. But I am just greedy for a reminder of when Avon was alive.

I pull at the ribbon with the greatest amount of gentleness. Guilt appears in my gut. That's how I felt when this gift was first given to me because I had already made the choice to leave Avon. And he knew, and gave the gift nonetheless. My best friend through and through.

The ribbon falls into my lap. I run my hands across it to flatten the wrinkles that have occurred over the years.

The paper is brittle as I attempt to tear it neatly from what it is holding within.

A book slips from the wrappings and I stuff it into my travel book as Luthias and his family enters my room.

"You don't expect us to go through the mirror, right?"

"I do."

I place my hand on the glass as I step through. Luthias and his family follow behind me. We exit the dragon mirror into the empty hall in Lithien.

"Where is my husband?" The morning light is just entering the windows of the castle. Laura seems to be impatient as I lead her through the castle and to the guest room that Sentier has chosen.

She knocks upon the door, awaiting an answer. I sense her excitement. When Sentier opens the door, he rubs his eyes and shrugs on a shirt. He stares at Laura for a long moment before he can process that she is standing before him.

He pulls her to his chest, kneeling down onto his knees. He rocks her slightly. "You were gone, but now you are here. You are warm. Your eyes are alive."

Laura grins, unable to make many words but simply three. "I love you."

Once they can make words, Laura looks at him with seriousness in her eyes. She then looks towards Luvon and Sentier's eyes follow.

"Is that my son?"

"Have I really changed that much? I don't think I got ugly, did I?" He turns to me, winking.

"It's just been years." Sentier rises from the floor to embrace both of his sons. "This is a miracle that I can never repay. My heart is filled with joy." He then reaches a strong arm out to me and Laura. "My family was once small and it grew. But some were taken away. But Death can be merciful and return them all."

The light in Sentier's eyes seems to be renewed, as if Sentier himself was resurrected from the Halls of Caolan. His spirit truly has. I hope that one day my father's spirit shall be renewed like Sentier's has. I wish for him to never be lonely ever again.

"I would like to sit down and speak with all of you." Luthias takes my hand. "The matter is very important."

Chapter 24

My teacup clatters in my hands as I sit next to Laura. She had once come to me during my time in Makya to reassure me that whatever was happening was intended to happen. She has reassured me that I needed to be strong and to hold hope for my future.

Seeing her in a not so celestial light makes her seem normal; makes her on the same level as me.

The same race as me.

The same titles as me.

She faces the same threats as me.

She places a box into my hands. "Open later. When you are alone." She grins at me, her almost green eyes shining.

Luthias looks at them all. He is seated next to Luvon with his father over his shoulder. "Much has happened since Laerune passed into shadow and then returned. Too much in fact to share in detail." He lowers his eyes for a moment. "LaRue was with child, but unwillingly the Electa took our child as a sacrifice." Luthias takes in a deep breath. "We still want you to know that you are still the grandparents and uncle to our child. That even though he grows with Death, that he is and always will be ours and yours. He will always be family."

There is a moment of silence and I see out of the corner of my eyes that shadow again. I keep calm and I refrain myself from drawing too much attention to that one spot. I fumble with the box in my hands. The wrappings are colored a light pink with a bow shaped like a flower holding the box together.

Luthias notices the slightest bit of my distraction and he leans forward to take my hand. "I hate to tell you all of this, but LaRue and our court plan on leaving Lenair in search of the stones. You are more than welcome to join us if you think that is the path rightly intended for you."

Luvon vigorously shakes his head yes. "I am not letting you out of my sight ever again."

Luthias grins, but then looks to his parents. "We shall see, Luthias. I do wish to return home." Laura turns her head to Sentier. His pale hand intertwines with his. "I think our kingdom is in need of its Queen. I have seen how dark it has gotten."

Laura rises from her seat, placing a hand on my shoulder. "LaRue, would you care to show me around the palace?"

"It would be my honor."

I open the gate to the gardens for Laura. A woman rises to her feet, wiping her hands on her apron and then bowing. "Do the flowers look nice, your majesty?"

"They look beautiful."

"Do you still care for music, Laerune?" Laura asks, her head not even turned in my direction.

"I do."

"Were you taught any instruments along with your studies? I know you practically spent years learning about the stars."

"Yes. I played the pianoforte."

"Ah, the pianoforte. The rarest instrument just because it is so large to transport. There was one in Thia, but it was destroyed during the war. There was something about the sound it made that frightened people."

"It sounds mournful sometimes."

"Tis true." Laura bends down to snip off a dead flower with her nail. "Tell me of this looking glass."

"I don't know anything about it."

"Was it gifted to you?"

"It was just in the castle hall."

She places a finger to her mouth. "I've never heard of such a thing. You could send hundreds of people to one place without any effort."

"An army to the front gates of its enemy." I fumble with the box still in my hands. "But, they meet us at the gates of Lenair."

Laura meets my eyes. "What are you saying?" She seems highly confused.

"The mirror could send an army to Elbonare's Halls. But I had a vision where the enemy met at the gates of Lenair." I tug at the bow holding the box together.

"It tears you apart that you don't know what's in that box, doesn't it?" She points at me.

"Doesn't the unknown scare you?" I spin the box around. "I am just scared it's going to be something that brings back bad memories."

"I have chosen this gift not to bring you down, but to raise you up, Laerune. My son had once bought a similar one at a black market once."

"It better not be jewelry. I tend to lose those things. You know, if people just kept their jewelry and pretty stones to themselves then we wouldn't be having this problem of the war of the world and such other things. And why me? Out of all the people, why did it have to be me to be the only one to find these stupid stones?"

"Because Death chose you." Laura stands taller. "Caolan knew that you would be able to pass his tests and withstand what the Electa will put you through. You are strong. Your heart is strong."

"There is so many people-"

"Would they sacrifice themselves for others? Would they return when the God of Death offered them so much?"

"You've followed my story pretty close, haven't you?"

"I've been at Death's side for years, Laerune. I know many things and so does Luvon." She points at my hand. "Your story is already being written in the stars."

Laughter enters the garden as three Elves come strolling by. Their arms are wrapped around each of their shoulders. Luthias, Tasar, and Luvon chuckle about whatever they were talking about before they entered this part of the garden.

"Hey LaRue! Tasar and I want to know where to find the prettiest ladies." Luvon leans on my shoulder. "The most stubborn you can find."

"Sorry, I'm already taken." I push him off my shoulder with a laugh.

"Luvon. Behave." His mother growls at him. "You can't go talking to every lady. It's impolite. You can't lead them on." She folds her hands behind her back.

"Yes, be like Lu and love the same girl his entire life." His eyes turn to Tasar with a laugh. "I'm not just talking to them either."

Laura seems highly displeased. "You are of the royal bloodline of both Thia and Lithien. If I ever hear you speak like that again-"

"You'll send me back to where we were?"

Laura grabs him by his pierced, pointed ear, dragging him down the pathway. She releases him and points her finger as a warning to him. Laura then shoves him forward and back towards us.

Luvon pushes Tasar, announcing him as the finder. We all knew this game very well. The point was to run and hide from whoever was the finder. The game was usually to entertain children, but it's known to entertain adults too. *But the adult version tended to be more violent and swords were usually involved.*

We all run in separate directions through the maze of hedges. I stop behind a bush of violet hydrangeas. My nightgown bends in with the bundles of flowers. I still hold the box in my hand, the thought of what is in it still itching at the back of my mind. I shove it in my pocket.

Tasar runs by and I hunker down in the bushes. I stifle a giggle as I run from the bushes and down another row of hedges. Luthias comes around a corner, now in front of me.

"You better run!" Tasar yells.

Luvon quickly dodges me as I pass him around the next corner. I quickly come up to Luthias' side, passing him. I haven't ran this fast since I was younger. They never wanted me as the finder because I could always catch them all so quickly.

There is a scream behind us and Amar and Tasar run as Chalsarda becomes the new finder. I find Elora walking through the roses and I pull at her sleeve.

I turn to take a different corner. One by one I pass them, the rest slowing down behind me. The garden is a straight stretch to the village market and then through the castle halls back to the other gate.

"Run!" Luthias yells behind me as my friends slowly tire out and get caught by Chalsarda. A smile is plastered on my face as I exit the gardens, turning the corner to the village.

"Is that the Queen running?"

"There goes the rest of her court too."

My hair falls over my back, flying in the wind as I rush past my surroundings.

"Run Laerune!"

I skid through the castle halls and right past Dehlin and Flavel. They step back with a grin. I look behind me as Chalsarda gains on me. I see the door in front of me and I aim my arms out to open it.

The sun shines as the doors are flung open and I run to the next gate. Once I get there I would be the winner. Just a few more steps. I prepare myself to stop at the gate.

I roll onto the cobblestone path, laughing as my lungs burn in protest. Chalsarda joins me, her red hair flying everywhere.

"I don't think any of us could've caught you." Chalsarda rolls onto her stomach, still laughing. "The look on every Elf's face was enough to make anyone slow down and laugh."

"How will I ever look at them again?" I chuckle. The rest of my friends catch up to us. It feels as if a bit of my heart is less broken from this chance to have fun and be myself.

I place my hand on the castle gate door. It easily opens. "Is this the maze?" This was part of the kingdom that I have not seen. The walls tower in the blue sky. All of us stand, admiring the great walls that seem to go on for ages.

"I wouldn't start it now, if I were you." Dehlin calls towards us. "Or ever."

I turn towards him. "Have you been through it?"

"No. Most people die. It's more of to see if the enemy can ever make it through. They usually try. We often used it as a type of torture tactic."

The grey walls seem to loom over me. They seem to talk and warn me of their dangers. Their thoughts whisper into my mind.

We know you are our new ruler.
We won't harm you.
You are our Queen.

The voices are all different. They seem ancient. I take a step forward, but the gates close quickly before I can take another step.

"Don't try it, Laerune."

I step away from the gates as Dehlin places a lock onto the large doors. "I should get changed." I tell the others with a smile.

I run back to the castle, finding my way back to the dead end hall. I stare at my reflection in the mirror. She smiles back at me and I cock my head to the side. "Take me to the center of the maze." I step through the mirror and to what I was imaging as a stone circle.

I spin around in amazement as the middle of the maze shimmers into a paradise. The pool is the mirror and I dip my hand into it, the water rippling. The box in my pocket seems to jingle in protest that I haven't opened it.

I untie the ribbon, letting it fall to the ground gracefully. Inside the velvet lies a music box. I turn the handle as tunes come out, filling me with happiness. *This is meant to lift you up, Laerune.*

This song was Luthias' most favorite song to dance to with me.

"I have seen you have found my Aquitaine's paradise." I meet Caolan's eyes.

"Is this where she lures her victims?" I grin. Aquitaine had a dark demeanor in the portraits she has been portrayed in.

"She is not wicked, Laerune. Her maze has protected this kingdom for hundreds of years. I have maintained it for your return."

"But what of her return? Is this why you are planning this war?" I spin around Caolan.

"It's not just for her, but for every living thing in this very world." His voice growls, sending ripples through the pool. "I have secured you a new ally."

"Who?"

"Navain. You had war with him in the past, but he has put those petty matters aside. I have arranged a meeting for the two of you. Just step through that mirror."

Caolan shoves me back through the pool and back into the hallway in front of the mirror.

I wonder if I could just wish to go to where the stones are and then they would be found and my task over. I shake my head at the thought, but I try anyway.

I just entered into blackness. There is nothing. No warmth. No cold. No smell. No taste. Not even a feeling. There is nothing. *Nothing.*

I step back out, relieved to feel the air around me. "Luthias!" I feel his presence in the hallway. He places his hands on my cheeks.

"What is wrong?"

"I have a meeting with Navain."

I go to step towards the mirror, but Luthias pulls me back. I am about to growl at him, but he simply smiles. "Not dressed like this." He says as he continues to pull me back to our room. "You have a big first impression to make."

Chapter 25

The gown glistens. Luthias matches me; the sword at his side set in purple jewels. My sword has been reset with not only red for Ambrose, but blue and violet for Lithien and Lenair as well as a small emerald and orange stone on the sides.

We stand before the mirror once again. Luthias pushes me forward slightly.

I close my eyes as I step through, scared to see what will appear in front of me. When I open my bright, curious eyes, I see nothing but a dark hall in front of me. My steps are silent as I walk down the hall. I run a gloved hand over the stone walls, feeling each piece of the wall that could be thousands of years old.

You are bright.

The walls whisper.

You are too good for here.

One voice hisses. *The Killer of Innocence.*

I stand taller as I seek the end of the hall. My hand still brushes the wall; still whisks through the voices' minds, like a hand whisking away the stars among us.

It's not my fault. I am not to blame.

Don't hurt me.

You are a monster.

The voices scream, but they don't seem to be aimed at me. I release my hand from the wall and they are then silenced. I turn my head behind me. Luthias nods his head; his pale hand resting upon the handle of his sword and the red ribbon tied around it.

I turn the hall into what I believe is the throne room. And upon that throne sits Navain.

I grin as he sits up in his seat. He is tall, his hair dark and his eyes blue with the slightest bit of gold. He is shirtless; his muscles clearly show through his abdomen. I bow and Luthias' hand grips tighter on his sword. Navain rises from his seat and places his hand over his heart and then reaches it out towards me.

"A proper introduction is necessary. I am Navain, King of Nadien. Fae child of the Electa."

222

"I am Laerune, Queen of Lenair." I reach my hand back for Luthias to announce his title. I ignore the title of Fae. I don't feel like it is the right time to ask that question.

"Luthias, King of Lenair."

Navain does not sit back down, nor does he move from where he stands. Luthias shifts his weight and then crosses his arms.

"I am surprised. I never expected you to be so small and young."

"It doesn't make me any less dangerous."

"Dangerous." His comment is snarky. "You are standing before someone who was once your enemy, yet you are calm."

I grin, lowering my head at the slightest angle. "It seems as if we are to be in an alliance."

Navain breathes in deeply. "So it seems. I would much rather see the stones in someone else's hands rather than Elbonare. I would rather not have them used to destroy the world and create it anew with a higher being of evil. But I am sure that if *you* fail that you can survive by being Elbonare's pet. I am sure you can get Luthias to join you as well."

My voice rumbles from deep within my throat. "I would rather die."

"Again?" Navain waves his hand in agreement. "I would too. I do think that another God should be on the throne. Or there not even be a throne. Kings and Queens are meant for these lands, not the ones of the higher beings. They ruin our kingdoms."

"I agree."

Navain's eyes are honest and true. He steps closer, pushing a piece of hair away from my ear. "I am surprised you still have these. I would've thought Nolan would have cut them right off and hung upon his wall as a prize."

Luthias growls behind me. The thought of Nolan brings back bad memories.

Navain politely backs away and returns to sit back down upon his throne. He hums a tune to himself and I pull the music box from my pocket. I turn the handle and he looks up to me with shocked eyes.

Navain rushes to me, pulling the box from my hands. "Where did you get this?" He growls.

"It was gifted to me."

"Do you know why that song is so enchanting?"

I shake my head.

"Because it is the ballad of the Fae children; children of the Electa." He sits back into his throne, slouching his back.

He yells for a servant and a hunchbacked Orc hobbles in. I try not to turn my face up into a grimace.

"Bring me the chess board."

"Yes master." The Orc leaves, returning with a box, two chairs, and a table.

"Nasty things, aren't they?" Navain sets up the chess pieces along the board and then motions for me to sit. "They were an experiment gone wrong. Elbonare corrupted humans and the ones still with souls remain here. It puts a bad reputation on my part. The ones that attack your kingdoms have no ties with me." Luthias stands at my shoulder, his hand still upon his sword. "I want to see your skills."

I move the white pawn forward and the game begins. Luthias watches each move that is played, but does not interrupt us.

I move my Queen forward. I look him squarely into his eyes. "Checkmate."

Navain has nowhere to move his King and he simply leans back into his chair. I knock the black piece off of the board and it shatters to the ground.

"You allowed your King to be made of glass, where I made mine out of Mithril."

I rise to my feet, but Navain grabs my wrist. "Don't let him be hardened to stone." He releases me. "But, don't let the Queen fall in the process."

I take the King and Queen chess pieces as a token of my victory. I shove them into my pockets. "Good day, Navain." I bow and Luthias ushers me down the hall.

"Don't die too early, Laerune. I look forward to the day we fight side by side together." Navain calls down the hall as we step back through the mirror.

Once we return to our room, I place the chess pieces upon the mantle of the fireplace. Luthias changes out of his leather armor, but I remain in my dress.

"You don't plan on going anywhere else, do you?"

"No." I find myself dropping onto the love seat. "Just need a minute to ponder."

Luthias kneels down in front of me and then places his head onto my lap. "The world seems calm for a moment just knowing that my whole family sleeps right down the hall."

"Someone is missing."

My husband raises his head to kiss me. "Lorindel watches over both of us."

I wasn't thinking of him. I was thinking of Avon.

Chapter 26

I pack my things neatly into my travel bag. I go through the list of things in my head over and over. *Warm clothes. Rations. Sword. Map.*

The list seems endless as I attempt to remember the tiniest of things I still need to pack into my bag. I don't know how long I will be gone for.

I don't entirely know where to start. I have an idea where to find the next stone. I am assuming that the Erutan Mountain range holds the second stone. Maglanor, the creator of the stones, was buried there.

The first stone, which Avon found, is safely in my possession.

I stare at Avon's book that had originally been giftwrapped in my closet back in Ambrose. I reach for it as I flip through the brittle pages.

The language upon the pages of Avon's book is far from what I have ever learned in my studies. And never have I heard Avon speak in an unfamiliar language such as this.

I flip through the hundreds of handwritten entries. There is a point where the penmanship changes in three different instances. I assume it was passed on through a generation or two as entries are dated on each page.

"Why would you give this to me as a wedding gift?" I growl into my hands before placing the book into my bag.

My gaze is drawn to the floor. I bend down to grab the paper that must have fallen out of the book.

I swear. Ruins and their translation is written across the single page. I slip it back into the book. It will take a lot of time to translate and I am not sure if I will have time on my side.

I decide to take one more trip up the stairs to say goodbye to Avon.

I kneel down in front of the stone slab he is laid upon. "I know I don't have to ask this. But please, keep all of us safe and protected."

My nose tingles as the threat of tears increases. "How will I ever atone for what I have done?" I find myself sitting here with my head in my hands struggling to not rip out my hair.

"Hey." Luthias enters the hall as he pulls my hands from my face. "We will get him back. You know that. We will get them all back."

"I am scared someone is going to die." I return my hands to my face.

Luthias simply sighs and sits himself on the floor next to me. He looks up at Avon and then runs a hand through his red hair. "We don't know the future. But we do know that Death is a friend. Caolan won't take someone unjustly." Luthias must have wanted to say goodbye to Avon as well.

"Unjustly or not, I don't think anyone in my company deserves to die."

"Does anyone?"

"Deserves to die? Yes."

My husband swings my bag over his shoulder as he motions for me to grab the rest of my belongings for the trip.

I turn back towards Avon.

"Protect us, Avon."

🪶

The grass is covered in dew as I lead the silver horse from the stables. It pulls at the reigns in my hand until I sink my shoulders in defeat. "You stubborn male." I drop the rope and walk away. But the horse follows me instead. "You just don't like to be led, do you?" I run my hand over his head. "But you kind of have to let me lead you."

I grab the reins in my other hand as I hope that the silver horse will follow me this time. And with no hesitation it does. I give it a few comments of appreciation.

"You're not the only one that is stubborn."

"I am sure I can handle a tough horse. It hasn't been the first time." I speak to Dehlin.

"No. That is something I trained you well in. But you always had a certain knack for talking to them. Like you connected to the horse on a whole different level." The Golden Lord makes one more quiet remark. "Just like your mother and how she could heal creatures simply by talking to them."

"Where is my mother?" I assume it is a much more complicated matter than death.

Dehlin opens his mouth in attempts to say something, but he bites his lip and pulls at his tunic. "I'm not allowed to tell you. I took an oath."

"Took an oath from who?"

"Your mother."

A pain in my chest beats rather loudly. "Is she dead?"

Dehlin shakes his head. "Your father and the rest of the court of Ambrose is sworn under a binding oath similar to your court's oath. If we break it, we could die. It is considered an unbreakable vow that only a being with higher power can create." He breathes in heavily as I imagine he is carefully picking his words. "But that oath has kept Ambrose safe and in peace for many years."

"We will continue this when I get back."

"You really think you will be back that quickly?"

I laugh nervously. "I thought you were going to ask me if I ever thought I would come back. I was a tad bit concerned."

"You'll come back. Don't doubt yourself on that one. Caolan won't let you die a second time."

"I like to think that he will kill me as many times as possible to get what he wants."

His face turns soft as he takes both of my hands in his. "This isn't goodbye."

"I know."

"Your kingdom is under the greatest of protection." Dehlin winks.

"I know." A real smirk shines through my face.

It sends my nerves on edge having to bring so much supplies for such a large group. Part of me wanted to tell them not to come last night. I tossed and turned at the fact all night.

Seven people, plus Oka. Someone is bound to get hurt. And for some random reason, I find myself praying to Lyraesel in hopes that if any injuries occur that they will be healed rather quickly by the Goddess of Healing herself.

I didn't think of her often due to the fact that my father has always been there to heal most of my injuries. And Luthias, Elora, and I have been trained in the healing ways.

228

Luthias has a knack for it. In our younger years he was trained by my father and that was the highest honor in my kingdom. My father didn't even teach me everything. If Elender picked you to be an apprentice, you earned the highest gift and honor from my family. And only two people have earned that in my lifetime.

Avon and Luthias. The two people I felt the closest to.

I assume my father had planned that somehow with his short glimpses of the future. Possibly he thought that maybe, just maybe, I would need a healer in my life.

But I think they healed me in different ways.

Friendship. Love. Those types of things. They healed my mental health, while my physical health had been trained into shape by Dehlin.

My father shaped my future. I make the realization that he basically trained me into a warrior. Sending me to certain places during troubling times to fight in small battles, sending me to dinners with Lords and Kings of distant lands. All of those things were just him shaping the future for me to become who I am today.

I owe my father everything.

And if my mother contributed to all of this and the peace of Ambrose. Then I owe everything to my mother.

Luthias grabs my hips as he places his head in the corner of my shoulder. "Stop overthinking."

"How can you just tell?"

"I have known you for quite a long time. I have a lot of experience on deciphering your facial expressions."

I shake my head as I wrap my arms around him. "It is impossible to get anything past you."

Luthias pinches my sides as he throws one more thing into the horse's saddle bag. "I do have one more thing for you to over think. Someone decided to join us."

Navain canters into the courtyard as my court's swords are drawn in his direction.

"Stand down." I command them. "We now have an alliance with Navain and the kingdom of Nadien."

Tasar bears his teeth. "You expect us to become friends with this monster? He imprisoned you. We fought him in war."

"Those things are in the past. I think you will find that King Navain has the same goals as us."

Navain nods his head. "Elbonare took away everything from me and my family. He has kept my mother locked away for ages." His silver eyes glance at mine. A quick smirk shines in my direction as he begins walking towards the gate. "Come on! We already have a late start."

"I am in no hurry Navain."

"Yeah, but Elbonare and his servants might be." He points towards the sky at the eagle soaring above us.

I pull on the horse's reins as the guards open the gates for us. "Why birds? The Electa could have been any creature, but they had to pick something small and smart and that's easily mistaken for any other normal bird."

"We can't change it." Luvon growls. "You should have seen how many of Elbonare's servants entered Caolan's Halls just to sneak about. They shouldn't even be allowed there. They said they were visiting the dead, but I called them out on that." Luvon gives a huff of frustration. "But they simply looked at me as if I was stupid."

The sun already beats down and Luvon wipes the sweat from his forehead. "But you can tell they are servants of the Electa. They are far more beautiful and over all they just have a haunting feeling to them. A powerful feeling, I should say." He swears. "Why does it have to be so damn hot?"

"I wouldn't be complaining if I were you. Once we get to that mountain pass it's going to be close to miserable. Your skin will be frozen. The weather changes quickly around here."

"You'll be thankful if you have toes left." Tasar jumps into the conversation. "I got lost in the Erutan pass for about a week. Thought I was going to die, but an old human managed to track me down and lead me out."

"What was an old human doing in the Erutan Pass?" Navain questions.

"It's a trading route for them. You go through my home kingdom of Ambrose. Ambrose is mostly surrounded by a mountain range. But the pass crosses over to the shore. There is a river connecting to the sea, but that isn't used often as large boats are rare. Men use it to get goods from an island off of the mainland. Elves don't really go near it as we have solid traders with our closer alliances on the mainland."

"The people on that island are a bit different." Amar enters the conversation. "But they supply the men with lots of goods and weapons that they can't really afford from us Elves." He looks towards Chalsarda. "We have both been there before. Elender sent us on a mission to make sure that nothing fishy was going on. Not much land surprisingly, but they are getting supplies from somewhere other than the mainland."

Luthias chimes in with a scholarly tone to his voice. "That island has been a mystery for ages, but a treaty was made way before our time that discloses any and all information on where they get their goods from. The Elves in Laquilasse have had no desire in exploring the sea. We have been content on protecting our homeland."

I ponder the thought of other lands being out there other than our own. Like what kind of people take residence there. Or maybe there is nothing past that bright blue sea other than the God's Land.

I am sure Avon would have some sort of answer to my questions. He would come up with an elaborate story for me about how travelers would explore the great ocean and fight sea wyverns. He was always good at elaborating everything into this great big story that would send my imagination wild.

Luthias grabs my shoulder as he whispers in my ear. "Everything okay?"

"I just miss him." I keep my eyes on the forest ahead of me as the gate closes behind all of us. My pointed ears turn red at the tips as Luthias speaks once again.

"I miss him too."

The gate finally creeks close and I shut my eyes at the sound. *Leaving home once again.* The sound is almost haunting as it continues to ring in my head.

"Another adventure is ahead."

"Or a long walk to our death." I can feel Tasar glare at the back of my head. He doesn't seem too happy that Navain is coming along with us.

I snicker. "I think both can be equally exciting." I look back at him. "Especially if Caolan takes a liking to you. Then things aren't so permanent."

"The Great Laerune can't be killed unless the God of Death takes her himself!" Luvon sings as he clasps onto both of my shoulders and prepares to jump onto my back. I tip forward slightly before he lands both feet back onto the ground.

Navain actually chuckles which surprises me. Seeing him as a normal Elf and interacting with the rest of us makes him seem less dangerous.

There seems to be a sort of excitement among my court. Most of us have travelled separately, so this is the first time we have gone adventuring all together. I just hope we all make it back.

Tasar loops his arms around the straps of his backpack. "Navain, weren't you the one that hid the stones in the first place."

"Yes. But, Elbonare wiped my memory clean of their location as well as most of my memories that I had when I lived on the God's land."

I play with a jeweled button upon my cloak. My court looks a bit odd venturing into the woods dressed in jewels and circlets. Even Oka has adorned a golden collar.

I would rather not be known as Queen LaRue, but rather traveling Lords and Ladies, merchants searching for new trades. We all have different stories and different names made up if we were to encounter anyone on the journey that wouldn't bat an eye at wealthy merchants.

I giggle as Oka runs ahead of us, her own pack strapped around her sides. I made sure that she had extra food packed with her and her own blanket just in case the weather turned bad.

I keep a steady pace in between my court. Amar keeps the pack going with Oka at his side and Luvon and Tasar take up the back. Luthias occasionally drops his pace to speak with them. I am tending to stay quite as Elora tells me more stories about what had happened when I was in the Halls of Caolan.

Elora smirks and giggles. A gloved hand hides her smile from my sight. Her eyes glance towards Oka. "She just kept on getting bigger and bigger. She has very interesting things to say, but I don't think she wants to show you her voice yet."

"Voice?"

Elora taps at her temple. "Oka is very wise. I never expected her voice to sound so...ancient."

It is odd to see how much Oka has changed. When she was only a pup she would prance around and slide around on the marble floors of the castle hallways. Now, the only sound she makes is the thundering of her great paws and the occasional growl from her throat. I never gave her a voice, I read everything through her eyes and actions.

"What can a Wolf God do?"

"We have yet to find out."

Oka's head turns, searching around the forest. Her silver coat blends in among the birch trees and I watch as she disappears amongst them. Oka is our scout and with a simple howl she can alert us of an incoming enemy.

Luthias seems more pale than usual and I grab his hand. His freckles stand out brightly upon his nose.

"What's the matter?"

He gives me a genuine smile as the muscles flex in his neck.

Luvon and Tasar chuckle behind us and I let go of Luthias' hand. "What are you two planning?" I want in on their plans. I didn't like the feeling of being left out.

The set of troublemakers were my kind of group when I was younger. You could say that Avon taught me well when it came to getting in trouble and working my way out of it.

"Just playing a game." Luvon crosses his hands behind his back, staring up at the sky to avoid my eye contact. But he can't keep that serious face on for long and spit flies from his mouth in laughter. His red hair bounces as he bends over and Tasar slaps his back.

"Don't tell her anything." Those earth brown eyes plead to Luvon. Luthias turns around, his own blue eyes pleading for a different answer.

"He's paler than snow. What are you making him do?"

Luthias turns to face forward and begins to stare at the back of Navain's head. But his eyes are drawn to a lower direction and then back to us.

"Just a simple game of dare."

"You are children." I roll my eyes, but Luvon points me back to Luthias. "Lu, don't do it."

Luthias sighs and then chuckles. "I thought you two were actually going to make me do it."

Luthias was always the more mature one out of the two siblings, but he always seemed to get pulled into Luvon's shenanigans.

"Fine. I'll do it then." Tasar struts forward, but before I can warn him not to touch the King of Nadien, his hand connects with Navain's backside.

Navain's dagger is pulled out faster than my eyes can pick up. "How dare you. I should have your ears for this, you rat." Navain pins Tasar onto the ground.

The dagger goes to Tasar's ears.

"Navain, stop. Tasar, apologize."

Navain rises.

"I shall not touch the royal ass." Tasar brushes the dirt off of his tunic and pants as the other males attempt to control their laughter.

Chapter 27

The cold of night begins to set in. My court begins to set up camp for the night.

After setting out my bedroll, I place myself closer to the fire in order to read from the book that was gifted to me by Avon. I rest my journal on my knee as I begin translating the last entry.

It is Avon's penmanship, without a doubt. I wonder what he knew and hid from all of us.

Luvon and Luthias whisper to each other from across the fire. "She rarely sleeps." Luthias confesses to his brother.

"That's what happens when you are dead for so long. You forget how to be alive and normal."

I sense both of their eyes upon me. I know that they think that I am too invested in this book to care what they are saying.

I rise up to sit beside them. "I translated some of it." I raise the paper closer to the light of the fire. "Binded am I to the shadow world. Find me in between life and death. Bring me back to life in the end. Send me back to death where I have been."

Navain raises his head. "You translated it wrong. Bound, not binded. I would have thought that you would be more educated, Laerune."

I certainly never thought that Navain, King of Nadien, would be so concerned with correct wording.

"It's an incantation. It allows you to cross over to, what some call, the shadow world. You can talk to whoever decides they want to be spoken to. You can only do this since you have died and sent someone you love to Caolan's Halls. Very few possess this ability. If you say the incantation correctly. Try it again."

"Bound am I to the shadow world. Find me in between life and death. Bring me back to life in the end. Send me back to death where I have been."

I look around me expecting my surroundings to change, but it all remains the same. Except for the Elf that now sits beside me. He is enveloped in a blue, celestial light.

"I've been expecting you, Laerune." Maglanor's voice echoes. I know what he looks like since many of his portraits reside in storybooks. "You never came to speak with me in Death's Halls."

Maglanor's hair is braided with gold ribbons which is the easiest indication of who he is.

"You are in search of my stones, aren't you?"

I nod my head.

"My heart and soul is a part of them. I am even buried with one of them." *I am right about something!*

I reach into my pocket to grab the stone that Avon had found in the ocean. Maglanor reaches his hands out to hold it. He shakes.

"I haven't held one for the longest time." He lets out a deep breath and hands it back to me. "I am sure you can feel its power surging through your palm."

"Yes." Even through my dress pocket I could feel it; like a steady heartbeat beside me.

"You have found the one that was once a part of the ocean. Now, the challenge is to find the other three. The mountain and stars will be the hardest. I had created a fourth in secret and had one of the Electa hide it. I am sure only her and her closest servant knows of the location." His eyes turn towards Oka's direction. He pauses.

There is a long silence and my court and I aren't sure what to do.

"Is everything alright?"

Maglanor closes his mouth. "No. I have just been told that Elbonare has found a stone. Sibylla knew of its location and is now being held prisoner within Elbonare's Halls."

"The one that is a part of the stars?"

"Correct." He lets out a shaky breath. "Still, continue on the path you are on. Follow your sword's blade point. Wherever it points, you shall follow." He smiles. "Till we meet again, young Laerune."

I unsheathe Laura-enth, the blade glistens in the light of the fire. "Well, at least we have some information."

"Horrible information." Navain grimaces.

"Yes, horrible, but useful."

236

As we get nearer to the mountains and closer to Ambrose, the mornings become rough. Today our blankets are covered in a thin layer of frost and Oka shakes the snow from her coat. She smiles, knowing that she has done her job at keeping Elora warm at night.

Tasar stirs up the cold embers in attempts to restart the fire, but there is nothing but smoke arising in the cold morning air. I breathe deeply and my exhaling breath drifts up towards the greying clouds. It intertwines with each member of my court's breaths. Our signs of life become one as it rises above the smoke of the fire.

Luvon and Luthias are still fast asleep, spread out across their bedrolls. I imagine that they awoke in the middle of the night and just talked like they have been doing on a regular basis. There's a lot that they have to catch up on.

An eagle screeches above us in the trees followed by the hoot of an owl. They sound as if they are arguing. Luthias awakes as he jolts forward with his hand upon his dagger. He looks around quickly.

I place a freezing hand onto his shoulder.

"Someone was screaming." His blue eyes flicker to each member of our court to make sure that each one is okay and not in immediate danger.

Navain gazes upwards. A look of disgust is written across his face. "We have a spy among us." He spits.

The eagle stands proud upon the branch while fluffing his wings out. The owl is now gone, leaving its territory to make room for the eagle.

"It could be Elbonare. We need to be more careful with what we speak about."

The eagle meets my eyes. It looks as if it is grinning back at me. His golden beak glistens in the morning sun. I grin back at him. His tail feathers ruffle.

Oka growls and stretches out her legs.

You think you are more powerful than me, Wolf God?

My eyes widen as I look at the voice that has escaped from the bird.

Oka growls once again, but a voice comes out of her too. A proud one with confidence and all the anger of the world. *I may not be as powerful as you, God of the Wind, but at least I have the decency of privacy.* Her tongue curls as she bears her teeth.

You don't think I know who you travel with? That your master is the one I have been looking for? I will spare her at the moment, knowing that she will be needed in the end. The eagle's eyes meet mine. *If she lasts that long. I have others to do my bidding, but I like to see how far one girl makes it.*

Go away. Another growl escapes from Oka's throat.

You were gifted to her. But by whom? What God gave you to the Earth? What Goddess gave you to this girl?

I was not gifted. I did so willingly.

From whom do you take orders? His feathers ruffle one again as if showing a sign of dominance.

"Buzzard." I meet his eyes, both dangerous and haunting. His screech echoes through the air as his wings spread. But his glare quickly falls to Oka.

Who is she, the one that freed you?

It's not my tale to tell, Elbonare. Oka lowers herself to her hind legs as her tail curls. *You already antagonize them. It won't be hard to get information from them. They are your trusted servants, aren't they?* It looks as if Oka is smiling. Her tail wags slightly as she taunts the God of the wind.

Elbonare spreads his wings as the branches bounce as he flies away. I doubt that he will go far. If he does, he is probably planning on interrogating the other members of the Electa.

No one says anything as we begin to pack up our things.

Navain pulls me aside. "Do you have any idea what you and that mutt just did?"

I furrow my brow.

He grabs at the clasp of my cloak. "My mother is the one that will suffer his wrath." Those grey eyes hold sadness. "Aquitaine is his prisoner. Of course he is going to think that she was the one that gave you that dog."

"That's why we must find the next stone as quickly as possible so we can free her and the others."

I feel that Navain doesn't have faith in my words. He shoves me backwards as he swings his pack to his shoulder and takes the lead of the group.

I swing my own pack over my shoulder as I unsheathe my sword. I toss it forward, waiting for the point of the blade to show me the right direction.

It points forward, continuing us on the path to the mountain range ahead of us. I sigh and Oka comes up next to me. Her silver eyes look up at me and then to the mountains.

It's going to get colder once we come to the edge of the mountain. I assume we have to cross over the mountain pass.

"I guarantee we will have to cross it. This journey won't be easy."

I knew him. I knew Maglanor. I look to Oka. I would never thought it would feel normal for her to talk. *Before I was released to the Earth. We were very good friends.* Her mouth again looks as if she is smiling. *But I was reborn and released. I've been starting to forget what I looked like in my Elf form.*

"What did you do in your past life?"

I was a servant for one of the Electa. A handmaiden you could say. I ran errands, attended councils, simple things. They dressed me in extravagant gowns and jewels. I was treated like royalty.

I want to make a joke about how she is now treated like a dog, but I don't feel like that is appropriate. I keep a silent smile to myself. "Did they send you here for a reason?"

Of course they did. I was sent to take care of you. Did you really think I was sent to this world to just be a wolf? Did you think I found you just on a whim?

"I wasn't sure." I smirk. "The limping puppy I found in the courtyard of Ambrose was simply a miracle to me. Simply a friend."

Oka looks forward. I watch her paws move forward with grace. All four paws used to fit in my single palm. Now, one could barely fit in my hand. It's odd to think that this thundering Wolf God used to be a helpless puppy in my eyes.

I look behind me at Luthias. His eyes wander endlessly over the trees. "Stop worrying." I shout back to him. He hates it when I say that and his glare back at me shows that I have annoyed him once again. "I will shoot every eagle in the sky if that will make you feel better."

Elora is clinging onto Tasar's back, her hands wrapped around the top of his shoulders. They laugh at each other; grins covering their faces. I feel lost in my own thoughts as snow starts to fall from the sky. We are close to the mountains.

My mind wanders into visions and they come to me like flashes of lightning within a storming sky.

I see myself cloaked in red, falling to my knees. Blood drips through my hands and I look up. My sword is pointed into the ground. A figure enters the glade. I shake as the vision comes in and out of my mind. I look up once again at the figure before me. He places his hands upon my blood covered face.

Blood drips down my face and then down onto his hand. I rise to my feet, trying to reach for my sword as he rises with me. "This is your death, Laerune Aduial." The vision disappears, leaving me feeling more lost.

The snow now falls heavier from the sky. The clouds are now grey and looming over us. The clouds take over the mountains.

I pull my hood over my head, the rest of my court adorns their winter clothing. The only thing I wish I had was gloves. I regret forgetting to pack those.

The most prepared one in our group is Navain. I watch as he pulls on another shirt. He clearly planned his bag very well, for it wasn't too full and not too empty. He hands me an extra pair of gloves and I thank him.

I lean in towards Luthias. "Do you think that at any point I will have to do this alone?"

"I wouldn't let it happen. Why?" His eyes widen, letting me know that he is there to listen.

"Just visions."

Luthias rolls his eyes. "You are still believing everything they show you? You have a very big imagination. It could be just that."

I pause in my tracks, the rest of my court stops with me. "I know the difference." My words snap. "I've seen them my whole life. I have seen them come true." My eyes look up to his as I continue walking. My court pauses for a moment. Their laughter ceases in the chilled air,

I shiver as my body cramps up from the cold. Oka continues to follow me. Her paws are silent over the snow.

You should listen to them more often. Oka doesn't look at me. She continues to point those silver eyes towards the surroundings before her. *Sometimes they know what they are talking about.*

"I know. I am just too stubborn to listen to them. I take what they say to heart though."

They don't see that though. They see someone that is hurting and stressed about the future. Not someone that's living in the moment. Not someone that is living the life they have left. They are scared, LaRue. They are scared they will die. Watch the moments they cherish. Learn to cherish those moments with them. Include them in plans, talk to them, and get to know them more. They are your family. Don't be afraid to lose them just because you have gotten close to them.

"I know." I lower my head, turning it slightly to look at my family behind me. I know they are stressed, but I am trying to keep them safe. "I am scared too, Oka." I whisper to her. "I don't want them getting hurt. This is my weight and I must be the one to carry it. And if I must be the one to die again in the process, then so be it. I know that I will be leaving behind a new future. A new future that my family can continue to build."

They can't do it without you, Laerune. They would be lost. Luthias would be lost, a new path for him would be far out of reach if he lost you. We've all seen this. I've seen them without you.

"Was Elbonare planning this when you were within the Electa's Halls?" I change the subject.

He has always been planning this. As long as I can remember. I was also a spy for my Lady. I heard many things. Many things that frightened me, that frightened my Lady.

"And who was she?"

Lyraesel.

"You speak her name in vain?"

No. I speak her name in proudness. I am proud to be her handmaiden. I wouldn't wish for anything different. It's just now, she is stuck within Elbonare's Halls. She is stuck in her mind and she is now his servant. I speak of Elbonare's actions in vain, not my Lady's.

I nod my head to say that I understand. I assume that many of the Electa are being punished by Elbonare. Even if they don't quite realize it.

Chapter 28

As we travel further and further, the weather begins to worsen. The snow picks up, the wind sending it in every direction. Elora clings to Tasar's back, but her face is tucked into the crook of his neck and her hood over her head. We all stay close together in a group to savor the warmth of each other while it lasts. Even Navain decides to keep close to us.

I assume this is also how we will be sleeping tonight because I doubt a fire will start in this much wind.

I would rather burn up in heat exhaustion than freeze to death. I can't feel my hands anymore and I bury them into Luthias' coat pocket, causing me to walk in a sideways direction. I can barely see Chalsarda behind me. Only her fire kissed hair is visible through the snow.

She stays close to Amar, making sure she doesn't lose her husband in the blinding snow. I reach out to grab her gloved hand, making sure the two of them stay with us. Oka turns her head to the side in attempts to shield her face from the burning snow. I have never realized that something so cold could burn so much.

My face and hands seem raw as the wind attempts to push us away from the sword I have just thrown forward. The metal seems to want to stick to my skin and I sheath it back into my belt.

"Let's stop here!" I yell to them while pulling them towards the thicker branches of the trees. I know their limits. I know my limits and this is where we must stop. We all sit down with our backs against a snow bank. I find myself seeking warmth from inside of my backpack, hoping that the warmth from the morning could've stayed in there all day. But I am only met with more cold. More freezing, cold air.

I dare not cry because the tears would freeze to my face and I fear they would be stuck there forever. I have never wanted a fire so badly. I would burn down the whole forest if I had to.

Navain attempts to light a match, but nothing comes from it but the howling wind blowing it out. He stricks it a couple more times, but throws the remaining matches into the snow.

We all try to stay moving. I wiggle my toes in my boots, panicking at the thought of them falling off. My court has never experienced a cold like this. We have had mild winters in the Elven kingdoms with light snowfalls and average temperatures. Although Ambrose is near the mountains, our valley holds warmth and provides cover from the wind and snow.

I don't know how or when I was able to fall asleep, but I wake up covered in a thick layer of snow. I shake it off my body. My whole being, inner and out, shivers nonstop. Even my heart feels like it is shivering.

I watch as Chalsarda can barely open her eyes. The snow covers her eyelashes. I even see Oka shivering slightly, not even her furred coat seems to keep her safe from this kind of cold. I release a breath. The cold freezes it instantly.

I take my sleeve and put it on my nose to warm it up. My breath warms my hands and I sigh, the cold letting up just a little.

"Are we able to find a town nearby? Possibly an inn?" Luvon asks. Nods from my court members follow.

I leave the comfort of my sleeves to reach my hand into my pocket. I flatten the map out on my lap. "There is an inn about… thirteen miles from here. But, I am not sure if they take too kindly to Elves."

"Lockton?" Tasar questions.

I nod my head.

"No. They don't like Elves. Claim that we invaded them at some point."

"Well, keep your hoods up and I suggest adorning your hair in a fashion to tuck your ears in." Of course tucking your ears is uncomfortable and sometimes painful, I would rather do that than lose my ears. Especially when my ears are worth so much on the black market.

The town is small as we arrive at the edge of its borders. The bright lights of the houses are welcoming. The inn shines bright at the end of the pathway. Sighs escape from all of us as I dig into my bag for some coins.

I want my friends housed somewhere warm before I plan on continuing my journey to Maglanor's grave.

We push open the door as the warmth of the inn burns our faces. A few tables are full of men drinking and playing cards with a few women sitting on the men's knees. A fat man with a grumpy face throws a rag onto the counter.

"I am guessing you need a room." He looks my court up and down. "Three gold pieces." He opens his dirty palm and I place the money within. "It's the middle door to the left. It should be enough room for all of you."

His sneer makes us escape into our room. There is a small space for the bathing room where the water comes from a faucet and flows into a bath.

"Who wants to take a bath first? I am going to go find us some food."

"I'll come with you." Elora pulls off her gloves. Her hands are already gaining a pink color to them.

There are only two steps to get back into the dining area of the inn, but it seems like a thousand. My body aches from shivering so violently. Elora stays close to me, still savoring the warmth.

"What do you have to eat?" I ask the woman who I suspect is the innkeeper's wife. The woman sneers at me and I back away slightly. She drops a set of bowls into Elora's hands, spoons, and a large bowl of soup. "Thank you." I start to walk away.

"Have you heard of the Gods coming down from their heavens in search of an Elf?"

"If I had the ability, I would kill that species. Elves are not good for our world. They think they are better than everyone else because their ears are pointed."

I continue to cross the room and to the stairs, but I am called out.

"Where are you from girl?"

"We are merchants." I say a little too quickly.

"That explains the fancy clothes and jewels." The customer sips his mead. "Those won't get you far here. Elves will eventually steal them from you. They are not ones to trade with us humans."

I turn towards him; luckily my ears are covered by my hair and so is Elora's. "Have you ever seen and Elf?" I ask with a genuine sense of curiosity.

"I did once when I was young. The thing was so childlike, but in reality it was much older. The ears pointed, but short. They simply ran away."

"Then why do you think they are bad if they run away?"

"My ancestors were killed by that kind by an Elf named Laerune. They praise her apparently. That's why when Nolan revolted, we all had to as well." He sips his drink once again. "Lucky for us she is now dead." He waves his hand to tell me to continue on my way. I lift up my skirts as I make my way back to the room.

I give each of us a bowl and Elora passes out the spoons as Luthias gives us each a serving of soup.

"I think we are too accustomed to royal life." Tasar blows on his soup to cool it down. "Our clothes are not fit for the cold weather. When was the last time we went adventuring? Have we grown too soft?" He takes a bite.

"Adventuring always used to seem easy in my mind, but it takes a lot of heart." I tell them. "It's different when you actually know your destination, but we have none. Only an object and a task."

I burn my tongue on the hot soup, but I don't mind at the moment. Warm is better than cold. Chalsarda sighs as she escapes the steamed bathing room. Elora quickly sets down her bowl to take her turn. I think they needed it the most. Even if they tried to pressure me to go first, I would still refuse.

Luvon still shivers as he holds the bowl of soup in his hands. He places the side of the bowl to his flushed cheeks. Oka is asleep near the fireplace.

There are only two beds and the second one sits a bit crooked. The window is cracked and a slight breeze whistles through it. The fireplace overpowers that slight breeze.

Tasar spills his spoonful in his lap and he swears. He licks his fingers and wipes it from his stomach. "I don't like to waste food." He chuckles at me. "That's all I remember my parent's teaching me. Teaching me to share food with others who weren't so lucky in life"

"And you remembered that at the age of four?"

"I remember a lot at that age. Probably too much." Tasar lowers his head. An heir grown into a simple Elf with nothing but what he travels with. "I was with my parents that day. The day Tion descended upon us."

Navain leans in closer. "Tion, the fire drake?"

"Yes. My parents ran towards the smith's shop, the closest stone building to us in the market. I watched as buildings were knocked down by both fire and Tion's tail." He continues to eat his soup in between parts of the story.

"My father was then caught on fire. There was no way to help him, no water in sight, only buckets of oil surrounding me. My mother screamed and screamed. And then she saw that small child across the market and her motherly instincts kicked in. it wasn't to protect me, but to protect that smaller child. Not me." Tasar puts a huge emphasis on the last two words. "And then she was knocked to the ground and never stood back up. I hid further into the smith's shop as the walls crumbled around me."

Tasar keeps his head lowered. "I felt like I was stuck in that shop for days until Dwarves decided to ransack the remains. And they took me with them."

We all wait a moment, thinking that he might continue with the story, but he simply stops and continues to eat what's left of his soup.

Navain chuckles softly. "I have Tion's head hanging in my sitting room."

Tasar's eyes widen. "Do you really?"

"When this is all over, I'll invite you to Nadien so you can see it for yourself."

Elora comes out of the bathroom. Her wet hair drips across her cheeks. She quickly finds a spot in between Tasar and Luvon. I look to each of them as they nod their heads, allowing me to take the next turn in the bathing room.

I lay my coat near the fireplace to let the cold chill melt away. Oka picks up her head as I walk towards the door. She follows quickly after me. I lean against the door of the bathing room. The steam is welcoming and healing

Lyraesel is here. Oka tells me as she grins.

The bathroom window shakes as a large owl perches itself on the sill. It gives a simple hoot before turning herself into her Elf form.

She places warm hands upon my cold skin. Her face is covered in gold paint. Her clothes are simple with earthly colors. Her golden hair is braided in patterns I couldn't even imagine making. Lyraesel is simple.

She grins at me.

"Your spirit has grown since we last spoke." Her mouth gapes open into a smile. "I have been watching you for so long. Waiting for you to grow into something powerful and dangerous." Her hands fall to my shoulders. "You are strong. Beautiful. Fearless. Everything I have ever wanted you to be."

Oka wags her tail. Lyraesel falls to her knees as she places her hands around Oka's cheeks. "And you. I am so proud of you. You found her and have been protecting her very well."

She once again rises and stands before me. "You have powers Laerune. You will need to learn them soon enough. It has been such a shame that your father neglected teaching you those essential things."

"What do you mean by powers?"

"You were given gifts by the Electa when you were brought into this world. You just only have to seek them out within yourself. You have only touched the top layer of my gift to you. And slowly, you are reaching for Caolan's gift."

"How do I master these gifts?" There is urgency in both of our voices.

Her eyes turn soft. "In time."

"I'm tired of hearing that. It's not very helpful, you know?"

She winks. "Till we meet again, my child." And with her simple words, Lyraesel turns back into an owl and flies through the open window.

Oka wags her tail. *She has much to tell you in the future.* Oka seems to be hiding secrets in her silver eyes, but I don't have the heart to break her grin and wagging tail.

I slip into the bath that Elora refilled for me. The heat burns at first as my body becomes numb with heat. I keep my hair up, hating the fact that we will leave tomorrow and my golden tresses wouldn't be dry by then. It would freeze and break.

"Can you imagine if I had short hair?" I ask Oka.

She shakes her head. *Never. Don't you dare cut it.*

"Never." I shine a smirk in her direction.

What did you think of Lyraesel?

"She is very simple." I look over the edge of the bathtub. "She is like a mother to you, isn't she?"

Very much so. She has taken care of me since I was first created. I was never a servant or a pet to her. I was a friend, a daughter, and her family. And she treated me like so.

I sink further into the tub. The warmth rises to the top of my head. The visions again flash through my mind like lightning. It comes in and out of focus and I hold my head as the sensation pounds through my mind.

They have never been like this. They have never flashed and blurred like this before.

"Evil passes through shadows unaccounted for in the ruins of this place." The vision speaks as I pull a tapestry from a stone table.

It fades away rather quickly. The whole memory of it causes a migraine to appear in the front of my head. I run my hands over my face as the water drips down my cheeks.

I return to the room. Most of the soup is now gone. Oka returns to her spot near the fireplace and soon falls back into her sleeping position.

Elora seems to doze off on Chalsarda's legs. The warmth of the soup and the comfort of the small inn's room seem to be drawing my companions into sleep. Even Navain's eyes seem to droop with tiredness.

"We don't have friendship on our side in this town." I tell the rest that are more awake. "Elves are hated and not welcome here."

Tasar bites his lip. "We get the bad side of every coin."

"I am surprised you aren't used to it by now."

Luvon stirs from his nap. "I don't understand how they can hate Elves. We are just like everyone else-"

"But we are immortal." Luthias adds to his brother's comment. "I don't think you realize that there are many differences between the two races. I can sense their unrest in the past one hundred years. They are harvesting Elves' ears more often."

I rub the sleepiness from my eyes. "I sort of understand. The Elves are kind and caring to their fellow kingdoms. But humans seem to get left out of all sorts of things. Just recently Everford has been included. But they can thank Eryn for that. They are never invited to councils, balls, and parties. I would be a little upset too."

I look to the beds that lie empty. None of us has the heart to take up the crooked beds. I pull my blanket from my bag and shift myself into Luthias' lap. He wraps his muscled arms around my waist and places his chin on my shoulder. Luthias places a kiss onto the side of my neck.

I run my hands through the ends of his red hair. I plan on leaving everyone behind because I care about their safety. I attempt to cherish my fleeting moments with Luthias.

"You're nervous." He tells me. "I can feel your heartbeat through your back." Luthias nuzzles his face in my hair as he speaks softly.

I lean my head back into his shoulders. I scratch at my palms, but Luthias silently tells me to stop by placing his hands in mine.

"You need to be open to us Laerune."

"I hate it when you call me that." I move my head away from his. "It makes me sound too-"

"Unlike yourself? Innocent?'

I pull away rather quickly from his arms as I lean back onto the floor. "You think that LaRue isn't innocent?"

"Well, LaRue is now being used in many of your black market papers. Saying Laerune makes you, makes us, seem little again."

I remain silent.

"I didn't mean it in a bad way."

Instead of returning to Luthias' arms, I lean up against the empty bed. I cross my arms and close my eyes. "You never used to call me that. You would always call me LaRue."

"I guess I am just following suit. You are a Queen now. I just figured you wanted a more professional approach to your name."

"Being Queen doesn't change who I am. I am still that little girl you met in the forest that day."

Luthias smirks and shakes his head. "You are so much more than that, LaRue." He makes an emphasis on my name. "You have grown so much compared to who you were that day."

"But this hasn't changed." I place my hand over my heart. "It won't ever change." I then place both hands over my chest. "But, here. This gets tired. My soul is tired."

"I know." Luthias whispers in understanding. "Imagine how our fathers feel."

"I missed out on so much life, Luthias. I don't think you understand."

He crawls forward as his face meets mine. "You don't think I died every day when you were gone?" Luthias leans in closer to pull me tighter against him. "You have never been so wrong." He places a kiss onto both of my cheeks and then finally to my lips. "When you are away, my heart stops. I don't live. You and I are connected."

"Stop." I push him away with a giggle. "You are being sappy."

He comes right back to his spot. He grabs at my waist and I pull away in laughter as Luthias attempts to tickle my sides.

"Shh. You'll wake everyone up." I giggle into his cheek.

My smirking husband misplaces his hand and both of us hit the floor with a thud. I bite my lip and close my eyes as the sound echoes through the quiet room. I can feel Luthias' cheeks curl upwards as he places his head on my stomach. "Shh."

I watch as Navain's eyes flutter open and then close.

Luthias sits up slightly to look me directly in the eyes. "My favorite color is blue."

251

"Well, I love yellow." I grin at him. A simple conversation like this is what we need. It makes our lives seem back to normal. *Back to the younger years.*

Luthias places his hands on either side of me and lifts me off the ground. His hair dangles in my face and I move it away. "I like your shirt. Is it yours?" He questions.

"I stole it from your bag before we left. It looked warm."

Luthias' eyes rest on my face. "I have a plan."

"A plan?" I raise my eyebrow.

"Once we find all those damn stones, I am going to fashion them into a shiny crown to fit right on top of that beautiful head of yours." His lips meet mine.

"And you think that we are going to be able to keep the Saryniti?"

"With how much Hell this has put us through, I think you would be more than deserving of those stones." Luthias' eyes turn away from me. "We never sleep, do we?"

"I have just accepted the fact that I will be sleep deprived forever."

I watch how his eyes wander around the features of my face. Luthias raises his hand to caress my cheek. "When all of this is over, I want to take you to see the High Elves of Castimier."

"If we-"

"No." Luthias places his finger against my lips. "Don't talk like that." He sets his hand back down. "They would appreciate how you use your voice."

I scoff. "You have a better voice than anyone I have heard, Luthias."

He rolls over and shuts his eyes. His rhythmic breathing follows with the rest of my sleeping court.

"You know that I need you to leave by yourself. Only you can enter Elbonare's grave." Caolan sits on the end of the lopsided bed. "I am sorry I have appeared on a late notice. Elbonare had me held up or I would have told you sooner." The God of Death lets out a soft chuckle. "I will guide them back home safely."

Chapter 29

I step outside. The wind blows through my hair sending snowflakes into my golden tresses. The sky is a pastel purple and the snow brightens the scene in front of me.

I take a step into the white abyss. The snow crunches under my feet. I pull my hood over my head to keep the cold from touching my skin and freezing my bones.

The land ahead of me seems far as I stare at the white dusted trees and mountains ahead of me. The sun begins to rise turning everything beyond and ahead of me into orange brightness. The snowflakes still fall like stars from the sky.

I turn back towards the inn where I had snuck out from my sleeping friends.

"They would be in more danger if they came with you." Caolan grabs at my hand. "This is what's best. You summoned Maglanor, not them."

"I know. I should have known that from the beginning."

Lyraesel brushes my hair to the side. "This is a journey that you must take alone."

🪶

The mountains loom above me; strong and fierce just as the Gods created them for; to induce fear. To make us haunt in their sublime power. To cower in their mighty wake, but yearn in curiosity to explore them further.

I, myself, am unsure if I actually feel the need to explore them further than the beginning of this mountain pass. But, I have no choice to turn back. Simply, I bask in their glory.

Pine trees litter the body of the mountain like great giants holding grip of the earth hidden below them.

I stick my sword in the ground as I kneel before the mountains that emerge before me.

A raven soars above me and then descends to rest on the pommel of my sword. My red cloak billows behind me.

"The Electa is close. You must hurry. Their stone is near. Run!" The raven flaps its wings as it returns to the sky.

I race across the snow covered pass in the path of the raven's flight. The opening of the mountain is now before me.

I enter into the darkness and Maglanor appears beside me. His smile is reassuring as we walk into the cave together.

The male doesn't say a word as I reach the dias his body had been laid upon. I pull the tapestry from his body and the dust dispearses around me.

The stone glows under the embrace of his folded hands. I carefully take it from him.

"Keep it secret. Keep it safe." Maglanor urges me from the cave as his spirit merges with his body.

The sun shines brightly as I exit the mountain. Snow meets my face as I shoved to the ground. "You thought you could get far, didn't you?" A gleaming Elf stands before me. "Elbonare gave me a task and how happy he will be that it will be finished."

I reach my hand out to grab a fistful of snow and the glowing jewel that I have dropped beneath. The Elf pulls my hair as he places his weight to my back. His blade goes to my neck.

"How stupid of you to keep three stones in your possession. One in your pocket." He points his blade to my cloak. "One in your hand." I can hear him chuckle as he points the knife to my heart. "And one here."

I grip the stone tighter in my hand as the snow melts around it. I throw my hand back to hit the Elf in the face with the stone. Her grabs at his eye as the blood seeps from his hands.

I scramble for my sword. My hand meets the pommel as the Elf attempts to grab at my feet.

"Bound am I to the shadow world. Find me in between life and death. Bring me back to life in the end. Send me back to death where I have been!"

I appear in The Halls of Death. I begin walking up the stone steps that open up to the great hall. I wipe the blood from my lip. *I didn't think that would work.*

Within the hall sits a large pedestal with a book on top of its expanse. Caolan's head lifts up as the bird on his shoulder caws at my arrival.

"I am glad you have returned. I do have to admit that I didn't think you were going to make it out of that situation alive." Death's silky voice floats across the warm air. His robes whisper against the stone floor as he takes my hand.

He leads me towards the book. The God of Death motions me to open to the first page. Lists of signed names are littered in front of me.

"Now, that you have two of the four stones, it is time to command your army."

The first name on the list makes my heart beat quickly.
Avon Halhen Orthien Elendir.

Acknowledgements

Although writing this book took a lot more time than I thought it would, I am thrilled to finally have it in my hands. The second book in *The Tales of the LaRue series* is by far my favorite. It has come a far way from the initial manuscript that I had written by hand back in 2014. *The Queen's Rebirth* was my companion through many years and while LaRue's story is in no way a direct reflection of my own experiences, there were moments in this book that I very much needed to write. I hope that some of the hardships that you have read in this story resonate with you, and will remind you, that you can get through anything.

I am grateful for all those who have supported me and who have contributed to my completion of *The Queen's Rebirth.*

To my editor and fellow friend, Caeley Terwilliger: Thank you for being so invested in my character's lives and willing to go through my awful grammar mistakes in a very timely manner. I am thoroughly impressed with the feedback you were able to give me. Thank you for your hard work and thoughtful ideas. I am forever thankful that I can come to you and "fangirl" about the world I have created.

To my cover artist, Jocelyn (Jodie) Yu: You create magic with your art and I will praise you a thousand times over for it. You put a face to my characters in a way that I could not. You put up with me and my want for adding small details and that is no easy task. The first thing people see about my book is what you have created and people are drawn to it. I have no doubt that you will accomplish everything that you have dreamed of.

To my parents: Thank you for trying to find an answer to my endless questions about the most random topics. I know it isn't easy and I don't make any sense half the time, but your answers are appreciated no matter if it is right or wrong.

To Alex Bianchi: Who continues to show me magical places that have provided a backdrop for this world I have created. I will always be thankful that you don't mind when I pull out my notebook on any occasion. You make sure that I have everything I need before disappearing into the world I have worked so hard to create.

To my readers: Thank you for bugging me about when my next book was going to be out. Here it is. Don't read it too fast because it is going to take awhile to finish another one.

About the Author

Sydney Lyn is the author of the series *The Tales of LaRue* and *Three's A Crowd, So Let's Add One More*. She is the recipient of the 2018 Honorable Mention in novel writing in the Scholastic Art and Writing Awards. She currently resides in Marquette, Michigan.